THE
NIGHT
WHISPERS

THE
NIGHT
WHISPERS

CAROLINE MITCHELL

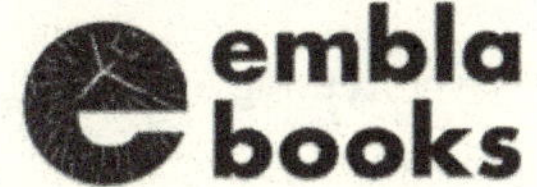

First published in Great Britain in 2022 by

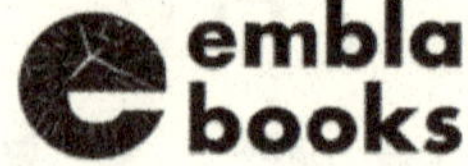

Bonnier Books UK Limited
4th Floor, Victoria House, Bloomsbury Square, London, WC1B 4DA
Owned by Bonnier Books
Sveavägen 56, Stockholm, Sweden

A CIP catalogue record for this book is available from the British Library.

eBook ISBN: 978-1-47141-163-2

This book is typeset using Atomik ePublisher

Embla Books is an imprint of Bonnier Books UK
www.bonnierbooks.co.uk

Praise for *The Midnight Man*

'One of the best opening chapters I've ever read'
Angela Marsons

'Terrifying, mysterious and suspenseful. A brilliant read'
Patricia Gibney

'If you like early Stephen King you'll love *The Midnight Man*'
Robert Dugoni

'Caroline Mitchell at her dark and twisty best'
Teresa Driscoll

'Will keep you on the edge of your seat'
Alice Hunter

'A spine tingling, creepy book'
John Marrs

'Creepy and intense'
Mel Sherratt

'A tense and deliciously creepy read'
D.S. Butler

'Twisty, tense and creepy as hell... I loved it!'
K.L. Slater

'A spooky, twisty mystery with a spine-chilling ending'
Susi Holliday

Also by Caroline Mitchell

Slayton Thrillers
The Midnight Man

Other works
Witness
Silent Victim
The Perfect Mother
The Village

The DI Amy Winter series
Truth and Lies
The Secret Child
Left for Dead
Flesh and Blood

The DC Jennifer Knight series
Don't Turn Around
Time to Die
The Silent Twin

The Ruby Preston series
Death Note
Sleep Tight
Murder Game

To the readers, writers and dreamers.

You hear them in the shadows
You won't know what they say
But when they turn their eyes upon you
It's too late to get away.

Beware the black-eyed children
Whose whispers never cease
They move with graveyard stillness
As only the good find peace.

Beware the knock on your door
As you lie in your bed
For if you draw back your bolt
You are already dead.

1

Monday, 2nd March 2020

My name is Mercy. I am twelve years of age. I haven't seen my family in twenty-five years. I don't have a grave. When I do, my headstone will be overlooked by a stone angel. Daffodils will grow there in the spring and snowdrops will rise through the winter snow when it crusts over the borders of my grave. My brother will be buried beside me. His name is Mikey. He is six.

Mother is calling our names. The faint sound of her voice used to be a comfort but now it makes me sad. She is both near and so very far away. I'm scared she'll stop looking for us. I'm scared I'll never see her again. You think about a lot when you're away for so long from the people you love. You think about things like graves, and being laid in the cold, damp earth. You think about the people who put you there. Mikey doesn't speak, but I know he feels the same. Perhaps I shouldn't say it but I'm glad I'm not alone. Will you help us, Elliott? Will you help us to find our way home?

Elliott's eyes snapped open and he blinked in rapid succession, gripping his duvet which was tumbling onto the floor. The digital clock on his bedstand glowed 22:22. His skin was cold and clammy and he rubbed his right ear to rid himself of the breath delivering whispers only he could hear. It was not the first time his sleep was invaded by the voices of the dead. But this time it was different. These were children, just like him. His long black lashes fluttered as he conjured up the girl's image while trying to keep her at bay. Mercy had been older, nearly a teenager, but the boy must have been six or seven, like him. The chalk-faced silent child, watching and waiting for Elliott to reply. Elliott's body trembled with an involuntary shiver, the thin cotton of his pyjamas doing little to protect him from the biting cold. Shadows lurked in every corner. His heart was beating too fast. Drawing his knees to his chest, he inhaled a few deep breaths. He'd been asleep, but not dreaming. The whispers in his ear were real. He fought the urge to call his mother, who had gone to bed early after working all evening at the Lakeside Hotel. Burying his head in his knees, Elliott whispered the alphabet backwards. 'Z . . . Y . . . X . . . W . . .' It was a trick Sarah had taught him to push the bad feelings away. Slowly, his bedroom warmed. The children were leaving. He was safe.

For the last few weeks, he had slept soundly. He'd almost believed it was safe to go to bed. He relaxed back into his pillow, staring at the stars floating on his ceiling cast by his new nightlight. His father's medal for bravery glinted on his bedside table. He didn't bring it to bed anymore. His daddy was too poorly to be a hero now. Besides, *real* heroes were brave on the inside; that's what Sarah said. She was a police detective. She should know.

He sniffled in the moonlight as his heartbeat slowed to its normal rate. The tip of his nose was freezing, and the tops of his fingertips too. He reached for his teddy and plunged his face into the soft fur. He didn't want to think about Mercy, but the image of the girl and her brother resurfaced just the same. Their mottled blue skin. The breath that smelled like the grave. But the real horror came when he looked into the hollows of her eyes. There was nothing there. Nothing but black tunnels echoing with screams. He snuggled beneath the covers. They were gone, for now. But a sick feeling in the pit of his stomach told him that they would return.

2

Rosemary's knees burned in protest as she rose from the sofa. It was as if moving from sitting to standing was the most unnatural thing in the world. Sighing, she brushed the scone crumbs off her dress. At her age, everything was a battle. Her sight had been the first to decline, rapidly followed by her hearing, and now her joints felt like they had given up the ghost. Her walking stick tapping against the wooden floor, she shuffled down the long, narrow hallway, pausing to turn the heating up a notch. She was meant to be watching the pennies but Geoffrey hadn't been sleeping. Best to keep the house toasty warm until the weather improved. Her son didn't have it easy. She had to put him first after everything he'd been through. Lingering outside the bathroom, she listened for signs of life.

She was rewarded with the sounds of a faint splash of water. Her hand hovered in mid-air as she readied herself to knock on the bathroom door. She bit her bottom lip. *Leave him. He'll only get annoyed.* Her inner voice was right, of course. Geoffrey did not appreciate her meddling, however well meaning. What normal man wanted to be living with his mother at his age?

Rosemary plodded back towards the living room. All the dreams she'd had about grandchildren . . . it was unlikely she'd have any now. Still. Monday night was fish and chips night and it had been nice, eating takeaway food while watching their favourite soaps. Funny, how when it was Geoffrey's turn to cook, they always ordered out. Her thoughts came to an abrupt halt as a soft knock rose from the door. It was gone half ten. Who could that be at this hour of the night? Why weren't they using the bell?

A rumble of thunder bellowed from outside. She froze in uncertainty as a feeling of ill tidings passed over her. It was as if someone had taken an ice cube and run it down the curve of her back. The last time she had felt like this, her beloved husband of forty years dropped down dead. She forced herself to breathe in . . . out . . . nice and calm. It was coming up to the anniversary of his passing and she couldn't get him off her mind. Sometimes it felt as if he was in the room with her. Last night she had thought she heard whispering, but when she turned around there was nobody there.

Another soft knock. *Get a hold of yourself, Rosemary,* she muttered to herself as she walked to the door. A crack of lightning sharpened her senses as she pulled it open. There were two small figures standing on her doorstep. Squinting, she looked behind them, but there was nobody else there. A howl of wind threatened to take the door off its hinges as she waited for them to speak. They stood in silence. Blinking, she made out the figure of a pale-faced boy and an older girl with straight blonde hair. They seemed far too young to be out alone on a night like this.

'Are you lost?' Rosemary said, softening.

'Please, missus, can we come in?' the little girl replied. Her words were a whisper, her eyes were shadowed, her face long. Rosemary cursed her vanity. She should have put on her glasses before answering, but she hated how the thick lenses distorted her eyes. She bent as she tried to take in their features. She didn't recognise them, but without her glasses it was hard to tell. But they were children, who seemed neglected and alone. A thunderous storm was brewing. They looked chilled to the bone.

'Of course you can.' Ushering them inside, she closed the door and guided them to the living room. 'Where are your parents? Has something happened?' But no answers came. The room filled with melancholy and a sense that something was very wrong. Perhaps they had run away from home? They could have been abused – or worse. She knew what her husband would say – call the police and let them deal with it. Right now, she felt his presence stronger than ever before.

'Why don't you sit down?' She gestured towards the sofa. 'You must be frozen. I'll make you some nice hot chocolate. How about that?' Obediently, they sat. The unnatural silence made Rosemary nervous. Her glasses were in the kitchen. She really should keep them on a neck chain.

Quietly, she took the cordless phone from its holder and brought it into the kitchen with her. Geoffrey would be out of the bath soon.

It took time for him to dry himself and get back in his wheelchair. There was no need to bother him, she could handle this on her own. Pressing on the kettle to boil, she slipped on her glasses and dialled her friend's number. Jemma was an ex-social worker. She would know what to do. But her relief as it rang faded when the answering machine kicked in. She dutifully left a message, explaining that two lost little children had turned up from nowhere at her door. 'I think they're in shock,' she continued. 'They asked to come in and haven't spoken since.' Rosemary sighed, her hand resting lightly on her chest. She should have waited for her son. 'They don't know I'm calling,' she added, feeling uneasy. 'I don't want to frighten them off.'

She heard the bathroom door close. 'Never mind, Geoffrey's coming. He'll know what to do,' she said before ending the call. Her thoughts wandered as she stirred drinking chocolate into two cups of warm milk. Perhaps they were hungry. She could make them a sandwich. She hoped the children hadn't been treated too badly. Carrying the hot chocolate on a tray into the living room, she tried her best to hold it steady as she manoeuvred without her walking stick.

They were still there. Staring. Seeing. Judging. Because she could see their faces now. She could see everything. 'No,' she gasped, the strength leaving her limbs. This wasn't real. It couldn't be. She didn't feel the shift in weight as the mugs slipped off the tray and splashed up the sides of her new beige sofa that she had bought just last week. The scream that followed was enough to curdle her blood. Then she realised it was coming from her. She couldn't make it stop.

'What's going on?' Her son's voice was coarse with worry as he wheeled himself in. 'Jesus!' The word fell from his lips as he stared, slack-jawed. His damp hair was stuck to his forehead, his tracksuit hanging loosely from his thin frame. Rosemary exchanged a look of disbelief with her son. Geoffrey had overcome the horrors of the accident which had left him wheelchair-bound. He had come to terms with living with his mother. But nothing could have prepared them for this. His face was ghostly, his mouth gaping as he took in the scene. Another roll of thunder. In her peripheral vision Rosemary saw movement. Her stomach liquefied as death stared them in the face.

3

Gerard couldn't remember walking out on his wife, Ruth, but it was done with such a sense of urgency that his sons thought he had lost his mind. Being a solid, understanding woman, Ruth told him to take the time he needed. He had simply been working too hard. But this wasn't a mid-life crisis. Darker forces were pulling his strings.

The proposed demolition of Blackhall Manor had not been publicised in the media, which is why his family were surprised when he insisted on travelling from London to Lincolnshire to save it. Given it was a listed building, he had an excellent case. But he couldn't tell his family why he'd come here because he didn't know. Lately, he didn't know a lot of things. His lapses in memory were growing worryingly frequent. It started with doodles; strange little stick figures next to a dense foggy woodland where birdsong was rarely heard. Then drawings of flint-eyed ravens were followed by moths with wings which seemed to dance on the page. Gerard drew until his eyes grew weary and his fingers were sore. Sometimes he would awaken from a dream-like daze with pages of illustrations scattered across his desk. Slowly, the outline of a building formed, its name a mass of jumbled letters. Blackhell. Darkhall. Blackmanor. The words tortured him as he grasped for their meaning. He was unable to concentrate in meetings, nodding to his colleagues as he pretended he was taking notes. Then he'd turn the page of his Moleskine notebook and continue drawing a mess of stick figures and words. He bought himself a pencil, as it flowed better on the page. Slowly the manor took shape. More words followed. Night Manor. Darkwoods. On and on the words came until it finally formed. Blackhall Manor.

Once the image and title of the manor were mastered, he began to draw maps. Then road names. Landmarks. A nearby town. In the night, when he could stand it no longer, he looked the place up.

His mouth had gone dry at the sight of it because it was a carbon copy of what he had drawn. Since then, his dreams were filled with whispers, the cries of children waking him in the dead of night. His heart thundering, he'd awake from lucid nightmares, the air thick with the smell of sweat and fear. It was accompanied by a sense of urgency that he could not ignore. It was as if his life depended on it. No. Not *his* life. The lifeblood of Blackhall Manor. To his shame, he allowed himself to be pulled in. He used his knowledge of legal procedures to stop the demolition and now the woman who owned the manor had been forced to put it up for sale. As an established property lawyer, he could have done it over the phone but after his first visit to Slayton he returned home, arranged a sabbatical from work and sorted things out with his wife. A psychotherapist, she was committed to her London practice, but not so busy that she wouldn't miss him after he'd gone. He'd promised his stay in the rented woodland cottage would only be for a month. But if he was done with Blackhall Manor then why was he here?

The gothic ruin stood on the highest point of Slayton, surrounded by a mass of thick trees. A network of barbed wire and brambles formed a barrier against intruders when the rusted gates were closed. Not for the first time, he wondered what had taken root in his brain. Sometimes he would lose whole blocks of time. He wasn't in control of his own mind and that was a frightening thought. 'Maybe you'll feel better when you get it out of your system,' Ruth had said. She'd seen the drawings of Slayton, expressed concerns at his lack of sleep. Then he had kissed her like he hadn't kissed her in years, because something deep down told him this could be the last time. But now he was naked, standing in his rented cottage on the cold, unforgiving tiles.

As he swayed on weak legs, he felt like he was on a tightrope – one wrong move and he would plunge to his death. His limbs ached with tiredness. He felt like he'd run a marathon. Goosebumps rose on his bare skin and his face creased in confusion. What had happened to his clothes? He touched the tight, dry skin of his face. Perhaps he had been about to get in the shower when . . . a noise from down the hall made his thoughts fall away. Someone was in the cottage. His stomach clenched. There was no point in trying to remember how he'd got here. That memory was gone, along with countless others which had evaporated into the ether, never to be retrieved. At least he was safe in the sanctuary of the cottage on the outskirts of Blackhall Woods. It was a small but adequate abode with the stench of stagnant water – or was that sewage? – hanging in the air. Tonight it was particularly strong, but that was the least of his concerns. He crept silently down the hall towards the knocking noise rising from the kitchen at the back of the property.

'Who's there?' he said, dread rising with each step. But there was no response, just a steady rhythmic knocking, then a slosh . . . He strained to listen, fear falling away as he realised what it was.

He opened the kitchen door, exhaling in relief as the sight confirmed his suspicions. The washing machine. That's all it was. An old, battered model knocking and sloshing in the corner of the room. Although why he'd needed to put a wash on, he didn't know. As for being naked . . . he peered at the glass door of the washing machine as his clothes went round. 'What the—?' The whisper left his lips as he bent closer for a better view. The water was crimson. His brow furrowed in a frown. It must be paint. Or a red sock maybe, something stupid like that. But he didn't have any red socks, or dirty clothes for that matter. He hadn't been there long enough. He stood, feeling as if his body knew exactly what had happened and was waiting for his dumb brain to catch up. The newly washed kitchen flagstones were damp, and he made out the sweet smell of lemon cleaning fluid beneath his feet. Had he just washed the floor? On auto-pilot, he returned to the bathroom, where he'd been heading when he came to.

It's alright, nothing to worry about, he told himself as he tried to calm his palpitating heart. *Shower and sleep, that's all I'd planned. I'd just cleaned the kitchen and was getting ready for bed.*

It was the not remembering that was freaking him out. The deep-buried feeling that something bad had occurred. He pushed the door open. Caught the unwelcome smell of sewage as he forced himself towards the only mirror in the house. Reaching out in the darkness, he pulled the long dirty string which dangled from the ceiling and activated the light above. He closed his eyes as it clicked the fluorescent light into life. He was shaking now, his eyes closed as he prepared to greet his reflection. He didn't want to open them but equally he had to know. To verify what was already screaming at him from the back of his mind.

Blood. The water in the washing machine had been tainted with blood. He opened his eyes and froze. It was smeared across his face, with flecks on his eyelids and his curly black hair that refused to turn grey, despite his age. 'Oh God, oh God, oh God,' he said finally, his trembling hands touching his face. The blood staining his cheeks had dried into his pores making his skin feel like stretched leather. It stopped abruptly at his neck, but flecks rested on his hair, his ears . . . he licked his lips and tasted it on his tongue. He checked his body for injuries, already knowing the blood wasn't his. But whose was it? A whimper escaped his lips as he dragged himself towards the shower. He had to get it off. It was all over him like a thousand red ants crawling on his skin.

Spikes of icy water made him gasp for breath as he stood beneath the rusty shower head. His head bowed, he tugged at each strand of hair as he tried to rinse it clean. He grabbed a bottle of shampoo from the shelf, squeezing it hard and lathering himself. Tearing at the sticky red coating, his eyes stung as the shampoo worked its way in. With frenzied movements, he covered every inch of himself. He watched as the water turned from brown to red, felt it turn from cold to hot, steam cloaking him as he discarded the shampoo bottle and grabbed a bar of soap. He could still feel it. In his pores, up his nose, in his ears. He scrubbed until his skin was bright pink. Closing his eyes, he took a deep breath before working up a lather on his face. His clothes must have been caked in it. But where had it come from? He glared at his feet, watching the water swirling around the plug hole turn clear. Any minute now, he expected the door to be kicked in as blue lights strobed from outside the window. But there was nothing. Nothing but the dull drip, drip of the shower head as he turned the water off. Wrapping himself up in towels, he glanced at his reflection once more.

*

His hands squeaked against the steamed-up mirror and he took a breath as it cleared. It was gone, all of it. Like it never happened at all. There wasn't a mark on him, apart from where he had scrubbed his skin. No defence wounds. No scratches. Perhaps it was an animal. Maybe he hit something with his car. He forced one foot before the other as he walked to his bedroom. Eleven minutes past eleven. He blinked. All he wanted was to put this behind him, and yet he found himself unable to leave. Just what was he doing here, and why? Why had he been drawn to Slayton? But a bigger question grew in his mind and it was sharply edged with fear.

What the hell had he done?

4

Sarah stared vacantly out of the office window, tired after her shift. The sky had clouded over, temporarily lit by flashes of lightning as the latest storm took hold. Her shoulders ached from being tensed, but each thunderous boom inched them a little higher. Last night she had slept on the sofa. She knew she was being irrational, but her fear of thunder was too ingrained to ease its grip now. Nobody else seemed bothered, and the impending downpour of rain did not stop the locals of Slayton from venturing out. On the streets below, a bearded man walked past wearing a thick woolly jumper, a pair of fluffy slippers and some teeny-tiny shorts which disappeared into the reaches of his considerable thighs. 'He must be bloody freezing,' Sarah murmured beneath her breath. In Slayton CID, no two days were the same. They received an above average number of strange cases, but then again, given the amount of odd people who lived in the area, that was hardly any surprise. *Perhaps eccentric is a more acceptable term?* Sarah thought. Her gaze followed the man, whose arms were flapping wildly as he appeared to argue with himself. *No,* Sarah thought. *Odd. Definitely odd.*

'It's time.' Richie's voice broke into her thoughts. Instinctively, she smiled. They had become quite the double act since their last big case involving the Midnight Man. It was much to the consternation of Yvonne, who disapproved of all work-based friendships apart from her own. Richie stood, hands on hips, his tie slightly askew from constantly tugging on it.

'Just a sec,' Sarah said, returning her gaze to Tiny Shorts Man, who was now trotting towards a hot-dog van which had pulled up against the kerb. Her eyes flicked to Richie, who was following her gaze. His beard was trimmed with the precision of someone who had too much time on their hands.

'It's not too late to back out, you know.' His Adam's apple bobbed as he tugged his tie once more. Their sergeant made no apologies for her high standards, and smart dress was expected. For male officers, ties were non-negotiable, and most female officers dressed in skirts or trouser suits. Today, the office was stuffy because it was too blustery to open the windows. Their budget did not stretch to air conditioning just yet.

'Now why would I want to back out?' Sarah gave Richie a patient smile before approaching the office mini fridge. She was normally not one for the limelight, or any sort of light, in fact. Sarah was a blend-into-the-background kind of woman. But today had to be acknowledged, and given nobody else was up to the task it had been left to her. Richie didn't seem at ease with the idea of presenting their sergeant with a celebratory cake.

'The timing isn't great,' he said, as Sarah rested the cake on her desk. Soon the icing would start to melt and all her efforts would be in vain.

'It's her birthday,' Sarah replied. 'The timing couldn't be any better!' Rifling in her drawer, she found the pack of candles that she had been looking for. 'Have you got a light?' Richie shrugged, but Sarah knew about the lighter in his pocket. 'Don't give me that, I know you're back smoking.'

'Is it any wonder?' he said, handing it over. 'Gabby's moods are driving me over the edge.'

He had a point. Their sergeant had been irritable for days and Sarah needed to get to the bottom of it. 'A nice bit of cake will lighten things.' She popped numerous coloured candles wherever she could fit them. In Sarah's mind, tea and cake were the answer to everything. It was a stellar effort, if she said so herself. The big square cake featured a marzipan figure of a woman sitting behind a paperwork-laden desk. She sported a small frown which Sarah believed captured Gabby's likeness quite well. Her short Afro hairstyle had presented more of a challenge, but Sarah was pleased with the overall effect. The words 'Happy Birthday, Boss' were emblazoned in police blue.

'Remind me why you're doing all this again?' Richie said, one eye on Yvonne who was waiting at the door, ready to signal their sergeant's return. Gabby was at a command meeting discussing team statistics and targets. Which was sure to compound her bad mood.

'Think about it,' Sarah replied, determined to remain optimistic. 'Soon she'll be too full of birthday cake to mention our performance last month.' Waving a hand, Yvonne trotted into the office on heels that were too high to run in. 'She's coming!'

'Action stations, everyone!' Sarah flicked the flint of Richie's lighter to each candle. The click of Gabby's expensive Italian leather shoes echoed down the corridor. She narrowed her eyes as she entered the office, immediately homing in on Sarah, who was holding her cake with both hands. 'Happy Birthday, boss!' she said cheerily. She wasn't brave enough to launch into song. If she did, she'd be doing it alone.

Gabby stared at the cake, her mouth downturned. 'That's a fire hazard. Put it out. You'll set the sprinklers off.'

'Don't you want to blow them out?' Not one to be put off, Sarah followed her to her desk. Apart from Richie, her colleagues had already returned to theirs. 'I couldn't quite fit fifty candles…' She took one look at her sergeant's frosty expression. 'I mean, forty-nine…' Gabby's expression was still rigid. 'Forty-eight?'

'Fine!' In one swift movement Gabby leaned forward and blew out the flames. 'Chop it up, dish it out and get back to work.'

Richie lingered long enough to give Sarah an 'I told you so' parting glance. But Sarah was not so easily dismissed. She acknowledged that she could be a major pain in Gabby's backside, given the number of times she'd told her, although she was never quite sure what she did to deserve it.

'Sarge…' she said, after Yvonne had taken the cake to divvy out, 'is everything alright?'

But her sergeant was leaving her desk. Another look from Richie, accompanied by a tight shake of the head. Sarah shrugged in response before following Gabby out the door. They had their own silent communication. In the police, you learned to develop your body language and recognise that of others. It was a safety mechanism. But today she chose to ignore Richie's warning.

She followed Gabby to the toilets. After checking the rest of the cubicles were empty, she knocked on the door. 'Taken!' Gabby thundered from the other side. But it wasn't that long ago that Richie had come to Sarah's rescue as he knocked on *her* cubicle door. That day, she'd been ready to walk out on it all. Today she was paying it forward. Spying a yellow hazard sign against the wall, she opened the main door and placed it outside. It would give them a few minutes' privacy at least. But as the door closed, Gabby emerged from the cubicle. Her eyes were moist with tears.

'I thought you were gone,' she sniffled, hiding her face as she blew her nose.

'Just setting up a diversion with the sign.' She watched Gabby splash her face before pulling a roll of paper towel and patting it dry. 'If you tell anyone you saw me like this . . .'

'I saw nothing,' Sarah said. 'And even if I did, I would never break the sanctity of the station loos.' Besides, they were friends. Neither would come out and say it, but their last big investigation had bonded them. A beat passed between them as Sarah shoved her hands deep into her trouser pockets. 'Sorry about the cake.'

'I told you all before, I don't do birthdays,' Gabby said flatly.

'And as someone who avidly ignores her own birthday, I respect that. But I couldn't let your fiftieth pass without . . .' She watched her sergeant's face crumple. 'Oh crumbs,' she muttered. 'I've really done it this time, haven't I?'

'It's not you,' Gabby sniffed. 'It's this bloody menopause. If I'm not sweating like a pig, I'm crying like a teenager. I can't control it.' Swearing beneath her breath, she dabbed her tears. 'Do you know how much sleep I got last night?' She didn't wait for Sarah to reply. 'Two hours. My sheets were soaked in sweat. These bloody hot flushes are driving me round the bend.'

'Is there anything I can do?' Having hit her forties, Sarah was not looking forward to the maelstrom of emotions which were surely headed her way. She searched her mind for some comforting words but came up blank.

Gabby blotted her forehead with paper tissue before checking the time. 'You should get going. You were due to go home over an hour ago. There's no overtime in the pot.'

'Will do,' Sarah said solemnly. She had only hung on to deliver the cake. The plan had been to give it to Gabby at the end of the day in case it went down like the forecasted lead balloon.

'Oh, and Sarah?' Gabby called. 'Do me a favour, will you? We've had a concern for welfare come in about a neighbour of yours. They're not answering the door and their car is in the drive. There was something about a couple of kids turning up at her door last night. Could you bring your radio and check it out? The PCSOs are on a training day and uniform can't spare anyone. She lives on the same road as you, so I thought . . .'

'Say no more.' Sarah raised her hand. She was secretly pleased. She would bring her police airwaves home and listen in on calls until her radio battery ran down. She'd have to mark herself as off duty, mind, otherwise control would be calling her up, sending her to God knows what.

She pushed the door open, ready to print off the police report and attach herself to the job. 'And Sarah?' Gabby said, clearing her throat.

'Yes?'

'Thanks for the cake.'

'You haven't tasted it yet.' Sarah grinned, before leaving her alone. She may be adept at decorating but her baking skills were lacking. She wouldn't be entering *The Great British Bake Off* just yet.

5

Yawning, Sarah pulled into her drive. Her home was situated on the corner in what had once been Slayton's old post office before they moved it into the heart of town. Sarah had come to love her little wisteria-covered cottage, which had a generous but somewhat neglected garden and warm, characterful rooms. As she learned to live on her own, she was making the place more homely, putting her stamp on things. It was a damn sight more loveable than Blackhall Manor which was situated on the way into town. Sometimes she wished she'd never inherited the place. For the last few months, she'd battled through red tape as she tried to have the place knocked to the ground. Thanks to some upmarket London lawyer, she was met with obstacles at every turn. It didn't help that it was a listed building, housing several species of bat. She jumped as a text notification rang out. An estate agent notifying her of a viewing.

'As long as it's not Simon Irving,' she said on the exhale of a sigh. Slayton's richest businessman had tried everything to purchase the manor house and its grounds. Another new development was on the horizon, which would mean chopping her woodlands down. Not on her watch. Slipping her phone into her pocket, she pushed thoughts of Irving and Blackhall Manor aside.

Her car door creaked loudly as she slammed it shut. 'Me too, old girl,' she said, feeling older than her forty-odd years. She brushed her fringe off her face. Her hair was too dark to be brown, but not dark enough to be black, somewhat like the storm clouds rolling overhead. *Bloody thunder can bloody well sod off,* she thought as she rubbed the back of her neck, trying to squeeze out the tension which had been building all day. All she wanted was to curl up on the sofa and watch Tom Selleck reruns on TV. But she had one last job to attend to first.

Rosemary Simmons lived at the end of her road, only five minutes' walk away. The concern had come in from her neighbour Jemma Foster, who had checked her voicemails and found that Rosemary had left her a message late last night. This afternoon, Jemma had rung her neighbour's doorbell and called her back, to no avail. Pulling back the sleeve of her jacket, Sarah checked her watch. It wasn't yet 6 p.m., but perhaps someone would be home by now.

A notification popped up from her Word of the Day app, *Cabal – a group secretly united in a plot.* She listened to the pronunciation before allowing it to roll off her tongue. She had always played with words. On some days it relieved boredom, on others it was a coping mechanism to ease her stress. But today she had no such concerns.

'Echo-November-seven-seven-three, TA,' she said to control as she recorded time of arrival on her airwaves radio. The call had come in hours ago and was updated low priority given Rosemary didn't live alone. Sarah reread the incident print-off that she had skimmed through before she left. It stated that in her voicemail Rosemary mentioned some neglected children who had turned up at her door. *Probably some scallywags messing around,* Sarah thought, scanning the page. *Or on the take for biscuits and lemonade.* But then parents kept a close eye on their kids in Slayton, especially late at night. Bad things happened to unsupervised kids in their town. Sarah scanned the rest of the short report. She didn't know Rosemary Simmons all that well, although Sarah was on waving terms with most of her neighbours. It seemed that Rosemary kept pretty much to herself. A woman in her eighties, she lived with her disabled son. They were more vulnerable than most on this street, and Sarah could relax once she confirmed all was well.

'Bugger,' she said, as rain fell in great fat droplets onto the broken pavement. She should have brought her umbrella. Holding her limp paperwork over her head, she glanced at the bungalow before her. A prickle of unease rose as she realised every curtain was closed. She slowed her steps. Good police officers didn't gallop up to the front door when attending a call-out, no matter how benign it seemed. They observed their surroundings. Took their time. At least, that's what her police training had dictated, not so long ago.

On the drive was a red Ford Fiesta which appeared kitted out for disabled use. She placed her hand on the bonnet. Cold. She glanced over her shoulder, noticing a net curtain twitch across the road. A sudden rumble of thunder made her shrink in her skin as each deafening boom shook the branches of a memory she'd spent her life trying to forget. The storm was growing in momentum as another flash of lightning tore through the sky. She pressed her finger against the stiff doorbell and waited, uneasy on the step. There was plenty of light left in the day. So why did it feel like shadows were closing in?

Fat drops of rain dappled the cement doorstep as she waited, shoulders hunched. 'Hello?' she called, bending to peek through the letterbox. The hallway was in darkness, all the doors closed. An eerie silence lay claim to the building. Sarah didn't like this one bit. She reached for her radio, alerting control. 'Echo-November-seven -seven-three, there's no response and all the curtains are closed. I'm going to check around the back.'

'Received,' the call handler replied.

It's probably nothing, Sarah told herself. *The kids have left and Rosemary has decided not to answer the door. Or maybe she caught the bus into town.* But still . . . as she walked the gravel path to the side of the house, she couldn't shift the lingering sense of unease. And then she heard it. A steady *thump thump*, coming from the back of the house.

The side gate was unlocked and the path opened out on to a vast mature garden. The sound was coming from the conservatory door, flapping open with each gust of wind. Rosemary's neighbour couldn't have checked around the back. Something was very wrong. Above her, darkening clouds chased day to night before its time. Sarah unclipped her metal baton and extended it with a flick of the wrist. 'Hello?' She wiped her feet on the grate before stepping inside to shelter from the rain. 'Mrs Simmons? It's the po—'

A flash of lightning illuminated the scene and the words died on her lips. She stared through the conservatory at a bloodied handprint on the far kitchen wall. It couldn't be, could it? Finding the light switch, she turned it on with the tip of her baton and stole into the kitchen. Her hand went to her radio. *Calm down*, she told herself. *See what's going on first.* Sarah was economical with her words when it came to updating control. On police airwaves, you were heard by all. In training school she'd stuttered nerve-stricken updates, her cheeks burning furiously with each mistake she made. It played in the back of her mind even now: make a tit of yourself over police airwaves and you never lived it down.

She had finally gained acceptance as a valued member of the team. The last thing she needed was her colleagues taking the mickey out of her. And now here she was, alone, staring at that red handprint, stark against magnolia walls. A rush of adrenalin flooded her system and her legs began to tremble. Blood. It was dried blood. On the counter was a tub of hot chocolate powder. A spoon lay on its side and a fly sucked on a sugar cube in a small glass bowl. She touched the kettle, knowing it would be cold. Policing wasn't just about doing. It was about feeling, hearing, sensing, smelling . . . and right now every fibre of her being was screaming at her to get out. She watched for shadows behind the glass door, her baton firmly gripped in her hand. Sarah knew these houses. The kitchen led into the hall and the living room was across the way. But who or what was waiting for her in there?

Her throat clicked as she tried to swallow. Her tongue felt glued to the roof of her mouth. She masked the feeling of dread by forcing confidence into her voice. 'Mrs Simmons? Rosemary? Are you in? It's the police. My colleagues and I are here to see if you're OK.' A small lie, but a signal to anyone within. With her baton raised, she entered the hall. The door creaked as she pushed it open, her training on forensics and Locard's principle firmly in mind. Powerful smells were being invoked in a house in which all windows were closed.

The metallic tang of blood filtered through to her nostrils. A weak gasp escaped her lips as the scene hit her with the force of a punch. The room looked like an abattoir. Splashes of blood patterned the walls, the carpet . . . Her stomach lurched as her lunchtime tuna sandwich threatened to make a reappearance. Behind the door was the body of a man, who had to be Rosemary's son, lying beneath an upturned wheelchair. He was on his side, his useless legs sprawled, throat slashed, one bloodied hand outstretched. But his eyes . . . A viscous substance oozed from his empty sockets as he lay, unseeing on the floor. Sarah's stomach dry-heaved at the sight. Staggering backwards, she bumped against the sofa and was confronted by the sight of Rosemary Simmons on the floor. Her chin tucked into her chest, she lay in a pool of congealing blood. Just like her son, her throat was an open wound, her eyes plucked from their sockets. Sarah could barely breathe as she took in the butchery.

Grasping for her radio, she backed out of the room. There was nothing she could do for these people. She needed to get the hell out of here until backup arrived. This time, there was no hesitation in updating control. 'Echo-November-seven-seven-three to control.' She waited for clearance to speak. 'Backup urgently requested. Both occupants deceased, their throats cut and their eyes . . .' She breathed through a wave of nausea. 'Their eyes are gone. Bring this to the attention of the duty DI.'

Her mouth had gone from being bone dry to pooling with saliva as the vision of the bodies loomed large in her mind. What sort of a monster had been here before her? Someone had taken sadistic pleasure from carving the victims up. She made it out the back door, gulping down breaths of rain-soaked air. The shower had abated and the garden was fragrant with petrichor. Two seconds of airwave silence was followed by multiple officers volunteering themselves to attend. Funny how it had been tumbleweed when the original call for welfare was updated on the system.

She walked down the garden path and tapped her retractable metal baton against the wall to shrink it back into position before sliding it into its holster. Her head was swimming. She wouldn't throw up, though. She wouldn't allow it. Another lurch. She could feel the neighbours' eyes watching her from the bungalows across the street as she swallowed back her horror. Her stomach stabilised, Sarah turned her thoughts to the vital next steps. She wished she had the duty car so she could secure the scene with tape. But all she could do was update the controller about what she had seen. Within minutes, the scream of sirens was cutting through the air.

Sarah's thoughts jostled for attention. She was no stranger to death. She had encountered cold-blooded killers before. But the brutality of the scene in that cosy cottage had floored her. She stood on the pavement, raising an arm as police cars drew close. The sky flashed overhead.

It was happening again. There was a killer in Slayton, and Sarah was right in the thick of it. But who would want to harm Rosemary Simmons and her son?

6

'Where have you put my boots?' Noah stomped around the caravan, wondering how a pair of size-eight Caterpillar boots could get lost in such a small space.

'There, out of the way.' His eighty-eight-year-old grandmother Olive cast a milky eye in his direction as she pointed to the cupboard next to the sink. 'Why? You off out again? Watch out for the gavvers. There's lots of 'em about.'

'Aye, will do,' Noah replied. Olive's cataracts may be robbing her of vision but her remaining senses offered more than most folks'. She could hear the scream of a police siren for miles. He plucked his boots from their resting place, careful not to deposit any crumbs of mud in her caravan. It was a garish affair, like many Romany trailers, all silver chrome and shiny leather seats. Her dresser proudly displayed her china on the left, and on the right, various Elvis plates hung from every spare inch of space. Every day her china ornaments were polished and placed in the exact position as before. To say she took pride in her caravan was an understatement.

'Just off for a ramble,' Noah said, running a hand through his mop of tousled hair. He wasn't fooling anyone. Olive knew where he was going. It was the only reason they were there.

'Aye, well, tread carefully.' She spoke on the breath of a sigh. 'You know what needs to be done.'

'I do.' Opening the door, he called his dog inside, commanding the Rottweiler to sit at Olive's feet. Storm was better than any security system. No harm would come to Olive in his care. Shaking off the rain, Storm gave a contented sigh as he settled at the old woman's feet. Needles of rain spiked the roof of the caravan. Noah was not one to run for an umbrella. He embraced the rain. He handed Olive her walking stick, his voice softening. Every day with the woman who raised him was a bonus, given her age. 'I won't let you down.' He spoke with conviction. A fiery determination to set things right. Because his grandmother wasn't the only person to have heard the children's whispers. He had heard them too.

Olive's hand rested on his. Her skin was like parchment but as soft as a newborn baby's. 'Mind yourself. I couldn't bear to lose you too.'

He thought about Olive as he walked the forest, taking trails only known to a few. Tiny droplets of rain sprinkled his skin, easing the humidity which had left the caravan like a sweatbox. Not that he'd spent much time in it. Like Storm, he preferred to sleep outdoors, and he had the insect bites to prove it. Taking a deep breath, he inhaled the scent of wet moss and the rich, sweet odour of hawthorn flowers beginning to bloom. It had been an odd year for nature so far, as flora and fauna bloomed weeks before their time. How anything grew in a forest so dank and dark was a mystery to him.

He walked beneath the dapple of leaves high up in the canopy. It was twilight all the time here. This wasn't a welcoming woodland, alive with birdsong as others he had stayed in. It was why his grandmother hated it here, only coming out of necessity and rarely leaving the safety of her trailer. But for Noah, each smell invoked a memory. And he did not shy away from them, no matter how painful they were. It was years since their last visit to Slayton, but he remembered each winding and crooked path as if they were etched into his skin. How could he forget, after everything that had happened here? He had left a piece of his soul behind that day.

Head down, he walked, the past playing a loop on an infinite movie reel. He thought about his son, a boy of fourteen. His mother was what Olive called a gorger, but that had never bothered him. But she couldn't hack the Romany lifestyle, and her need to settle was stronger than her love for him. He wondered what Josh was doing now and made a mental note to call him. He used to think that when he was forty, he'd have a whole brood of children who would also enjoy roaming the land. He should have known more than anyone that life never worked out as planned. He darted behind a tree as a passing van rumbled by. He was coming to the outskirts of the woods now. Evening was closing in, and the weather was moody.

Anger bloomed, raw and relentless, as he walked on, avoiding the main road, and saw the cottage in the clearing. He knew exactly who lived there. Its occupant, Arnold, had not been able to stay away forever. If he'd come back to face what he did, then Noah would gladly assist. But not yet. Such things had to be planned. He could not get caught and leave Olive and Storm on their own. There were a few cottages of this kind dotted about the woods. Most were standing empty, some were rented to holidaymakers who didn't know any better. He'd heard Arnold's cottage had fallen into disrepair after standing empty for so long. But nothing had prepared him for this. Vine leaves snaked up every spare inch of the walls, and the roof, once a slate grey, was now thatched with tufts of moss. Thick brambles surrounded the pathway, almost as tall as himself. It was as if the woodland wanted to reclaim it.

Arnold had always been a recluse, but now his wife had died, had he come home to face up to the pain he had caused? He'd been back for a year or more, but word had trickled out to Noah at a snail's pace. Better now than not at all. People still remembered. They did their best for his family, even after all this time. That's the way it was in the traveller community. They had long memories and looked after their own.

Shielding his face with his arm, Noah chose his footing carefully as he fended off the brambles. The front path had been cleared for its occupant but braving the hedgerow at the back of the cottage was a safer bet. He slunk behind the house, peering in through the tiny window which was thick with grime. The cottage was small and poky. The sort of place that was easy to forget. Noah took each window in turn. He was beginning to think he was on a fool's errand when he saw him, sitting in an armchair. Noah's jaw clenched in disgust. This Arnold was a smaller, shrivelled version of the man he remembered, but his hatred for him burned like a furnace, despite the fact that the two men had never met. Should Arnold look up, he would not recognise him. Not now; not back then.

He sat in the shabby armchair, staring blankly at the television. Noah thought about that night when the rain hammered against the roof of the caravan. His father's face, white with worry. It had been hard enough, bringing them up without their mother to help. He ground his back teeth. It never should have happened. He knew why the children were whispering. He could feel their malevolence skimming beneath the surface of this world. Too long had passed without answers. Yes, he knew what needed to be done.

7

'Jesus, Sarah, you don't do things by halves, do you?' Gabby stood, hands on hips as she watched officers cordon off the scene. 'I send you out for a concern for welfare and you bring me back a double murder.' They were standing outside the cordoned-off cottage as evening closed in. It was only 8 p.m., but the streetlamps had come on automatically as the sky faded to murky grey.

Sarah was about to reply when Daniel McGuire's tall, lean frame loomed over them both. 'So, you're the one I have to thank for this?' Tutting, he unzipped the hood of his forensics bunny suit. While his words were jovial, his features were grim. A DI from MIT, he was several years younger than Sarah, but he seemed to have aged since surveying the murder scene.

'Boss.' Sarah delivered a half-smile as she acknowledged his presence. The Major Investigation Team worked throughout the area but she'd heard the lilt of his Northern Irish accent on the airwaves from time to time.

'What's this about two wee kids?' He looked intently at Sarah. 'You live near here, don't yous? Have you seen any out and about?'

'No, boss,' she replied. 'We've got a bit of a stray dog problem, and some teenage joyriders in Lower Slayton, but kids don't go out unaccompanied. Not since . . .' Her words hung in the air. They all knew she was talking about the Midnight Man. But their last big case had been put to bed. Whoever murdered Mrs Simmons and her son was an unknown entity.

A thought occurred. 'You don't think the kids could have done *this* . . . do you?' It was with relief that Sarah had heard children's bodies had not been recovered from the scene.

'Doubtful.' McGuire shook his head. 'Whoever it was unleashed all sorts of holy hell. I'm not sure any wee bairn would have the

25

stomach *or* the strength for that.' His deep blue eyes seemed to probe her mind. 'You look shook, Noble. Why don't you go home? Get a stiff drink. We'll take it from here.'

Sarah cursed her inability to hide her emotions. She was a good cop but not a tough one. Good because she listened. Paid attention to the little things. Or at least, that's what she told herself. But tough . . . no. A born empath, she absorbed other people's pain. Hitting upon the scene without any prior warning had knocked the stuffing out of her. But admitting to it would make her look weak in the eyes of her sergeant . . . wouldn't it?

Unsure of how to reply, she stole a glance at Gabby. Her default expression was deadpan, but the look she was giving McGuire was glacial. Sarah's eyes narrowed as she absorbed the atmosphere between them. Gabby's dislike for the man was radiating from her in waves. Sarah cleared her throat. Her sergeant was the stiff-upper-lip type and normally, she'd have Sarah conducting door-to-door enquiries with the rest of the team. Right now, she didn't even acknowledge DI McGuire's concern.

'I presumed *we* were taking ownership of this case.' Gabby straightened to her full five foot seven height, still looking up at McGuire, who was watching crime scene officers enter and exit the scene. Something told Sarah that McGuire didn't miss much. He turned on a smile, going from serious to cheery in less than a second as he turned his attention to Gabby.

'I've given Saint Bernard the heads-up. He took a bit of persuading but he's happy for us to take control.' He switched his gaze to Sarah as Gabby failed to reply. 'You look knackered. Away with you, it's an order. Go home to your bed!'

Sarah raised an eyebrow as she absorbed the dynamics between Gabby and McGuire as McGuire ordered her to go home. He was not in the least bit ruffled by Gabby's obvious displeasure. Sarah didn't know many people who were prepared to go head-to-head with Gabby, but there was nothing she could do here. She was outranked. Their boss DI Bernard Lee was a rotund, good-natured sort who had taken Sarah under his wing. But lately he hadn't been himself. It wasn't like him to be going home early or handing over prime investigations, retirement looming or not.

Gabby conceded and nodded to Sarah to go.

'That was very gracious of you, Sarge,' Sarah said as they both left the scene. It wasn't like her to give up without a fight. They walked shoulder to shoulder to where Gabby had parked her car, which was near Sarah's home. The street was alive with twitching curtains, and several neighbours had ventured to their garden gate to watch the entourage of police and specialist teams. Both Gabby and Sarah were careful not to make eye contact. There was nothing they could tell them at this stage. The locals would learn more from the press once they got hold of it. Sarah only hoped the police managed to tell the victims' next of kin first. It didn't take a genius to work out that something awful had occurred. Crime scene tape flapped in the wind as it cordoned off some of the road. At some point the black van marked PRIVATE AMBULANCE would arrive to take the bodies away, but not before the coroner had viewed them in situ. An image of Rosemary Simmons' dead, empty eye sockets rose in Sarah's mind. She sniffed her sleeve. The smell had clung to her clothes. There was no way she was getting any sleep tonight.

'How are you feeling?' she said to her sergeant, not forgetting her outburst in the ladies' toilets.

'Nothing a dose of HRT won't fix,' Gabby replied staunchly. She was not one to stay down for long. The stink of car exhaust fumes grew as the road filled with traffic. Police were in the eye of the golden hour and Gabby would no doubt return to the station to assist. As if sensing her thoughts, her sergeant glanced back at the cottage with regret. 'If Bernard's given the case to MIT then he's the one in control.' She descended into low-level muttering, but Sarah could just about make her words out. 'The sooner he retires the better. He's taken his eye off the ball.'

Sarah nodded in agreement. Murders like this were high-profile and solving a case worked wonders for the team's reputation and morale. There was more to life than dealing with the endless burglaries and fights which had broken out in town.

'Should I come back to work?' Sarah said, as they drew level with Gabby's car. 'I don't mind . . .'

'Go home.' Gabby activated her central locking before giving Sarah the once-over. 'You look like shit. People around here are scared enough as it is.'

Sarah gave a weak smile. The quick and brutal follow-up was a defence mechanism. Gabby didn't want her thinking she was going soft because she had sent her home. 'See you in the morning, then.'

Sarah stepped onto the kerb as a police car drove past. Gabby was already in her car fastening her seat belt, her usual frown in place. It wasn't Sarah who was the cause. It was McGuire, she could tell. Gabby was not a fan. An Oxford graduate, he had risen up the ranks through a fast-track scheme rather than having the benefit of experience beneath his belt. Plus, he'd stopped her from entering the crime scene. But Sarah could see his reasoning. If CID weren't taking charge, then Gabby didn't need to physically see it. Soon there would be a wealth of photographs, exhibits and videos back at base.

Sarah walked the path to her house, uneasy in her skin. It seemed like a lifetime since she'd pulled up on her drive, planning her evening. She shoved the key into the lock, listening for sounds of life. She was greeted by her orange tabby, who delivered a low miaow of disgust. 'Sorry, Sherlock, are you hungry?' Sarah bent to welcome him into her arms. But her embrace quickly became a hoop that he jumped through. Sherlock was not one for cuddles and he ran ahead of her into the kitchen, his tail waving loftily in the air. It was just like any other evening, if it weren't for the image of two savaged corpses branded on Sarah's brain.

She picked up the post from the mat. It was junk, apart from one official-looking letter. She recognised the headed paper as soon as she opened it. It was from Simon Irving's solicitors, making another offer for Blackhall Manor. As the CEO of Irving Industries, he was one of the richest men in Slayton and well known to all. Tutting, Sarah threw it in the recycling bin. She wouldn't sell to Irving if he was the last person on earth. Discarding her jacket and shoes, she dished out a helping of stew into Sherlock's bowl. The thought of eating reheated chunks of meat made her stomach heave. She cast her eye at the floor that needed washing and the crockery gathering in the sink. It would have to wait. She was bone-weary but sleep was far off. She rested Sherlock's food bowl on the floor, then groaned as an alert for a Zoom call pinged on the laptop she'd left open and charging.

She'd forgotten all about the online meetup. Grabbing a bag of crisps, she settled on the sofa, her hand hovering over the invitation to join. She wanted nothing more than to find the TV remote, but she had only recently reunited with her schoolfriends. She shouldn't let things slide. She clicked accept, getting the tail end of Elsie's conversation.

'Why is it that brain cells, skin cells and even hair dies but my stubborn fat cells have been granted eternal life by the Lord?' Elsie's shiny pink face peered out from the screen as she noticed Sarah's presence. 'There you are. I thought y'all weren't going to show.' She was sitting against her headboard, adorned with the cats who shared her large bed. Given she was morbidly obese, it was where she spent a lot of her time.

'Sorry, I forgot,' Sarah groaned. 'I'm afraid I'm not great company tonight.'

'Rough day at work?' Maggie replied, glass of red wine in hand.

'Shoo!' Elsie interrupted as she shouted at her cat. 'Git your ornery butt away from the camera. Nobody wants to see that.' Her Southern American accent always made Sarah smile. It was nice seeing Elsie getting to grips with Zoom, even if her cats did get in the way.

'You'll hear about it soon enough,' Sarah said, unable to share the details of the crime until it hit the press. 'Just . . . don't answer the door to anyone you don't know, yeah?'

She watched her friends' faces fall. Elsie grabbed her mobile phone, no doubt searching her local neighbourhood groups – her online grapevine. 'Oh, Lordy.' She paled as she turned back to the screen. 'Is it true? There's been a double murder in Slayton?'

'Not again.' Maggie shook her head, before taking a large sip of wine.

'You don't know the half of it.' Months had passed since the Midnight Man. The town and its occupants were beginning to heal.

But this . . . this was unlike anything Sarah had ever seen. And as for lost children knocking on doors . . . Her friends' expressions reflected her own fear.

'Are you OK?' Maggie's frown deepened. 'You look a bit green around the gills.'

'I was first at the scene.' Sarah stared at her friends, each face etched with concern. 'It was awful. There was blood everywhere and . . .' She bit her lip, hastily stemming her words. The fact that the victims' eyes had been removed was being kept from the press. 'Sorry. I'm not meant to talk about it. Don't tell anyone, will you?' She directed the question at Elsie as she scrolled for news on her iPhone.

Elsie raised an eyebrow. 'Well, missy, common sense may not be a flower that grows in everyone's garden but you don't need to worry about me.'

'I know what you're like, Jessica Fletcher!' Sarah countered. But the quip was good-natured, and Elsie did not disagree.

'It'll be all over the papers soon.' Maggie filled the silence. 'You can tell us about it then.'

As Sarah plumped her cushion, a thought occurred. She hated to ask, but did so just the same. 'Has Elliott had any nightmares lately?' It was a loaded question. This was about far more than dreams. Elliott was an insightful little boy with an uncanny sensory ability that could not be explained in a rational way. But Maggie was shaking her head as the question left Sarah's lips.

'No, and I'm not going to ask him. Sorry, Sarah. You're on your own with this one.'

Maggie's gaze was on her wine glass. She would not meet Sarah's eye. And Sarah did not blame her for being protective of her child. Given Slayton's history, she had every right to be.

8

'Now now, y'all, quit your fussing.' Elsie greeted each cat in turn as she gave them a last saucer of milk. It had been quite the day. From the excitement of Sarah's news and the obesity clinic's pool session, she was all tuckered out. Despite having washed her hair, she could still smell the faint whiff of chlorine from her long mousy brown strands. Water therapy was one of the new methods of weight loss she had been encouraged to participate in. She enjoyed sitting at home writing, but getting out to the clinic was now part of her once-weekly routine. She'd felt like a walrus when she first waded into the pool, but the buoyancy that enveloped her when she was deep in the water was bliss. It was more than therapy. It was a lifesaver.

She approached her bed, peeking through her living room window for good measure. She wasn't ready to sleep upstairs just yet. The last time she walked up those steps she nearabout broke her neck falling down them again.

Keep movin' forward, she reminded herself, as she always did when her thoughts pulled her down. Sliding beneath the duvet, she took her laptop from her bedstand. Her son Christian was due to call. They were both night owls, and she would check out the black-eyed children as she waited to hear from him. Word on the street was that two strange kids called on Rosemary Simmons before she died. Her neighbour Jemma said Rosemary sounded spooked when she left her voicemail. But when the police called to the house, the children were nowhere to be seen. Elsie wriggled her toes beneath her covers as three of her six cats settled down at her feet.

A yelp escaped her lips as her computer's Skype application chimed and she smiled as she accepted the video call. She barely recognised her son these days. With his smart clothes and tidy haircut he was a world away from the nerdy young man who spent each night in his room. Christian would always be quietly spoken, but Irving had found him a flat to stay in midweek and a job in their Lincoln office which offered him respect. Nobody wants to piss off the boss's son, after all. As for her . . . she didn't speak to her baby daddy. Irving wouldn't give her the time of day. But she didn't get her panties in a bunch over that. He'd paid generous child maintenance, and for her treatment at the clinic. As a teenager, Simon Irving had made a bet with his friends that he could take her virginity – and won. She couldn't regret his cruel joke. Without it, she wouldn't have her boy, and he was her reason to get out of bed. The Simon Irvings of this world didn't do things out of the goodness of their heart – they thought the sun only rose in the morning to hear them crow.

'I heard about the murders.' Christian's voice was filled with concern. 'Are you OK?'

''Course I am, doodlebug. You don't need to worry about me.' But death had cast a shadow over Slayton once more.

'You're very pale,' he said, unconvinced. 'Are you sure you don't need me to come home?'

'Oh, *that*!' Elsie moved her laptop as her cat Felix joined her on her bed. 'I was researching black-eyed children and y'all made me jump.' She would have loved nothing better than for her son to come home. But he'd spent most of his life looking after her. She would see him soon enough.

'I've heard of them.' Christian sat up, interested. 'Wait . . . why are you looking them up?'

Elsie told him about Rosemary Simmons and her alleged visitors, stroking Felix as he settled down on her lap. 'Now everyone in Slayton is talking about black-eyed kids. I've read that if they follow you home, you're in deep do-do.'

'Pretty much,' Christian chuckled. 'But they're just an urban legend. You know how these things go. They're as real as the computer games I play.'

It was good to hear Christian sounding so sensible, but they both knew from experience that he was easily manipulated and some legends *could* come true. But she didn't want to talk about the Midnight Man today. They had agreed to leave him in the past where he belonged.

'Did you hear the story of the old couple in Vermont who answered their door to a strange boy and girl one night?' Felix purred rhythmically as she recalled the story. 'They asked to come in, saying their parents would be back soon. But the minute they stepped inside, the owner's cat kicked up a fuss. The woman said she made the kids hot chocolate while the man tried to tease out who they were.' Elsie grew serious. 'But when they asked to use the restroom, he saw their eyes were as black as the night.' It gave her chills to imagine it. 'Then the man's nose started spurtin' blood, and all the lights went out.' She shuddered as she recalled the tale. 'After the kids left, weird things kept happening. One by one, their cats either disappeared or died. Then the man got cancer. He said he'd never been so scared as when he looked into their eyes . . .' She stiffened as the radiator behind the bed emitted a long, low gurgle.

'I heard stories of them hitchhiking or asking for a lift,' Christian joined in. 'There have been sightings in Texas and in a pub in Staffordshire. It made front-page news.'

'Yeah, I read about that Texas reporter. They wanted to get into his car. He said they carried this feeling of impending doom. He couldn't get away quick enough.'

'You'll find lots of stories if you look for them online,' Christian replied. 'But maybe you're better off leaving that stuff alone. Especially now I'm not there . . .'

'Christian Abraham, hush your mouth. I'm not alone. My cats keep me company and my friends keep an eye on things. Besides . . .' She tapped the side of her nose. 'Sarah's a cop. She keeps me in the loop.' She treasured her friendship with Sarah and loved being kept in the know.

Christian scratched his chin. 'OK, Mom, just be careful. Make sure you lock up every night.'

As the call ended, Elsie warmed at her son's protectiveness. Reading between the lines, there was homesickness there too. He may only have been a short drive away, but it would do them both good to learn to cope on their own. There was a time when she depended on Christian for everything and felt the bitter edge of his resentment in return. Now he had a flat in the city, things were better between them when he came home.

She shifted in her bed, her breathing shallow as she listened for the slightest sound. There were no whispers outside her window, just the soft purring of her cats and the reassuring tick-tock of the clock on the wall. All the same . . . she closed down her laptop. She would leave the black-eyed children alone for tonight.

9

Wednesday, 4th March 2020

Elliott sat at the kitchen table, his feet swinging beneath his chair. Dust motes danced around him in a shaft of amber sunlight. They seemed to hold a life of their own. Elliott noticed the little things. He liked their little kitchen. It was small but warm, unlike his cold and unwelcoming bedroom which cast shadows on the walls. In the kitchen, his mummy's paintings brightened the space and his drawings were stuck to the fridge with turtle magnets he'd bought on a school trip. But today the room felt unsettling, the sound of his mother's humming feeding his unease. Usually, they listened to Smooth Grooves Radio at breakfast time. Elliott liked waking up to the sound of Maggie singing her favourite songs. But this morning the radio was off, and Maggie was humming a soap opera theme tune instead. Something was wrong.

He glanced at the empty wine bottle ready for recycling. Another bad sign. Elliott had learned about 'tells'. It was the way people leaked how they were feeling without knowing they were doing it. His mum's tell would have been funny if it didn't worry him so much. Not that he would let her know. She tried to keep bad things from him. But bad things had a way of finding him, no matter what. He searched his mind for a comforting thought.

'Did you know that tortoises live between eighty and a hundred and fifty years old, while turtles only live between twenty and forty years?'

'No, I didn't know that.' A smile rose to Maggie's face as she lifted the saucepan from the hob.

He wrinkled his nose at the smell of scrambled egg as she plated it up for them both. He would have been just as happy with Coco

Pops, but he liked it when she sat with him to eat. 'Everything OK?' she said, watching him closely as she sat and picked at her food.

Elliott nodded, shoving a forkful of scrambled egg into his mouth.

'It's just that . . .' Maggie sighed, lowering her fork onto the plate, 'last night, something bad happened in Slayton. You might hear people talking about it. I don't want you to worry. It has nothing to do with us.'

'Was it the children?' Elliott cleared his throat. But the question on his mother's face suggested he was wrong.

'What children?' Maggie tilted her head. 'Did you have a bad dream?'

Elliott shrugged before pressing his glass of juice to his lips. Thoughts of Mercy and Mikey made him feel a stone was stuck in his throat, and Mummy wasn't ready to hear about them. Not yet.

Outside, a car alarm pierced the air. 'When is Auntie Sarah coming round?' He wiped his mouth with the back of his hand. Sarah knew all about scary stuff. Sarah didn't think he was weird, like the other kids in school. He stared at his plate as he waited for a reply.

'She's very busy at work.' Maggie picked up her fork and jabbed at a piece of egg. 'You can always talk to me.'

Elliott chewed methodically, his gaze fixed on his plate. But his thoughts were with the hollow-eyed children and their sharp, cold breath on his skin. How could Maggie understand? But Sarah would. She knew what it was like to be on the outside of things. *Will you help us, Elliott? Will you help us to find our way home?* The memory of Mercy's words gave him goosebumps. Last night as he slept, he had seen Mercy and her brother, both veiled in red. But it wasn't just red for blood. It was red for anger too. What did they want from him?

10

An air of gloom hung over Slayton. Driving to work, Sarah watched townsfolk walking with heads down, wearing the same bleak expressions as when the last murder rocked Slayton. Today, parents held tightly onto their children as they walked to their school's breakfast club. A line of people waited at the bus stop, their faces long as they watched her drive past.

Dammit, Sarah thought as the police station security gates rolled open on their runners to allow her in. She had forgotten her watch. It was stupid, but not out of character. She'd been distracted, her thoughts on a loop as the murder scene replayed in her mind. Was it like this for other police officers? How did any of them get any sleep? Asking them would no doubt only highlight how young in service she was. She glanced at the building before her and chased the self-doubt away. If the last few months had taught her anything, it was that she was as good as anyone else in there. But there was still room for improvement. She needed to eat healthily, for a start. Given she'd left the house fuelled by toasted crumpet smothered in jam, she wasn't winning on that front yet. Some of her colleagues would have been in the office since dawn. Murder investigations demanded everything you had to give and more.

As she got out of her red Mini Cooper, the roar of a motorbike entering the car park drowned her thoughts. It was Richie, and she watched as he pushed the kickstand into place. She waited for her colleague to attach his helmet to the back. Security was tight in the police car park, with activated electric gates on runners which you needed a tag to pass through. Cameras were everywhere, more for the SERCO vans transporting prisoners to court than for them. In Slayton police station, suspects were called prisoners, regardless of whether they were attending court or being released on bail.

37

'You look tired,' Richie said, giving her a curious eye. 'Get any sleep?'

Last night, the forecasted dump of rain had finally shed, bringing an end to the thunder at last. The sound of rain against her windowpane had provided a backdrop to Sarah's thoughts as she'd lain in bed with her ginger tabby at her feet. 'A little,' she said, feeling guilty that she hadn't been able to stay on and help. Richie had worked late into the night helping officers with door-to-door enquiries, briefly checking in on her as he canvassed her road. All she had done was give him an umbrella to protect him from the apocalyptic downpour.

She looked him up and down, taking in his casual attire. It was not a look that Gabby – AKA 'the ball-breaker' – would approve of. 'What's with the tracksuit? Shouldn't you be wearing leathers?' It was how they started every day: he asked how she was and she found something to worry about in return.

An easy-going smile spread across Richie's face. 'I've just come from the gym. Suit's in my locker.' He pointed to her cheek. 'You've got some, um . . . Jam for breakfast, was it?'

'Crumpets, actually.' Grateful for the heads-up, Sarah rubbed at her cheek before entering the building.

The second she walked into the office she felt her sergeant's stare. Sarah's hand rose to check her face for a second time. It wasn't jam catching Gabby's attention, so what was it? She mentally recounted her movements at the crime scene yesterday. Had she left too early? Done something wrong? The air around Gabby felt charged as she drummed her red-varnished nails against her desk. The rest of the team were busy working but there was no mention of last night's case now that MIT had taken over. She approached Gabby's desk, which was near her own.

'Have MIT turned up yet, Sarge?'

Gabby raised her coffee cup in the air. It was emblazoned with the words BOSS LADY. 'Empty. Fill it. Then we'll talk.' Sarah swiftly set about the task. Coffee took precedence over most things, and the newest person in the team was responsible for keeping her sergeant's mug replenished. Although Gabby was wearing different clothes, she looked as if she'd been up half the night. Maybe it wasn't just newly qualified detectives who lost sleep when a murder came in.

Having made coffee for her team, Sarah finally took a seat. It felt good to be in the office. The place she once dreaded was finally feeling like home. She looked to her sergeant as she awaited news.

'MIT will be working out of our office.' Gabby nodded towards their DI, who was in conversation with Richie. 'They've requested outside help, so I'm giving them two of our most capable officers to assist with the case.'

'Oh. Right.' Sarah nodded, deflated. Usually when a big case came in, she would be taking statements and knocking on doors, but by the sounds of it, she may not get the chance. There was always plenty to do in Slayton, but she realised she had a vested interest in this case. The killer had been on her street.

'How friendly were you with the victims?' Gabby's words pierced her thoughts.

'Why?' Sarah's eyes widened. 'You don't think *I* had anything to do with it, do you?'

An uncharacteristic chuckle escaped Gabby's lips. 'I wonder what goes on in your head sometimes, Noble, I really do. I'm asking if you knew your neighbours, not if you finished them off.' She paused to sip her coffee. 'You can't work the case if there's a conflict of interest.'

'Work the case?' Sarah echoed Gabby's words. Was she one of the capable officers Gabby had been talking about? 'There's no conflict of interest. I barely knew them,' she quickly added.

Gabby leaned back in her chair. 'Then familiarise yourself with the case. McGuire will be here soon. I can't have that lot saying we're not up to scratch.'

A spark ignited in Sarah's chest. This was turning out to be an interesting day. She tugged at her knee-length black skirt, which she'd paired with a starched white shirt. According to her book on power dressing it made her appear authoritative, but now the day was under way she felt more like a waitress. Still, she could not contain her grin.

'You look like the cat that's got the cream.' Richie looked her over as they strode down the corridor to the briefing room where MIT were setting up. At least now he was wearing his suit, complete with a small silver pin in his lapel. Richie was a member of the British UFO Research Association. It had taken him almost a year to be accepted. It fostered a scientific examination of unexplained sightings as well as investigations into reports of 'high strangeness'. He'd explained it all to her one evening over a glass of wine. 'Most reports are complete BS,' he'd said as they'd chatted in the pub. 'It's the military sightings I'm interested in. Those guys have no reason to lie.' Sarah had absorbed it like a sponge, fascinated by his findings, particularly his thoughts on hypnosis and memory regression. Sarah was glad he trusted her enough to show her a side known only to a few.

But today their focus was on the murders and integrating with MIT. The team comprised half a dozen people who dealt with high-profile murders, along with outside help from specialist officers who hot-desked throughout the county, going to where they were needed. While they would be sharing the CID office, briefings would remain separate.

'Did you hear what Gabby said about us?' As they passed the intelligence posters and notifications of sports and social events, Sarah basked in the glow of her sergeant's words.

'Do I want to?'

'This time you do. She said she was giving the case to her two most capable officers. I didn't think for a second I was one of them.'

Richie snorted, his footsteps echoing down the hall. 'Don't be taken in by that. She said most *capable* officers, not the best. She knows that if anyone can deal with this weird shitshow, it's us.'

Sarah's smile faded. 'What do you mean?'

'It's not your run-of-the-mill crime. It's a high-profile case. If we don't get the result the public want, consider yourself thrown under the bus.'

'No. Gabby wouldn't do that.'

'Maybe she wouldn't, but if things don't go to plan McGuire will need *someone* to blame, and it won't be a member of his team.'

Sarah slowed her pace, sobered by his words. Suddenly she wasn't in a hurry to get to the briefing room anymore. She nodded at a couple of officers as they passed her in the hall. She would make the best of the situation. She would not let Gabby down. 'You managed to get someone to take over your caseload?' Most officers kept their case files for the purposes of continuity and victim care.

'Yeah,' Richie replied. 'Yvonne's been given the stuff that couldn't wait. She's well pissed off.' Yvonne wouldn't appreciate being left behind, but now that Sarah thought about it maybe she was the lucky one. Sarah's nerves bubbled up as they entered the briefing room. She'd been excited to work with MIT. But now she was wondering what she had let herself in for.

11

The briefing room was bustling as the officers set up the landscape for a busy day ahead. The space was large enough to hold several teams of officers, with generous windows flooding the room with light. The room buzzed with a sense of urgency. This was a fast-moving investigation. Every resource would be offered up for a quick result.

'Alright, Gav? Need a hand with that?' Richie approached a harried-looking middle-aged man as he updated the boards.

'Richie, me old mate, how the hell are ya?' Gav responded enthusiastically, shaking him heartily by the hand. Their banter quickly steered towards football. Sarah envied Richie's popularity as she stood, arms folded, waiting to be told what to do.

''Scuse me!' A young man bustled towards Sarah holding two chairs. 'Sorry.' Sarah sidestepped him, feeling like a spare part. She turned to DI McGuire who was speaking to an officer connecting a laptop to the briefing equipment. She'd heard Rosemary's next of kin had declined a family liaison officer, who could have established full victim background and created a detailed family tree. Sarah presumed that task would now be passed on to her, along with the usual house-to-house enquiries.

'Ah, Noble.' McGuire took her to one side. She followed him obediently to the corner of the room. 'I hear you're embedded in the community.'

She *did* feel at home talking to regular people – well, as regular as they could be in Slayton.

'You could say I understand them,' she replied, reminding herself to be more forthright. If what Richie said was true, she'd have to stand up for herself, particularly when embroiled in an investigation as serious as this.

'Good.' McGuire stood, hands in his trouser pockets. 'Revisit whoever wouldn't answer their door last night. Get yourself out there later today and see what you can find out.'

'Do you have any suspects in mind?'

'All the answers are out there.' McGuire winked. 'We just need to find them. They're a nosy bunch down that road. Someone out there knows who called on Rosemary and her son last night.'

Sarah folded her arms. The residents of Lower Slayton had a right to be nosy, given what had gone on. 'Have you made any headway with forensics?' Sarah spoke forcefully as McGuire turned to walk away. She cleared her throat, her cheeks flushed as Richie glanced over.

McGuire checked his watch. 'Briefing is in ten minutes, you're staying, aren't you?'

'I am?' Sarah coughed. 'I mean, I am. Yes.' She hadn't expected to be asked. Given she was still on restricted duties, she spent most of her time outdoors.

'There's just one thing . . .' McGuire lowered his head. 'Everything you hear in this room is private. The case has been updated as sensitive. You can only share what we release to the press.'

'Absolutely.' Sarah nodded furiously. But it wasn't her colleagues she was worried about, it was Elsie and Maggie, the armchair detectives of Slayton who had a way of prising things out of her. She would have to be on her guard.

'Good!' He clapped his hands, making Sarah flinch. 'Because after briefing, you and Richie can revisit the Simmons house. CSI are done with it but the scene is still secure.'

'Sure thing, boss.' Sarah swiped her fringe from her face, trying to sound positive. But she knew what awaited them. Dried blood, flies, and the return of earlier memories. If someone *had* turned up at Rosemary Simmons' front door, her neighbours would not have missed it. It was just a matter of getting them to talk.

She tuned back into McGuire's narrative. 'Then before you clock off, call in on the travellers camped up in Blackhall Woods. See what they know. I'd send someone from the team, but we don't want to go in mob-handed. It's better coming from you.'

'With all respect, boss, why me?' Sarah tilted her head, trying to figure out his angle.

'You own the land, don't yous? You don't have to mention you're a copper, best not to get their backs up.'

'How did you know I owned the land?'

McGuire tapped the side of his nose. 'There's not much that gets past me, Noble. Not much at all. It's not a problem, is it? You've not had trouble with them in the past, or you would have called it in.'

'No, I haven't. If it's the Coopers, they stay a few days and clear up before they leave.'

'Good!' McGuire replied cheerily. 'Put some feelers out and report back to me. If we need to visit them in a police capacity later, then at least you'll have built up a rapport.'

Sarah tried to look happy about it as she clutched her notebook and pen. She had just joined the team; she couldn't very well say no. But the truth was, she barely knew the travellers who occasionally visited the woods. It *had* to be the same family, nobody else stayed there for long. The woods were too dark and unwelcoming, with high trees blotting out the light and leaching any warmth from the day. The security company Sarah hired kept an eye on things, and travellers were welcome if they respected the land. Sarah would not visit in her capacity as a police officer. Nor would she question them about what had occurred.

She watched McGuire as he strode away. One thing was sure: he was thorough. How had he known so much about her? But he wasn't behaving like your typical DI when a murder investigation came in. He wasn't just calm . . . he was positively cheery. No wonder people were wary of him. She exchanged a look with Richie and knew he was thinking the same thing.

12

Sarah hurriedly approached the Tesco Metro, her bag for life in hand. She didn't have long. Normally she didn't come to the far end of town, but it had been worth the extra distance to nip home and pick up her watch. She'd missed the little beeps and reminders to hit her daily step count goal. If she was going to eat sandwiches and crisps, she could at least try to burn them off. She pulled on her face mask, inhaling the tang of antiseptic as she pushed open the door. Recent news reports were worrying as they discussed the virus hitting the world with force.

Sarah fiddled with her colleagues' cash. If she wasn't buying syndicate lottery tickets, she was on the sandwich run. The team may be under pressure, but they still needed to be fed and Slayton police station did not have much of a canteen. Besides, it was a relief to escape the crime scene images on display in the briefing room. It wasn't that she couldn't cope with the sight of the hollowed-out eye sockets – it was the itch at the back of her brain telling her it was going to happen again. There was no evidence to suggest it, but she couldn't shake a sense of impending doom. She looked at the people around her, heads low, shuffling through the aisles. Perhaps her perspective was tainted but Slayton felt off-kilter today.

Her spirits brightened as she heard a familiar booming voice in the next aisle, but as she turned the corner she hadn't expected to see her DI, Bernard Lee, pushing a wheelchair.

'Hello,' Sarah said, her smile fading as she approached and saw the troubled look on his face. Sarah hadn't seen Bernard's wife in months. Not only had she aged since Sarah had last seen her, she was also wheelchair-bound. She looked so small and vulnerable next to her husband's chunky stature. Helen couldn't have been any more than sixty years old.

'I want to go home,' she groaned, tugging at the elastic of her mask.

'And you will, my love, in a second. We're here to get milk, remember?' Bernard gave Sarah a pained look. 'Sorry. I'm afraid you've caught us at a bad time.' Lately he had been taking extended lunch breaks. Now Sarah could see why. No wonder he'd been happy to hand over the investigation. It seemed he had a lot to contend with.

'Hello, Mrs Lee, how are you?' Sarah said, but Helen seemed agitated. She raised a bony finger and beckoned Sarah in. Sarah bent to hear her whispers. Her breath was stale, her teeth coated in a film of plaque, a world away from the slim, well-groomed woman Sarah had encountered in the past.

'Call my husband. I want to go home.'

Sarah looked at her quizzically. 'Your husband?' she echoed, checking she had heard right. The woman nodded fiercely, staring at Sarah with red-rimmed eyes.

'Darling, I *am* your husband.' Bernard squeezed his wife's shoulder. It sounded like a well-worn response.

'You're an old man!' Helen snorted, growing agitated as she flapped his hand away.

Sarah gave Bernard a knowing look before turning back to his wife. 'Tell you what, why don't I grab you the milk, then we can get you home.' Helen replied with a tight-lipped nod.

'Why didn't you tell me?' Sarah followed Bernard as he pushed Helen towards the dairy aisle. She was quiet now, her eyes vacant. Sarah had seen this before. Her grandfather had Alzheimer's before he died.

'Helen wouldn't want people's pity. What good would it do?' Bernard walked with the stance of a defeated man. Only now could Sarah see the toll his wife's illness had taken on him. His face was lined with worry, his clothes creased. Everything clicked into place. This was why he was considering taking early retirement from a job that he loved.

'Here you go,' Sarah said, passing Helen the milk. She returned her attention to Bernard, keeping her voice low. 'You should have told us. We could have helped.'

Bernard's words were stern. 'I know you mean well, so don't take this personally, but I'd rather handle this alone.'

But Sarah was not so easily dissuaded. 'Is this why you're taking early retirement?'

Bernard sighed. 'Nothing's set in stone. If Helen settles into her care home then I might stay on.'

'Can we go home now?' Helen craned her neck to look at them both. 'I'd like to go home.' Sarah looked down and saw she was wearing two different shoes. Both black, both slip-ons, but one had a bow and the other did not.

'Of course we can go, love, whatever you want.' Bernard smiled at his wife. Sarah's heart felt heavy as she watched them both. 'There must be something I can do . . .' she began to say, but Bernard cut her off.

'There is. Do your shopping, get back to work and don't breathe a word of this to anyone. I mean it, Sarah. This is a private family matter. You know how people talk.' It was most likely why Bernard had taken his wife shopping on the far side of town.

'You know where I am.' Sarah squeezed his arm. 'Bye, Mrs Lee, nice to see you.'

Helen's gaze had turned inwards as she sat clutching her litre of milk. *Poor Bernard*, Sarah thought. Helen was fading like an old photograph, and Bernard was struggling to cope with her care. Alzheimer's was a cruel mistress. When the person you loved looked at you with the eyes of a stranger, two different shoes were easily overlooked.

13

As the day progressed, Sarah compartmentalised her encounter with Bernard for another time. She would try speaking to him later when he was more receptive. Right now, she was standing on the road outside Rosemary Simmons' bungalow, channelling all her focus into the case. Today, time had slipped through her fingers as effortlessly as sand. With each hour that passed, her frustration grew. Time was their biggest enemy in cases such as these. Evidence eroded, memories faded and perpetrators got further away.

'You OK to go in?' Richie watched as Sarah slipped on her forensics bunny suit. Sweat was beading her forehead as she wrestled her way into what felt like a giant plastic bag. It didn't help that she was wearing a skirt. She swore as she pulled it up while trying to retain her modesty.

'I'm OK,' she grunted, zipping the suit over her chest. 'Why wouldn't I be?'

'No reason.' Richie grinned. 'But I'm not sure those suits were cut out for skirts.'

'Tell me about it.' She approached the officer in charge of scene guard and threw him a sympathetic glance. She knew the boredom of standing at a scene for hours on end. The backs of your calves aching. Trying not to think about going to the loo. Then handling the never-ending questions of neighbours and passers-by.

Her thoughts evaporated as she stood at the front door. Had the children knocked or rung the doorbell? The plastic buzzer was dusted with dark fingerprint powder. CSI had recovered fingerprints after blitzing the scene in record time. But nothing matched police records – not even the bloodied handprint on the wall. It had not belonged to either occupant – or to a child, for that matter. The possible presence of children added a bizarre twist to the case. She followed Richie

48

inside, inhaling the distinctive smell of decay that could only come from a corpse even when it had long been transported away.

Sarah balanced on the stepping plates, taking in her surroundings. Silence had a different quality after such brutal violence, and the house felt muted in the wake of the double tragedy. The hall was small and narrow, each wall covered with family photos which were a timeline of events. Births, communion, confirmation, marriage. But photos were snapshots of the life people wanted to portray. They did not reflect reality, or the secrets their keepers wanted hidden from the world. According to briefing, Rosemary's son divorced from his wife not long after his workplace accident. He had no children of his own, no relations in the area, or friends with young children. Enquiries were still ongoing but there was no explanation for the visitors at their door. According to intel, Rosemary's eyesight was failing and her glasses were found where she fell. The sound of passing traffic filtered through. The crime scene cordon had been shrunk, allowing cars to pass by. But the house was still their domain – for now.

She knew why McGuire had sent them here. Briefings were good, as was the video recording of the scene. But nothing could beat physically being inside the home. The last time she was here, her presence was tainted by a mixture of horror and panic. Today's visit would sharpen her senses and motivation to do everything she could.

'The conservatory door was open.' Sarah's voice broke the silence. 'They could have come in the front door and escaped out the back.'

'Jesus,' Richie gasped, taking in the scene. It was as if someone had dipped a paintbrush in blood and flicked it up the walls and ceiling. 'That's some spatter. They must have cut a main artery.'

'They cut, they gouged.' Sarah shook her head. 'It was like walking onto the set of a horror movie.' She thought of Maggie and Elliott, of Elsie and her sergeant, Gabby, all living in the area. All vulnerable to attack. And what about her, just a few doors down? She stared at the blood-encrusted carpet, sucking in a deep breath and instantly regretting it. The bodies had been removed, but their outlines were visible. A skid mark suggested the killer had slipped as they made their escape. It explained the handprint as they steadied themselves. To Sarah's left, two thin red tyre marks stained the carpeted floor.

'Geoffrey's wheelchair?' Richie said, following her gaze. Sarah responded with a nod. Early forensics suggested Rosemary had been murdered in front of her son. Even the light fitting was dotted with red. He must have felt so helpless, watching the horrors unfold. *To think, that one human could do this to another.* Sarah imagined the scene. *And for what?* She raised a finger to her nose to stem the stench lingering in the air.

'Geoffrey's throat was cut, just like his mother's. But their eyes . . .' Her gaze was haunted as she stared at Richie. 'Why did they take them out?'

Her colleague's face was pale but composed. 'Because they're a monster.'

The moment lingered as Sarah continued to process the scene. Richie approached, his suit rustling as he touched her arm. 'We'll catch them. They're not above the law.' Sarah nodded, not trusting herself to speak. This had happened just a short walk from where she lived. Was the killer a stranger to Slayton, or were they home-grown?

14

As he trudged along the outskirts of the woodlands, Arnold kept his head down. His balding scalp was wet with perspiration beneath his peaked cap. At least it was cooler in the forest. There were no peering eyes to recognise him, no awkward questions from townsfolk. His gaze roamed over the treetops as something scurried overhead. *No human eyes, anyway*, he corrected himself. Tizzy, his Yorkshire terrier, was yapping incessantly. She was his wife's dog as far as Arnold was concerned, but Mary had died some time ago. Tizzy was too highly strung to be a decent companion, but at least she forced him out of the cottage for her daily walks.

He glanced over his shoulder as he ambled up the path to his cottage. His wife's words rose from his memory banks, as they did each time he ventured out. *Nobody's looking at you, Arnie. Don't be so paranoid.* Mary thought he was unhinged, but then Mary hadn't known the truth. In Ireland, it had been a relief to walk down the street without fear of being recognised. Even then, he'd half-expected one of the travellers to catch up with him. And now with Mary having met her maker, he was back where it all began.

Why had he come back here? The same reason why he hadn't sold his old cottage, he supposed. He hadn't been able to stay away. Decades had passed since the incident, but the guilt he harboured was a parasite burrowed under his skin. It was twelve months since he'd returned to his cottage in the woods. Twelve months of waiting for a knock on the door that never came, but the whispers did. He heard them each night as he drifted off to sleep. Sometimes they came through his keyhole when he was kicking off his shoes in the hall. It was enough to give him a heart attack. But when he stared through his grime-streaked window, there was nobody there. Now the town was alive with gossip, and he had made his way to Rosemary's house to see if the rumours were true. The sight of the crime scene tape told him all he needed to know. The past was knocking, just not at his door. Not yet.

Negotiating his overgrown path, he mumbled his discontent as he tried to balance his bag of shopping, the dog lead and house keys to let himself in. His face grew slack at the thought of what awaited him. Rosemary and her son were dead. They had not gone into the night quietly. Their demise had been far from the blessed release he imagined himself facing one day. Yet he remained, just the same. He unclipped the dog lead, dropping his bag of bacon, eggs and bread on the kitchen counter. He plodded into the living room, taking comfort in the soft ticks and chimes that were a kind of music to him. Clocks of every variation and size surrounded him. They sat on the mantelpiece, his carriage clocks and decorative ornaments with embedded timepieces. The bigger clocks hung on the wall: cuckoo clocks, novelty clocks and clocks which told you what time it was anywhere in the world. In the hall, his grandfather clock chimed with precise regularity. His collection had grown over the year. Anything was better than silence.

It did not take long to get the open fire going, and the faint spits and crackles offered further comfort in the desolate space. He sat, watching the flames flicker, Tizzy snoozing on a newspaper at his feet. A dart of fear shot through the moment of peace as the doorbell rang. Tizzy yapped furiously as the doorbell emitted a sudden *brrring*. 'Shush!' Arnold gestured, flapping his hand to shut her up. He rose from his armchair and squinted through the lace curtains as he felt a presence nearby. It was a woman, by the look of it, someone official in an ill-fitting suit. A charity collector? No. They didn't come this far out. She had to be police, and she was walking to the window, having given up on the door.

Ducking away from the glass, Arnold pressed himself against the wall. There was no way he was talking to the police. He knew how these things worked. They would be making enquiries with Slayton townsfolk, but they didn't usually come this far out. Had they worked out the connection? The thought made his stomach churn. They couldn't have. The palms of his hands lay flat against the wall as the woman peered through the glass. He looked around the darkened room, the weak lamp in the corner barely enough to help him find his way. It was years since the curtains had been fully opened. He couldn't remember the last time a window had let in some fresh air. Satisfied the intruder had gone, Tizzy finally calmed down. Arnold had gained a reputation as a loner over the last year. The crazy old man with the dog, who didn't answer the door. He shuffled back towards the window and watched the woman leave. *Peace for now*, he thought. But she would be back. His legs felt weak as he found his way to the chair. His gaze fell on the picture of Jesus which hung on his wall. Arnold cringed beneath the judgement of what he had once seen as a kind and loving deity.

'Stop looking at me,' he whispered, his words an anguished whine. 'I said, stop looking at me!' He grabbed a doily from the sofa and hung it over the frame. That was better, for now. But he was enslaved by a guilt he would never escape. God would judge him when his day of reckoning came. He fell down in his chair and buried his head in his hands.

15

Elliott didn't know where the whispers were coming from. He woke from the smog of sleep to hear faint scratching at his windowpane. He pulled his duvet up to his chest as if it were a force field. The sudden extinguishing of his nightlight made him whimper. They were here.

Mercy and her brother stared with hollow eyes from the end of his bed. 'Help us,' she whispered. 'Help us find our way home, Elliott.' They raised their hands towards him, their fingers lavender white. Elliott's eyes rolled to the back of his head as he became part of their world.

Taking a sudden breath, Elliott jolted awake. His heart was thumping too fast, his pyjama top damp with sweat. His nightlight stars still floated on his ceiling. It had been a dream. He sucked on his bottom lip, peeping at his window. Slipping out of bed, he drew the curtain across, his tummy in knots. But there was nothing there apart from a tree. Had the branches been tapping against his window? He hated this house, where it felt like winter all year long. It was just him and Maggie now that Daddy was gone. Sometimes when he couldn't sleep he heard her crying in her bedroom, and it made him want to cry too.

He turned away from the window as he caught the sound of a TV theme tune coming from the hall. His spirits lifted instantly. It was *Blue Bloods*, which could only mean one thing. Slipping on his Gruffalo slippers, he trotted quietly down the hall. His friend Jahmelia usually babysat, but she had a cold. The sight of Sarah in front of the television flooded him with relief. She caught his eye as he lingered in the living room doorway and immediately grabbed the TV remote.

'Oops, sorry,' she said, turning it down as the credits rolled. 'Did I wake you?'

Elliott shook his head. His gaze crept to the clock on the wall. The big hand was on the twelve but the small hand was on the ten. Mummy had made him go to bed early and now he knew why. She didn't want Elliott to talk about the bad things happening in Slayton. But Maggie didn't understand. Bad things were like rainstorms. They came if you talked about them or not.

He took his place beside Sarah on the sofa. Some grown-ups didn't like his quietness. But his Auntie Sarah didn't mind. They spoke without words. He watched her face change as she took in his. That was the way it was with Sarah. Whatever you were feeling, Sarah felt it too. Mummy called her a 'fixer', but she was more than that.

'Bad dream?' Sarah said, tilting her head. Elliott nodded, the words stuck in his throat.

'Would you like me to make you a hot chocolate?' She smiled. 'I quite fancy one myself.' But the image of two mugs of hot chocolate on a tray brought forth cold dread.

'No!' Elliott squeaked, grabbing her by the wrist. 'Don't go.'

Elliott relaxed as Sarah sat back down. Her hand was warm as it rested on his back.

'Sweetheart, what's wrong? You're safe here, you know that, don't you?'

Elliott nodded in response. Mercy and Mikey weren't coming to hurt him. He did know that. They wanted to go home. But their eyes were so dark, their cold hands grasping to pull him in. Elliott couldn't help but feel scared.

'The children,' he said. 'They're lost.' His head bowed, he tugged on his pyjama sleeve. Mummy had told him not to talk about his dreams.

'Sarah's my best friend,' Maggie had said one night, as though warning him. 'But she's a detective too, and that will always come first.' But Elliott thought police were there to keep you safe. He rubbed the sleep from his eyes. Sometimes grown-ups made no sense.

'Who are the children, Elliott?' Sarah brushed her hair from her face.

That was her 'tell'. Sarah tugged her fringe when she was worried. Elliott's heart fluttered. The last time he told Sarah secrets, she nearly died. He shrugged instead.

'That's OK.' Sarah smiled. 'You can talk to me when you're ready. Now how about we get you to bed?' Elliott yawned, taking her hand as she offered it.

As she went to put him in bed, Sarah shivered. 'It's freezing in here. Do you want to sleep on the sofa until Mummy gets home?'

Elliott brightened. 'Yes, please.' He looked at Sarah in wonder. She knew. This was the room where the bad dreams came. He followed her back to the living room as she set up a bed on the sofa in front of the TV.

'There you go.' She stroked his hair as he snuggled beneath the duvet. The lights were dimmed and the room was warm. He was safe. But Mercy had stepped inside his body as if he were a onesie and zipped him up. In his dreams, she had made his mind her home.

Elliott blinked as he awoke to voices in the doorway. Maggie was home from her shift at the hotel. He squeezed his eyes shut as he listened to their whispers. 'I'm grateful, Sarah, you know I am. But Elliott's had a tough year. It's important to keep him in a routine.'

'Why didn't you tell me he was having bad dreams?' Sarah replied.

Maggie sighed. 'They've only just started. I was hoping it was a one-off. Is that . . .' She paused. 'Is that why he's sleeping on the sofa?' Elliott couldn't see Sarah's face but he guessed she was nodding in reply.

'Have you ever thought about moving out of this place and starting afresh?'

Elliott listened as his mother took off her coat. 'Leave Slayton? I couldn't. I have a support network here.'

'God, no, don't you ever leave Slayton. I meant buying a house for yourself. My next-door neighbour is putting her place up for sale. I think they were spooked by the murders.'

Maggie's dark chuckle seemed to warm the room. 'And you think that moving *nearer* a murder scene will make Elliott sleep better at night?' Elliott strained to listen to the reply.

'Fair point,' Sarah said, her voice low. 'But wouldn't you like to move somewhere a bit closer to work?'

'This is all I can afford to rent until my divorce is settled,' Maggie replied. 'As much as I'd love to be your next-door neighbour, I'd never scrape up enough cash for a deposit.'

It made Elliott sad to think about his parents splitting up. He missed his daddy a lot, but Maggie said he needed the doctors now, and all the other people who were helping him. He wasn't the same person anymore.

Elliott sank back into his pillow as Sarah pulled a throw from the armchair. 'You don't mind if I kip here tonight, do you?'

'You'll never sleep on that battered recliner,' Maggie whispered, hovering over Elliott on the sofa. 'Take the spare room.'

'I'd rather get into your fridge,' Sarah chuckled, her boots thudding against the floor as she kicked them off. 'You look bushed. Get to bed. I'll keep an eye on Elliott.'

He settled back under the covers. There would be no more nightmares tonight.

16

Thursday, 5th March 2020

Sarah stepped carefully through the woodland, the early morning breeze playing with her hair. The people she needed to see were deep inside the forest and you could only come so far by car. She grimaced as her foot skidded in the black, slippery earth. She'd woken with a crick in her neck this morning but at least she'd managed to get some sleep. It had warmed her to see Elliott happy and bright as he readied himself for school. Sarah had taken his words from the night before to heart.

Was it coincidence that he had dreamed of lost children the same time two people were killed? He could have heard about the murders at school. Word had spread of Rosemary's nocturnal visitors, who were possibly the last to see her alive. Elliott may not have told her a lot, but it was enough to spur an early visit to the travellers on her land. Yesterday she had visited Arnold Smith, sure he was inside. But as she knocked on the door of his woodland cottage, an unwelcome feeling grew. His dog kicked up a fuss, but there was no sign of Arnold himself. Hopefully she would begin her working day by ticking off at least one outstanding task. She knew a little of Noah Cooper's sad family history but had not linked it to recent events until now.

She trudged on, the smell of rotting moss rising around her. This was jeans and wellies terrain. In the police, you never knew where the day would take you, which was why her wellington boots were kept in her car. She paused at the sight of a chrome caravan parked up in the clearing next to a shiny grey van. A small fire emitted a plume of smoke which danced up to the high treetops. Next to it was timber chopped from fallen branches which had been made into home-made seats. At the side of the caravan was a small washing-line, its clothes hanging limply in the dead morning air. They would not dry quickly under the gloomy canopy. The air felt different in this part of the woodland. Sarah's flesh crawled as she was overcome by a sudden chill. She rubbed the back of her neck. Above her, tree branches were thick with crows. Their caws were low and grating as they communicated in the language of the forest. It reminded Sarah why she didn't come here. She felt like an intruder in the very place that she owned.

She returned her attention to the washing-line, and the men's jeans and plaid shirts hanging next to a string of women's black dresses and old-fashioned slips. Would the locals assume the travellers were somehow involved in the case? It seemed like quite a coincidence, them turning up prior to the murders. Given their history, they had every reason to feel animosity towards Slayton. Sarah could imagine the town meetings and the accusations which would fly as scared locals lashed out.

Approaching the camp, she was welcomed by the sweet smell of burning timbers as they crackled their last breath. Her attention was drawn to a stocky black Rottweiler, whose hackles were raised. 'Hello, boy.' Sarah extended her hand as she approached. But the dog did not appreciate strangers on his patch. He sat on his haunches, a rumbling growl escaping through his teeth, and didn't break eye contact as Sarah stepped to the side. Did he belong to the pack of strays that wandered around Slayton, or were his owners inside?

'Hey there,' Sarah said softly, taking another sidestep towards the caravan. 'I come in peace.' But nobody was coming to her rescue as the dog vocalised his discontent. *Bloody hell*, she thought as he stood, teeth bared. *What am I supposed to do now?* Any sudden movements in either direction and he may pounce.

'Hello?' she called out to the occupants of the caravan. 'Anybody there?' She sensed movement inside, but it seemed nobody was in a rush to answer. She had walked all this way; she wasn't going home now.

'Can you call your dog off, please?' she shouted. 'It's me, Sarah Noble. I own this land.' She caught movement of a net curtain and exhaled an exasperated sigh. 'There's no problem, I just want a quick word.'

She hadn't realised the dog had closed in on her until she looked down. His large honey eyes were unblinking as they locked on her. His coat revealed a criss-cross of silver scars, but he was obviously well fed. 'Easy, boy . . .' Sarah tried to mask her nerves. 'You've been through the wars, haven't you?' Without warning, the dog lunged at her extended hand. Sarah's yell echoed around the forest as his sharp teeth punctured her flesh. 'You little sod!' she gasped, trying to stem the blood that trickled from the bite wound. At last, the caravan door creaked open.

'Storm!' a male voice boomed. 'Come in with you!' The second the dog heard its master's voice he turned and ran inside. The man's glare at Sarah was thunderous before he turned to close the door.

'Excuse me!' Sarah called loudly, remembering his name. 'It's Noah, isn't it? Your dog just attacked me!'

The back of her hand throbbed as she tried to stop the blood. The man paused in the doorway, glancing at her wound. 'If he had *attacked* you, you wouldn't be standing. It was a warning nip for trespassing, nothing more.'

'But it's not his territory,' Sarah countered, 'it's mine. I own this land.' She was lashing out as she was in pain, her pride wounded as much as her hand. Noah considered her with a calm, measured gaze.

'Come in, then, let's have a look at you.'

Sarah paused. This was what she wanted, but now she was rooted to the spot. 'I'm not going near that horrible hound.' But the man before her smiled, his dark eyes crinkling at the corners.

'Storm won't hurt you. Not with me around.'

'Storm needs to learn some bloody manners,' Sarah retorted. 'Have you got something I can put on this?' She was still reluctant to enter the caravan, but she needed to disinfect her hand and stop the bleeding.

'Olive has some gauze.' The man waved her in. 'Come.'

Sarah peeped inside to see a woman sitting in the far corner. Storm was at her feet, eyes closed as the woman petted his forehead, as if he'd done something good. Sarah tried to hide her annoyance but it must have been written all over her face.

'Don't be cross with t'auld dog,' the woman said, as Sarah stepped tentatively in. 'He was trying to protect us. The same way he protected his last owner who beat him to within an inch of his life.'

It was then that Sarah understood the scars on the animal's haunches. 'I didn't know he was a rescue,' Sarah said, the heat leaving her words. The last time she'd attended was over a year ago and there were no dogs in the area then.

'I remember you,' Noah said as he wrapped her hand in a muslin gauze. There was a gentle calmness to Noah's movement as he treated her. 'Best to get a tetanus jab, just in case.' He was a handsome man, smelling of sweet burning wood, outdoor camps and roll-up cigarettes. It wasn't a bad smell as far as Sarah was concerned, and she admired his nomadic ways.

Sarah was about to say she was up to date, but then remembered her audience. He didn't need to know about the hepatitis B and tetanus jabs she'd received because she was in the force.

'It's only a graze,' he added. 'But I'll keep a better eye on Storm until he settles down. I thought he was coming round.'

The dog approached, giving her a sniff before allowing Sarah to gently stroke his head.

'So you own this land?' Olive removed a whistling kettle from the gas hob.

'I inherited it from my family . . . I've no problem with you being here, by the way.' Sarah paused, remembering the real reason why she was here. 'Are you here for the anniversary, or stopping off on your way to somewhere?'

Noah didn't give his grandmother a chance to respond. 'Why do you want to know?' he said warily.

'Just making conversation,' Sarah responded, thanking Olive for the steaming tea as it was handed to her. 'I'm selling the place. It won't be in my hands much longer.' She admired the delicate china cup which had been taken from the dresser.

'And you're scared we'll devalue it?' Noah's words were blunt. 'Is that what this is? You want rid of us in case we drive the price down?'

He was suspicious, and offensive with it. But to be fair, he had good reason to be on edge. Twenty-five years ago two of his younger siblings went missing from these woods. But the anniversary of their disappearance wasn't marked by flowers or ribbons. Nor were they mentioned in church or on the local news. The residents of Slayton had shown little concern over the years. The thought filled Sarah with shame. 'Look,' she said, resting her cup in the palm of her hand. 'I think it's awful how your family were treated. More should have been done. I just wanted to let you know what was happening with the land. I can't see the place selling quickly, not with everything going on in town.' She sighed, remembering her DI's advice to build up a rapport. 'And now . . . what happened to that poor woman and her son . . . it's awful.'

Noah fell quiet as he leaned against the counter.

'Have you heard about it?' Sarah looked to Olive, who was sitting again, stroking the dog. But Olive gazed through her, as if she was seeing into her soul. A breeze whistled through the caravan, and Sarah fidgeted on her seat. 'Anyway . . .' her cheeks flushed as no response came, 'here's my mobile number. Any problems, give me a call.' She rested the piece of notepaper on the coffee table before her.

'You think we'll have problems, then?' Noah watched her intently as she rose.

'No.' Sarah's brow furrowed. 'But if anyone does have any issues, refer them to me.'

'Thanking you kindly,' Olive said, as Sarah turned to leave. Storm stayed where he was as Noah opened the caravan door and let her out.

'I feel like I've offended you,' Sarah said, glad to be back outside. Even the gloomy forest had a lighter atmosphere than the caravan. Truth was, the jury was out as far as Noah was concerned.

'We are quiet people,' Noah replied. 'We don't bother folk and all we ask is the same in return.' He folded his arms over his chest. 'But I'm sorry you got hurt. We won't darken your door much longer.'

'I'm sorry about what happened, before . . .' Sarah said earnestly, both meaning the words and digging for information with the purpose of her visit in mind. 'It must be hard, not having answers after all these years.'

'Well now, Miss Noble . . .' Noah began, 'you of all people should know that the ties of the past don't easily let go.' Noah didn't linger long enough to elaborate. Without saying another word, he let himself back into the caravan.

Sarah contemplated their meeting as she returned to her car. From what she had read about his siblings' disappearances, Noah's family had not received much support from the press. Then there were the 'missing' posters, which were ripped down as fast as they went up. Police were under no pressure to solve the disappearance of the missing traveller children and the case ran out of steam. Now Noah and Olive were back, clearly haunted by the past. It was strange, though, how they had shut down when Sarah mentioned the recent deaths.

She sat in her car, recalling their tight expressions . . . the suspicion in their eyes. Were they here to mark an anniversary, or was their presence more sinister than that?

17

Craig's Cakes & Coffee Shop was a welcome respite from the cold. The morning had been a busy one, and it was a relief to sit down. Sarah dabbed at her sandwich crumbs with the pad of her finger. 'I can't stay much longer,' she said, smiling at her old friends Elsie and Maggie. 'The only reason I'm here at all is because I said I had a dental appointment.' She squirmed in her chair, resisting the urge to tug at her black trousers which were digging into her waist.

Maggie gasped in mock horror. 'Really? Officer Sarah Noble veered off the straight and narrow to have some lunch?' She arched a blonde eyebrow as she switched her gaze to Elsie. 'It's you, isn't it? *You're* the bad influence.'

Elsie chuckled. 'Heavens to Betsy, if the cat had kittens y'all would blame me for it.' She was sitting in a reinforced mobility scooter, the only one big enough to accommodate her girth. Elsie was trying hard to lose the weight that had confined her to her home for the last year. Getting out of the house was a huge step forward for her planned independence.

'You gotta eat,' Elsie continued, patting Sarah's hand. 'I'm sure the Lord will forgive you this once.'

Sarah relaxed into the padded circular chair. It wasn't the Lord she was worried about, it was DI McGuire who she was hoping to impress. She could put this down to community enquiries. It wasn't as if Elsie or Maggie were short of things to say. The three of them made a unique trio. Despite her prudish ways, Elsie was a closet steamy romance writer, under the name of Caroline Brookes. Maggie was an artist, and raising Elliott, a seven-year-old boy with inexplicable insights. Sarah valued her time in their company, which was why she couldn't bring herself to cancel today.

'What in tarnation is going on in Slayton?' Elsie asked. 'My life has turned into one big calorie counter and I need a change of subject.' For the last ten minutes they'd talked about Elsie's treatment at the obesity clinic, where she was making slow progress.

'I wouldn't know where to start,' Sarah replied. 'There's always something going on in Slayton. Never a dull moment and all that.' She clasped her fingers around her coffee cup and stared at the remains of her drink. She knew what they were after – insider info on her latest case. McGuire's warning had been clear. She wasn't allowed to share.

'I think Elsie's looking for the lowdown on the black-eyed children,' Maggie said knowingly.

'Black-eyed what?' Sarah heard her but it didn't make sense.

Elsie's face lit up as she prepared to tell all. 'They've been sighted in Slayton around the time of the murders.' She waggled her fingers for spooky effect. 'With their deathly white skin and blacked-out eyes.'

Blacked-out eyes? Sarah turned to Maggie as a chill enveloped her. This was too close to the bone. 'What's she talking about? Please translate.' Elsie was known for embellishment, and this was Sarah's good-natured way of asking for it straight.

'She's telling the truth.' Maggie rested her hands around her own coffee cup as she relayed everything she had learned. 'If they follow you home, great harm will befall you.'

'Befall?' Sarah scoffed. 'Have I stumbled into an episode of *The Twilight Zone*?'

'Well, it's all over town.' Elsie looked dolefully at her mineral water, most likely wishing it was a latte.

'The internet is alive with it too,' Maggie continued, scrolling on her phone. 'This fellah called Roger Newman makes YouTube videos about them.'

'I saw that. It's been shared in the Slayton community group on Facebook.' Elsie sniffed. 'News like this travels faster than a burp in a sandstorm in these parts.'

'Why haven't you mentioned this before?' Sarah groaned, reaching for Maggie's phone. But Maggie responded with a shrug. Was it connected to Elliott's unease? Sarah watched the video on mute, reading the accompanying subtitles. Newman talked enthusiastically about black-eyed children calling to a house in Slayton and crying to be let inside. He went on to say how mother and son had been murdered but the children were nowhere to be seen. Content like this would make her job harder as local pressure mounted and panic set in. Slaytonites weren't just superstitious – many were gullible too. Soon the station would be hounded with calls. 'Maybe it won't get that many views.' Sarah handed Maggie her phone.

'Are you kidding?' Maggie laughed. 'No one's talking about anything else.'

'Fan-bloody-tastic.' Sarah sighed. Slayton was a magnet for all things strange as far as she could see.

Elsie threw her a curious glance. 'Have y'all figured out who did it yet? I need to know if I'm safe in my bed.'

Sarah's expression tightened. 'Now, Elsie, you know I can't talk about the case.'

'Doggone it, Sarah, I'm asking as a concerned citizen. If I stopped you on the street you'd have to tell me somethin' . . . wouldn't you?' Elsie fixed her friend with a glare.

'I'd offer you some reassurance and tell you our best officers are working on it.'

'In other words, you don't know diddly-squat.'

Sarah glanced around the coffee shop, which had mercifully gone quiet after the lunchtime rush. There was a man sitting at the table behind her filling out a crossword puzzle. In the corner, a middle-aged couple were having what appeared to be a muted argument about a mother-in-law. Staff were making the most of the downtime to clear tables and wash cups. Leaning forward, Sarah spoke in hushed tones.

'Motivation is the hardest thing to prove. The children turning up could be completely unrelated. Or they could have been a distraction during a burglary gone wrong.' She wasn't going to say it, but she didn't believe that for a minute. The image of the victims' empty eye sockets was haunting her. No burglar would have gone that far. Mention of black-eyed children left her with a sense of unease, but she mustn't get carried away just yet. Sarah looked directly at Elsie, who was hanging on her every word.

'Have either of you got any sensible theories? Seeing as you're so keen to talk about it.'

Elsie took a breath. 'I hear tell Rosemary's son moved in with her after he was injured, and she nursed him back to health. Poor fellah. He worked for Irving Industries, but he was medically retired some time back.'

The mention of Irving Industries made Sarah prickle. When anything bad happened in Slayton that name always came up. But it wasn't big news that the victim once worked for the company owned by Slayton's wealthiest entrepreneur. With the amount of building developments being launched, lots of people in Slayton did.

'You don't think Simon's involved, do you?' Maggie turned to Elsie, who knew the Irvings better than most.

'He wouldn't dirty his lily-white hands.' Elsie grunted as she shifted her weight. She blotted a tissue to her forehead to absorb the beads of sweat which had gathered there.

'And murder is not good for business,' Sarah added. 'Not when he's selling Slayton as the safest place to live.' The 'choose safety for your family' campaign was still being pushed, despite everything that had happened in recent months.

'*And* it's not that long since he lost his daughter,' Maggie agreed, on the breath of a sigh. 'If it's not Irving, then who? And why?' She crossed her legs, her features taut with worry. 'It's awful. All of it. I hope you find whoever's behind it soon.'

Sarah squeezed Maggie's hand in a small gesture of comfort, as memories of the Midnight Man were stoked. The last year had been tough on them all, but Maggie had felt it the most. 'Believe me, I want nothing more.' She thought of Maggie's son, and how his uncanny intuition had helped her in the past. 'Elliott hasn't said any more to you, has he?' She hated to ask the question, but she could not rest easy until she did.

'Nothing.' The tone of Maggie's words relayed that the conversation regarding her son was closed. She was trying to protect him and Sarah couldn't blame her for that.

'What happened there?' Maggie was looking down at Sarah's hand, which had a large skin-coloured plaster on the back.

'Dog nipped me.' She looked from Elsie to Maggie. 'I paid a visit to the travellers camped down in Blackhall Woods, and their Rottweiler didn't exactly give me the warmest of welcomes.'

'A Rottweiler?' Elsie exclaimed. 'You should be more careful.'

'It was a misunderstanding,' Sarah added. 'Nothing to worry about.' She didn't want to elaborate. Noah and his family deserved some peace. But at the same time her intuition nagged at her to delve deeper into the story of his missing siblings. She glanced at her watch. 'I'd best be off. If you hear any more gossip, let me know.' She rooted in her handbag for her purse.

'It's all paid for,' Elsie said, before Sarah could take out her debit card. 'My treat. Lord knows when we'll get out again if the government lock us in. I was talking to the woman behind the till in the health shop and she reckons it's only a matter of time.'

Sarah smiled her gratitude. She didn't want to think about this virus from China that was doing the rounds. She had her hands full with her job. She slipped some hand gel from her bag and sanitised her hands. 'I'll get it next time. And really, well done. I know how hard it must have been for you, getting here.'

'Worth it,' Elsie said. And it was. She knew Elsie would walk through hot coals to be part of their newly formed group of three. In school, Elsie had been an outsider, but now Sarah couldn't imagine not having her and Maggie in her life. Their regular meetups were better than any therapy. But as she waved her goodbyes, her mind was racing ahead.

Just who – or what – had visited Rosemary's house? There had been no signs of forced entry. Young people were much more likely to be invited inside. Were these black-eyed children killers in disguise?

18

Gerard sat in Craig's Cakes & Coffee Shop, absorbing the community around him. It was ages since he'd had the luxury of people-watching, but it was more than curiosity which brought him here. He'd consumed as much as he could from online news and social media. Two people died on the day of his blackout. On the day he'd come to in the cottage, naked and bloodied, with his clothes swishing in the washing machine on a boil wash. It couldn't have had anything to do with him, though – could it? The idea was ridiculous. Yet it was there, that tug on the gut. That knowing. The childish urgent whispers. But Gerard couldn't believe that he had killed those people. How could he forget a thing like that? He didn't have it in him to commit murder, and he didn't even know the people involved. But then, he hadn't known about Blackhall Manor either, until he'd discovered the place existed in real life as well as in his head.

But murder? No. He was a father, a husband. He was the man who bought his wife roses once a week. The person who chased a bee around his office with a glass and a piece of cardboard to ensure it left unharmed. He wasn't capable of it. There must be someone else in the frame.

Last night, sleep had evaded him. Had the voices he'd heard come from his own head? The absence of streetlights was unsettling and the woodland had been graveyard dark. The screeches and cries which had risen from the trees had made him keep the curtains tightly shut. He didn't know what he was more afraid of: the noises in the woods or another blackout. He had pulled each deadbolt, shoving furniture up against the door. But if he could drive a car during his blackouts, then he could quite easily undo those deadbolts. Perhaps it wasn't the only thing he was capable of.

This morning, his wife had called him and it had taken all his self-control not to break down. He'd told her it was a bad line, cupping his hand over the phone as he cleared his throat. As always, Ruth was understanding, patient and kind. It was another reason why he couldn't bring his problems to her door. She didn't deserve whatever shit was about to rain down on him. Not to mention the kids. Not that they were children anymore. He stared unblinking at the newspaper as his thoughts went to them. At least he'd taken out life insurance. If anything happened to him, they would be well provided for. Was that what this was coming to? He examined his nails. He had scrubbed every inch of his skin, but it still felt like someone else's blood was sinking into his pores.

He felt bone-weary as the thought gnawed at his brain. It came from the dark place, the part of himself that scared him. He should leave. Turn his back on Slayton and never return. But he knew he would only get a mile down the road before turning back. This wasn't an impromptu holiday. This was dangerous. His head low, he sat, pen in hand. The newspaper crossword helped him blend into the background as he listened to the people around him. He stared at the puzzle, chewing the top of his pen before filling each box.

H-A-R-V-E-S-T. He stared at the question for a second time. *To reap what you sow.*

There were a couple of coffee shops in Slayton, but he'd instinctively known that this was the place where the locals hung out. He had struck lucky with his choice of seating. The woman who had just left had sounded like a detective. From what he'd gathered, the police didn't have a lot to go on. From the corner of his eye, Gerard watched the larger of the three women press a napkin to her forehead. He detected the hint of a Southern American accent as she passed the time with her friend. She was sitting on a wide mobility scooter. The owner of the coffee shop seemed happy to see her as he'd opened the double doors to allow her vehicle in.

'I don't know what Slayton is coming to.' Her voice was brittle with worry. 'Makes you scared to go out at night.'

'Makes you scared to stay in too,' the woman across from her replied.

Gerard listened closely as the women sat in uneasy silence. The blonde woman's spoon clinked against her cup as she stirred her second cup of coffee. 'Sarah wants to talk to Elliott about what's going on, but he's only a little boy. Just when I think we have a handle on things . . .' A sad exhale left her lips. 'People still look at us funny in the supermarket.'

'Oh, hun, if I worried about people looking at me funny I'd never leave the house.' The larger woman spoke in good-natured tones. Gerard felt like a voyeur. What was he doing here, listening in on private conversations? A year ago, he wouldn't have contemplated such a thing. He thought about leaving when the woman spoke again. 'Do you think Sarah knows more than she's letting on? About the murders, I mean.'

Her blonde friend sipped her coffee. 'I can read Sarah like a book. I think the police are baffled by this case. I mean, who are these kids, and why are they knocking on people's doors?'

'Ugh.' The Southern lady shuddered. 'I'm getting one of those Ring cameras. If any creepy rug rats turn up at my door, I'll be telling them to back the hell off!'

Her friend chuckled at her response. 'Can you imagine it? Wouldn't want to be a Girl Guide selling cookies right now.' Their laughter broke the concern that was etched on both of their faces.

Keeping his head down, Gerard moved quietly between chairs as he exited the building, but he was leaving with more questions than he had when he entered. How much truth was there in this small-town gossip? What did children knocking on doors have to do with a double murder? Whatever it all meant, it provided a frisson of hope that there *was* someone else involved. There was nothing to say that the blood on his skin was human after all. It could have belonged to an animal. It could have been any number of things. Perhaps the children's presence *was* a distraction tactic for a burglary gone wrong . . . It could be nothing more than a coincidence that he'd returned in such a state that day.

But why couldn't he remember? That was the biggest mystery of all. He should see a doctor, but he was afraid of what they might find. No, the most important thing of all was not to say a word. To anyone. As he parted through the double doors, he inhaled a breath of fresh air. Passing a nearby bin, he glanced at the unfinished newspaper crossword puzzle before tossing it in. Some things were better left untouched.

19

McGuire loomed over Sarah as she typed up reports on the system. It was a blessing that she'd learned to type, given the amount of admin involved in her role. It was coming up to five o'clock, and as she was still on restricted hours, she was due to go home. But Sarah didn't want to return to her empty cottage, with nothing but her cat for company. She frowned as McGuire continued to look over her shoulder. Sarah was used to DI Lee, who left her and the team to it. McGuire's hands-on style of leadership was taking a bit of getting used to. Sarah shifted, waiting for him to leave.

'Did you not hear the tannoy?' he said at last. 'Front desk is calling you.'

'Bugger,' Sarah muttered. She had been so immersed in her work she hadn't heard the call. 'I mean, thanks, boss,' she said, as McGuire turned and left. Locking her computer, she headed down the corridor. She still hadn't worked McGuire out. He was certainly a different kettle of fish from Gabby.

'Sorry, I didn't hear the tannoy,' Sarah said, as she spoke to a glum-faced Patricia, today's front counter staff. She sat, picking at her chipped nail varnish, her flowery perfume filling the room. 'I rang but yer phone lines are jammed.' Patricia was from the Black Country and did not suffer fools gladly.

'Yes, sorry,' Sarah apologised for the second time. 'They've not stopped ringing all day.'

'Tell me about it!' Patricia shook her head. 'Bleedin' black-eyed children. Folk round 'ere have too much time on their hands.' She exhaled a disgruntled huff as her phone rang for her attention and Sarah waited as she dealt with the call. Front counter was a depressing place, situated behind a sheet of safety glass, with holes and a small microphone to aid communication with the outside world. Being a police officer, she had access to front office, but members of the public had to speak behind the glass. Slayton police station was open twenty-four hours, so it wasn't unusual for people to wander in drunk off the street and cause trouble. Then there were the disgruntled girlfriends who came in to complain about their other halves being locked up. Fights had often broken out as feuding families came together to enquire about the family member who had been taken in. It was the reason why the hard plastic seats were bolted to the ground.

There were four basic interview rooms off reception and the main door into the station for which you needed a security pass. Clasping her hand over the phone, Patricia pointed to the door on the left. 'A Mr Irving wants to speak to you. I told him to wait in there.'

'Irving?' Sarah replied. 'I'm not expecting any Irving. Unless . . .' Her eyes widened. 'It's not Simon Irving, is it?' The untouchable Simon Irving wouldn't be interested in the likes of Sarah . . . would he? Patricia responded with a crisp nod before returning her attention to the phone.

'Sorry to keep you waiting,' Sarah said, entering the side room. She didn't like or trust the intimidating Simon Irving but she would still be polite.

'Ms Noble.' He rose from the plastic chair, giving her a five-star smile. 'I'd shake your hand, but we have to be careful these days.' He was talking about Covid, and Sarah didn't disagree as they sat. He was immaculately turned out, wearing a suit so well fitted it had to be made-to-measure. People like Simon Irving didn't wear off-the-peg.

'Indeed,' she replied, grateful she had escaped physical contact with the man. 'What can I do for you?'

'I'll get straight to the point. I'd like to buy Blackhall Manor and the surrounding woodlands – today.' He gazed at her intently. He may have been smiling but it wasn't reflected in his eyes.

'Oh. Right. Well, the thing is, I'm on duty.' Sarah forced a smile. 'And . . . that's a personal matter, so now is not the time to discuss it. I assumed you were here on police business.'

Irving was wearing the same stiff expression, his posture taut. This was a man who wasn't used to hearing the word 'no'. 'My lawyers have written to you several times but we've had no response. I'm willing to make a generous offer. We have plans to regenerate Lower Slayton. You don't want to be the one to stand in my way.'

Sarah prickled at the words. For months she'd complained that Lower Slayton was left behind, and now here was someone promising to inject some much-needed cash, starting with the land she owned. As for Blackhall Manor . . . it was a millstone around her neck. 'You know there's a protection order on it, don't you?' She had planned to raze the building to the ground but Gerard Baker, a property lawyer from London, had turned up out of the blue before Christmas and slapped the protection order on it. She'd thought it was strange at the time, how he had appeared from nowhere just to stop her tearing the old place down.

'My dear . . .' Irving said, with a dollop of condescension, 'there are ways and means around everything.'

She pushed back her chair and stood. She couldn't listen to any more of this.

'I'll think about it.' She glanced at the clock on the wall. 'Now, if you don't mind, I need to be getting back to—' But Irving blocked her exit as he struggled to contain his growing annoyance. She caught a whiff of mint on his breath as he stood closer than she was comfortable with. He flashed her another five-star smile.

'I'm sure we can come to a mutual agreement. Why don't you give me your mobile number? My receptionist will schedule us in for a meeting at my offices in town. Or lunch?'

Sarah swallowed, unable to think of any number of comebacks which would line up in her thoughts once he had left. She wished she had the guts to stand up to him, but by the second or third round in the ring with the Simon Irvings of this world, she turned to water. Sarah was aware she had issues with male figures of authority. Given her background, it was hardly any surprise. It was why she worked so well with Gabby. As a female, her sergeant wasn't a threat.

Sarah ground her back teeth as Irving refused to budge. People like Irving sensed weakness and she was positively reeking of it. Pulling her phone from her pocket, she reeled off the number on her screen. With a sly smile of satisfaction, Irving said goodbye and immediately left.

Why did he want the building so badly that he had made a personal visit to her workplace? More to the point, why hadn't she bitten his hand off? Sarah would finally be free of the building that had been in her family for years. And there was the money, which would go a long way.

'Right.' She slipped her phone from her pocket. 'Time to sort this once and for all.'

Joan, her estate agent, seemed sympathetic as she explained the need for a quick sale. 'Funnily enough, I was about to ring you. We have had an offer but it's fifty thousand pounds below what Irving Industries is offering.'

'Take it.'

'Are you sure? It's a lot of mon—'

'I said, take it,' she snapped, not wanting to change her mind. A beat passed between them. 'Sorry. I have a lot on my plate. Please accept their offer. What do they want it for?'

'They're twins, a right pair of old dears. They have links to Slayton and they'd like to turn it into a hotel. Nothing ghoulish, they want to restore the place to its former glory rather than make money out of its history. Cash buyers – not short of a bob or two.'

She explained the offer was lean because of the amount of money they'd need to plough into the place.

'Fair enough,' Sarah said. 'As long as they're not connected to Simon Irving, we can go ahead. Then the next time he bugs you, tell him the place is sold.' Sarah afforded herself a smile. The number she'd given Irving was Joan's, not hers.

Thoughts of the manor clung to Sarah as she walked down the corridor. Would she finally be free of it? More importantly, was she ready to let it go?

20

Noah lay on the ground outside his caravan, inhaling a breath of crisp, night forest air. His cot bed was slightly raised to keep the insects from crawling into his sleeping bag. His skin was oily from the home-made concoction Olive insisted he slather on himself, which repelled the horseflies and midges that flew in swarms this deep in the woods. That, and the smoke from the fire which crackled and spat next to him.

He enjoyed living off the land. Noah didn't need a television screen when the sky above him was clear. His hands clasped behind his head, he stared through a clearing in the trees at the stars above. Memories of days past danced and bobbed, raising a host of emotions. He wondered what sort of reception he and his grandmother would receive from the people of Slayton. He had never encountered such a superstitious bunch. He had pitched up on many sites over the years, faced many forms of prejudice, but it was nothing compared to the mixture of dread tinged with hope which he encountered each time he returned here. Hope that they would find closure this time. Dread that they would leave without answers, the same as every other year. But this year was different. Arnold was back. And according to his extended Romany family who were also searching for answers, Arnold knew what had happened that day.

He watched as the bats above him flitted between the trees. They lacked the grace of the ravens who swooped through the skies with ease. Bats skittered to and fro like drunk drivers, calling to each other in a frequency that only they could hear. He felt a kinship with the forest creatures that may be unappealing to some. The whole foundation of the Romany existence was built on being free and untethered to the modern world. These days, they were hidden people, which suited him just fine. It seemed that he was not the only

76

restless soul tonight. He had paid Arnold's cottage another visit, and the old man was out. Where was he at this late hour?

Noah would need to tread carefully. A trip into town had revealed his instincts had been right about Sarah Noble. Not only was she the landowner, but she was a police officer. Her rusted red Mini Cooper was a distinctive little car as it drove into the police station car park through the staff entrance at the back. A little more digging was all it took to confirm what she was doing there. Sarah had seemed decent enough, but Noah's mistrust of those outside his community was deeply ingrained. Bring the police into the mix, and all his walls went up. She was sniffing around for a reason. When it came to Arnold, he would need to cover his tracks. It was a shame, as he had liked her. She seemed too nice to be part of an establishment he could never trust.

He was no angel, but neither would he hurt someone who didn't deserve it. He rarely started fights, although he wasn't afraid to finish them. He left a campsite better than he found it. Kept his head down. But he couldn't spend the rest of his days returning to this place. His grandmother was getting too old to live without running water and electricity.

Arnold's presence here reinforced his determination. For years he had hunted for answers, putting up a reward for information – no questions asked. Finally, his patience had earned him Arnold's name and little else. But a name was all Noah needed. He would get the rest out of him soon enough. This had to be their last visit. This time he was not leaving until he got what he came for.

Reaching out beside him, Noah stroked Storm's fur. Violence did not come naturally to him, but he would see this through. Then they could pack up and leave. He would do whatever it took to find answers. Because someone knew what had happened to his little brother and sister on the night they ran away. It was his job to catch up with them and find out exactly what.

21

Tizzy was so excited to see other people that she danced in circles on the pavement, almost tripping Arnold up. It was much to the amusement of a bunch of teenagers passing by. Yanking the lead, Arnold kept his head down, grizzling to himself as the teenagers' laughter faded behind him. *Blasted long-haired layabouts with their stupid gadgets. They should be drafted into the army, the lot of them. That would sort them out.* Muttering under his breath, he gave another tug of the lead as Tizzy continued to yap and bounce all the way to the churchyard.

'I need to speak to you, Father!' he demanded, hammering on the local parish priest's door. The cottage was situated behind the church, in the grounds of the graveyard. The priest had finished his duties for the evening but he would make time for Arnold, who continued to thump his fist on the door. Today the priest appeared dishevelled, which was unlike him.

'Arnold,' he said, running a hand through his thinning auburn hair. 'Is everything alright?'

'Shush!' Arnold chastised the little dog as he strained to hear the priest. But Tizzy wasn't having any of it. She was in quite a flap.

'There, there.' Father Aloysius bent down to the little dog. 'May I?' he asked, before scooping Tizzy up in his arms and murmuring comforting sounds.

'Do what you want,' Arnold grunted. 'I've had enough of the annoying little sod.'

'She's trembling,' the priest said, cradling the dog like a baby. He was used to Tizzy, given the number of times he had visited Arnold's wife before she moved to Ireland for the last year of her life.

'Then take her,' Arnold handed over the lead. 'She's nothing but a pest!' A sense of relief washed over him as he parted with the dog.

'What? I couldn't possibly . . .' The priest's eyes widened, yet he folded his fingers over the tartan lead just the same.

'Then give her to the dogs' home!' Arnold retorted. 'I've had enough of her.' He watched the priest calm the whining Tizzy, who was visibly shaking.

'You didn't come here to talk about Tizzy, did you?' Father Aloysius was nothing if not perceptive as he stroked the dog's fur. 'Do you need to talk?'

'I need confession,' Arnold uttered, feeling a little happier now he was rid of the annoying mutt. 'In church.' He wasn't taking no for an answer. He turned on his heel and approached the grey stone building. As his feet scrunched on the gravel path, he knew Father Aloysius would be palming Tizzy off on his unsuspecting housekeeper. Maura was live-in, and she had a thing about little dogs. Which suited Arnold just fine.

He took his place in the confessional. From the moment he entered the small dark box a sense of calm washed over him. He bathed in the quiet hush. He could be anywhere in the world. The musty smell and the creak of the wooden seat beneath his weight brought back so many memories. How many times had he sat here, begging for forgiveness yet unable to say the words? His crime was too horrific for anyone's ears, even a man of the cloth. But he lived in hope that one day he would be able to share the burden of what he had done.

Father Aloysius was a good man. He would honour the sanctity of the confessional. Arnold thought about Rosemary Simmons. Had she sat here too, tortured by the knowledge of their actions? The thought sent a flare of fear through his soul. He wasn't ready to die, but he *did* need absolution. He could not escape the feeling that the children were coming for him next. Father Aloysius pulled the small hatch across, his voice low and comforting as he instigated confession.

'Forgive me, Father, for I have sinned.' Arnold blessed himself reverently. 'It has been one week since my last confession.' He could not see the priest's face as he recited the opening words he knew so well. Arnold had heard them so many times before they had become a soothing balm. When it was his turn to fill the silence in the dark space that had held the secrets of so many, he confessed to having unkind thoughts about the teenagers he'd encountered on his way. About wanting to snap Tizzy's neck when he'd had enough of her barking. But it didn't come close to the real reason he was here.

The priest fell silent and Arnold's heartbeat accelerated as the box began to close in on him. It was beginning to feel more like a coffin than a place of peace. He could almost hear the ghostly cries of the children who occupied his thoughts. He inhaled a deep breath, but the usually comforting scent of old timber now rose in his nostrils like the stench of decomposing flesh.

'Is there anything else?' Father Aloysius made Arnold jump.

'You know there is, Father.' As he wrung his hands, Arnold's voice was raspy with despair.

'Then repent of your sins.'

'I . . . I can't.' Rocking on his seat, Arnold closed his eyes tight, trying to find the strength to carry on.

'You've held onto this for years. Do you mean to carry it to your grave?' The priest was talking about Arnold's unspoken secret, the one he hadn't been brave enough to share.

'No, Father, I can't.' The truth felt like a flare in his chest, burning his insides and turning him to ash. Year on year it ate away at him, taking another piece of his soul. A thought occurred. If he could not talk about it, he could at least skirt around what happened.

'The children, Father.' His voice trembled as he whispered. 'They're coming for me.'

'What children?'

'The ghost children. I hear them, whispering at my window. Asking to be let in.' It was the first time he'd told another living soul about the voices which woke him from his sleep. It had started only a couple of weeks ago, and was already driving him to despair. What did he expect, given it was their anniversary? Some souls would never rest.

'And what would these ghost children want with you?' The priest sounded somewhat exasperated and Arnold could tell he wasn't taking him seriously. He dragged both hands over his face. As if it were that easy to wash his sins away. He opened his mouth to speak, but all that came was a miserable whine.

'Are you ready?' Father Aloysius insisted. 'Is now the time to talk about what's bothered you all these years? Or will you be taking your secret to the grave?'

Arnold knew what the old priest was doing – showing him the idiocy of the situation. This secret was killing him and yet he clung to it like a raft in a storm. His silence was heavy as Father Aloysius waited for his response. He took a deep breath.

'No, Father. I can't do that. Not anymore.'

'Then you are ready to confess?'

'Soon.'

'Very well.'

Arnold relaxed back on his seat as the priest absolved him of his sins. All except one. He would stand by his word. He had made progress today. Soon he would be ready. He would deal with the shame of his actions. The next time he came to the confessional, he would tell all.

22

Sarah waited patiently for DI McGuire to conduct the last briefing of the night. It felt odd to be at the station now that darkness had closed in. But McGuire seemed in no hurry to send her home. She used to think that restricted hours suited her, but perhaps that was more to do with her lack of confidence than needing to leave work on time. Working with MIT, Sarah felt like she mattered. She may not have as much experience as her colleagues, but she did have insight. She watched the rest of the team filter in. None had been particularly friendly, but they were too busy with the investigation to acknowledge her. At least she had Richie, who approached, popping his top shirt button and loosening his tie.

'What are you still doing here?' he said, removing her notebook from the spare seat she had kept for him. 'I thought you'd gone home.'

'I've been manning the police helpline.' Sarah spoke in a low voice. She'd managed to pop back and feed Sherlock earlier in the day so she was in no hurry to leave now. 'It's quite nice, catching the last briefing of the night.'

Richie snorted. 'Come back to me when you've worked ten days straight. Then we'll see how nice it is.' His words broke into a yawn as he stretched in his chair. 'I've been interrogating the intel system for the last hour. I'm bushed.' Richie had been tasked with checking for crimes with a similar MO in the UK. 'The only cases involving the removal of eyes are gangland-related crimes.'

Sarah couldn't see a connection. 'I think the Simmons family were more into hot chocolate than cocaine. Nice waistcoat,' she added, glancing over the black material. She liked his taste in clothes. Unlike Simon Irving, he didn't have to try hard to look good.

'Thanks.' Richie delivered a warm smile, their eyes locking as Sarah's stomach did a little somersault. She cleared her throat,

82

inwardly chastising herself for thinking of Richie as anything more than a colleague and friend.

They both watched as McGuire took long strides into the room, casting an eye over his audience before standing in front of the board.

'How are we doin', folks, are yous still with us?' The room fell into silence. 'I'll take that as a yes, then. Right. As predicted, rumours of black-eyed children have spread through Slayton and our police helpline has been jammed with random calls.' He eyed Sarah up. 'Anything to report there?'

Warmth spread to Sarah's cheeks as all eyes turned on her. 'No positive leads, and very few actual sightings. Most calls are from people digging for information. They're scared to go to sleep at night.'

'I had a feeling you'd say that,' McGuire replied. 'We're wording a press release which will go out in the morning.'

A deep voice rose from the back of the room. It was Gav, the officer Richie had spoken to previously. 'We're wasting our time with all this black-eyed child bollocks. We're MIT, not bleedin' Mulder and Scully.'

'I know,' McGuire replied. 'And you're probably right. But we'll explore every avenue as this is a particularly gruesome case.' His hesitation made Sarah sit up in her chair. By the look on his face, he had news. 'The search team have found the victims' eyeballs discarded in a dog litter bin in the next street.'

Sarah's stomach churned at the thought. Those poor people . . . not to mention the officers who had to search through piles of dog-dirt to find their eyes. The discovery gave them something new to think about. Why remove them in the first place?

Between forensics, the autopsy and the blood spatter report, McGuire pieced together a series of sinister events in the Simmons family home. 'Let's recap what we know so far. Geoffrey had been taking a bath, and at some point his mother made hot chocolate for four.' McGuire talked about the voicemail that Rosemary had left with her neighbour. 'The drinks were probably for the children, which suggests she was comfortable in their presence. The question is, *who* were they and *why* were they there?'

A bearded officer named Dan spoke up. His hair skimmed his shoulders, and his blue striped shirt was open at the neck. 'Well, it wasn't a distraction burglary, because they would have kept Rosemary in the living room, not in the kitchen making drinks.' Distraction burglaries were common in Lower Slayton, and the trick was to keep the homeowner talking at the front while someone crept in through the back and grabbed items of value such as handbags, phones or laptops.

'Aye,' McGuire replied, his features grim. 'They usually avoid direct contact, and it's rare for anyone to get hurt.' He nodded at Martin, their head CSI. Martin wasn't just small in stature, he was quietly spoken and Sarah strained to listen as he pointed to various photos.

'From piecing together clues, we've worked out that Rosemary was attacked when she was carrying out a tray of hot drinks from the kitchen to the living room. This was around twenty to eleven, not long after she left the voicemail on her neighbour's phone. Time of death is also backed up by the autopsy report, due to the partially digested fish supper they'd had a couple of hours before.' Silence descended as officers listened to Martin replaying the scene. 'As Mrs Simmons was attacked, her son wheeled forward, to protect her. But he didn't stand a chance. The killer cut his throat from behind.' Martin pointed to the images on the board. 'You can see the blood spatter here . . . here . . . and here as it rises in an arc. He would have bled out quickly, once the jugular vein was severed.'

'Yet the killer persisted,' McGuire said. 'First with Geoffrey and then back to his mother, removing their eyes. But why, if they weren't kept as trophies? Was it a symbolic act? Or a ritual of some sort?'

Martin continued, head bowed. 'We've got no definitive shoe prints, only the imprints of covers worn over them. They took care to cover their tracks, yet left a bloodied handprint on the wall.' The image of the blood-red handprint appeared stark against the whiteboard.

'It's sloppy, which suggests they were no trained executioner,' McGuire added. 'Not that Rosemary was likely to be on anyone's hit list. Any hired killer worth their salt wouldn't have left a trace.'

'What about a domestic incident gone wrong? Or a serious falling-out with the neighbours?' A blonde woman with dark roots spoke up. Sarah had never heard of a neighbourhood dispute ending up with the victims' eyes being plucked from their sockets. She steeled herself and spoke out.

'I've talked with neighbours at length, and I live on that road myself. Neither Rosemary nor her son set foot outside their door, apart from going to church, and according to family, they were very close.'

McGuire thanked her for her input before speaking to a member of the tech team. According to him, there was no evidence of any untoward communication, dating apps or social media profiles on the victims' laptops or phones. Sarah stared into space as she turned things over in her mind. The only other motivation she could think of was money, but neither party gambled nor owed debts.

All that was left was the unwelcome prospect of a random killer with a bloodthirsty streak. But if these were spur-of-the-moment murders, then where did the children come in? Then there were the rumours of people hearing whispers. Of spooky children sighted in the local park at night. Slayton's teens were joyriding scallywags but they weren't capable of this. From what Sarah had gathered anyway, the children who had called on Rosemary Simmons were younger than that.

Regardless of DI McGuire's cheery disposition, he would feel pressured for results just the same. Sarah wondered if Gabby was relieved the case hadn't landed at her door – but she knew her sergeant too well for that. She would still be smarting, and looking into things herself. People in Slayton were scared, and it was only natural. The victims were just like them – regular people, on a regular street. Heaven knows how locals would react if they knew the full facts. If Rosemary and her son could be so brutally violated, then what was to say it couldn't happen again?

'DIU are compiling a list of violent offenders within a twenty-mile radius of Slayton who've been released from prison in the last year.' McGuire would work closely with the Divisional Intelligence Unit, who were invaluable in cases such as this. Enquiries would be made with psychiatric units, bail hostels and drug rehab units too. As the topic of potential suspects was discussed, Sarah's thoughts wandered to Noah, guarded and wary, as he had watched her every move. Did he know more than he was letting on? She recalled his expression, the determination on his face which was etched with his loss. How many more lives would be taken before answers were found? She would not be the only one in Slayton uneasy in her bed tonight.

23

Pinpricks of white light flashed behind Gerard's eyes as he rubbed them with his fists. He sat at the splintered dining table, his paperwork spread next to his laptop and printer as he tried to focus his thoughts. It was a far cry from his swish London office and his ergonomic furniture. In London, his office was flooded with light and smelled of jasmine and patchouli. Here, he inhaled a concoction of damp mingled with sewage as he sat at his dingy workspace. The dining table was old and splintered, with enough room for his laptop, printer and paperwork. It didn't matter if he spilled his coffee or littered the wood with sandwich crumbs. The same could be said for the rest of the grimy cottage, which needed a deep clean. It was at least an open-plan space, living and dining rooms combined, with a small functional kitchen down the end of the hall.

He could have booked a suite in the Slayton Lakeside Hotel, but something told him he couldn't afford to bring attention to himself. At least here he had privacy. His eyes flicked to the dirt-streaked window, through the gap in the limp orange curtains which hung from a yellowed rail. The woodlands were alive, from the bats flitting in the skies celebrating twilight to the foxes emitting screeches when the moon was high in the sky. He felt a deep understanding of the creatures who lived here. He foraged in his mind for answers. It was like dipping his tongue into a cavity where a rotting tooth had been. All that was returned was an empty, sour taste. He should have been happy. He had achieved what he came here for. He'd thrown a stick in the spokes of progress. Blackhall Manor would not be demolished on his watch – but why did he care if that rotting old building survived another day? And if he had achieved what he'd set out to do, then why was he lingering in Slayton?

A sense of unfinished business returned. Something which would put all his work regarding Blackhall Manor in the shade. Far away, in the parts of his mind where long-forgotten memories lay, a child's urgent whispers were delivered on an icy breath. He could not make out the words, nor did he want to. His Adam's apple bobbed as he swallowed back the feeling of being uneasy in his skin. His mind felt at odds with his body, like he was wearing someone else's shoes. Had Blackhall been a ruse to draw him in? He glanced at his notebook, realising he had drawn two stick figures, a boy and a girl. Groaning in frustration, he scrunched the paper into a ball and sent it flying into the corner of the room.

It was going to happen again; he could feel shadows closing in on his peripheral vision. His blackout wouldn't be immediate, but soon. His stomach clenched at the thought of losing control. Just who did he become? He shifted uneasily in the hard chair. It felt strange to think of himself externally. To fear his own actions. Every time he searched for answers, he only found a dead end.

He glanced around the room at his efforts to keep himself inside. Tonight, he'd taken every precaution, locking the doors and barricading every exit. The windows were tiny and surely too stiff to open without waking himself up. He thought about setting up a tripwire – an early warning system. Dammit, he'd tie himself to the bed if he had to. If there was any way of waking himself from his living nightmare then it was worth implementing. But it wasn't as easy as emerging from a dream. He froze as his phone rang in his pocket. It was Ruth. A low breeze whistled through the cottage as the night air found an entrance through a crack in the windowpane.

'Have you been feeding yourself?' she asked, after they greeted each other. 'I worry about you in the middle of nowhere, all on your own.'

Gerard's grip on the phone tightened. Ruth hadn't worried the whole time he was snowed in in a chalet in Switzerland, and back then she hadn't heard from him for a week. If Ruth was concerned, it was unsettling. She was never one to cling to his shirt tails. There was more to this than she was letting on. Her voice brittle, she skirted around the subject, confirming his suspicions. His wife thought he was losing his mind. 'I'm fine,' he said, at last.

'Then when are you coming home?' Ruth swiftly replied. 'People are asking questions.' Gerard rose from his chair and rested his hand on the radiator, which was stone cold.

'Since when did you care what other people think?' Silence filled the line. 'Ruth, if you've something to say, I'd rather you came out with it.'

'Alright, then,' she replied. 'I'm worried about your health. I want you to see a doctor. You're not yourself.'

In those three words his astute wife had touched on the heart of the problem. For once in his life, Gerard didn't know what to say. He was tired. Too tired for any of this. All he wanted was to go home, but he was caught in an invisible web. He pulled a blanket from the back of the sofa and wrapped it around his shoulders. The temperature was plummeting as night drew in.

'I'm coming out there.' Ruth's voice was forthright as he failed to respond. 'We can travel back together. I'll set it all up.'

'No,' Gerard said flatly. 'I need to do this alone.' The turn of phrase surprised him. It was the first chink of insight he'd had all day. So he needed to do something more – but what? He could not involve Ruth, whatever it was.

'Need to do what?' His wife echoed his thoughts.

'To rest and recuperate.' Gerard sat back on the old leather sofa which had seen better days. 'I'm a grown man, for God's sake. Can't I have any peace?' He hated the sharpness of his words, but he could not risk Ruth turning up. He stared out the window and saw only blackness. This was not a good place. It would not end well.

'Are you sure that's all it is?' Ruth's upper-class accent was imbued with concern. 'Because I'll be happier when you get yourself checked out.'

'I will when I get back,' Gerard lied. 'A full MOT, if that's what you want. But I'm fine, honestly. I think it was the pressure of work. Everything got to me. It's peaceful here. I'm feeling better every day.'

'And you'll come home soon?'

'Absolutely. I've not been here a wet week. No need to panic yet.' He forced a laugh, as a feeling of dread wrapped itself around him. The crumpled piece of paper mocked him from the corner of the room.

24

Friday, 6th March 2020

It was a treat to start the day in the lounge of the Slayton Lakeside Hotel. Sarah was moved by the sight of the water as dazzling slices of orange reflected the rising sun. A sunny day was promised, and the hotel's wall-to-wall windows provided a breathtaking panoramic view. Sarah was no stranger to the lake. As teenagers, she and Maggie had splashed in its waters, swinging from ropes attached to the overhanging trees. The memory was a happy one, but the smile faded from Sarah's face as she remembered why she was there.

Something dark was looming over Slayton and the mystery of the whispering children was one she had still to unpick. She tore her gaze away from the lake as she greeted the woman she'd arranged to meet. Lou Simmons was Rosemary's only daughter and had flown over from the States. She was Florida-tanned, with glossy black hair and a set of white teeth that Simon Cowell himself would be envious of. Introducing herself, Lou extended a jewelled hand.

'Sorry for your loss.' Sarah shook her hand firmly, but the words seemed inadequate given what had occurred. It was more than a loss. It was devastation of horror movie proportions.

'Thank you.' Lou spoke from behind a large pair of sunglasses undoubtedly hiding puffy eyes. She scooped her navy dress beneath her as she took a seat. Staff at the hotel knew Sarah well. This area was known as the 'chill zone' with cosy chairs and a selection of books and newspapers to choose from. A small bar served speciality coffees and muffins while the bigger bar served alcohol at the other end of the room. The first floor housed the hotel's restaurant and nightclub. They would not be bothered here. Sarah depressed the plunger on a pot of coffee she had ordered for them both.

'Is coffee OK? Or would you prefer something else?'

'Coffee's fine.'

As they settled into their conversation, Sarah probed Lou on what life had been like for her mother and brother as gently as she could. 'Did you keep in touch much? It can't have been easy after your brother's accident.'

'I've been so busy getting my business off the ground, I didn't have time to call home.' Lou sighed, her words heavy with grief. 'When we did speak, all Mum would talk about was Geoff. Even before he was injured, her life revolved around him.' She delivered a sad smile. 'Sorry. That sounds bad.' Her accent was more American than English as she talked things through.

'Don't apologise,' Sarah replied. 'Families are complicated. No judgement here.' She sipped her glass of water. 'Did you get on with your brother?' What she really wanted to know was if Geoffrey was easy to live with, but she skirted around the question, conscious that Lou was at the early stages of getting to grips with the loss of her brother and mother.

'He had a real chip on his shoulder.' Her features taut, Lou tore her gaze away from the lake. 'He worked for Irving Industries until the workplace accident which put him in a wheelchair. He struggled to cope with it all. He found fault in everything I did. Like life was so tough for him, and nobody else.' She slipped off her glasses and dabbed a tissue to her watery eyes. 'He had these awful bouts of depression, and then Mum would expect me to get involved. It's partly why I left Slayton.' Her words faded as she gazed out at the lake again. 'Sometimes I forget how beautiful it is here . . .'

'You live in Florida now?'

Lou nodded. 'Mum never visited. I bought them both plane tickets after Dad died. Thought they'd come back with me for some sun. They wouldn't step outside of Slayton.' She shook her head. 'It's like the place has . . . *had*' – she corrected herself – 'a hold over them.'

'But not you?' Sarah drained her glass. She understood the power of Slayton more than anyone.

'I can't stand the place. It's always felt so closed in. And the people . . . they're so narrow-minded.' Her gaze flicked to Sarah. 'Sorry. No offence.'

'None taken.' Sarah smiled. She couldn't disagree. The hiss of a coffee machine interrupted their conversation as a barista got to work. 'What about Geoffrey's wife? Did you get on well with her?'

Lou shrugged. 'They weren't together that long. I didn't know her very well.' Police had already spoken to Geoffrey's ex-wife, who had been shocked by her ex-husband's death but was clueless as to why anyone would want to hurt him.

'You mentioned a business in America,' Sarah continued. They were going off at a tangent, but people opened up more over an informal chat.

'I run a British chauffeur service,' Lou replied. 'The celebs love it out there. We're in LA, Hollywood, Miami and Manhattan too. They can't get enough of us Brits.' Her expression brightened as she talked about work. 'You should hear my phone accent. I sound like the Queen.'

'That's impressive,' Sarah replied. 'The business, I mean.' She paused, gently steering the conversation towards what she needed to know. 'And business is going well? You don't have any adversaries? What I mean is . . .' she continued, carefully orchestrating her words, 'there's nobody who would wish your family ill? Anyone you owe money to?'

Lou's hand fell to her chest as the conversation took a turn. 'God, no. People think I come from Windsor. They don't know anything, apart from the story I feed them. Social status is everything over there.'

Slipping her police-issue notebook from her bag, Sarah made a note of her website as Lou provided details. 'And your mum or brother weren't worried about anyone?'

Lou shook her head. 'Mum wouldn't hurt a fly. She devoted her time to church and Greg. Her world revolved around him.' She paused for thought. 'But after his accident it felt like they closed ranks.'

'What do you mean?' Sarah tried to read her expression but she was giving nothing away.

'I don't know . . . I couldn't quite put my finger on it. I remember

I came over once and sometimes they'd be whispering, like they didn't want me to hear. When I asked what it was about, they'd look at me funny and deny it. You know, I haven't thought about that until now. But that was years ago.' She slid her glasses back on her face. 'I can't believe they're gone.' Her chin began to tremble and Sarah passed over a pack of clean tissues. She always carried a pack for interviews such as these.

'I'm so sorry,' Sarah said. 'I know how hard this must be for you.' She spoke with some authority. 'You've been offered a family liaison officer, I take it?' But Lou shook her head.

'No need. I fly home tomorrow. My wife will come back with me for the funeral as soon as their bodies are released.'

It made sense under the circumstances, as the bodies may not be released for some time.

'Why would anyone do this?' Lou leaned in towards Sarah as a couple walked past. 'They weren't robbed. They didn't have any enemies. I don't understand.'

She wasn't the only one. Motive was their biggest problem right now. 'That's what we're trying to find out.' Sarah sipped her coffee, which was welcome as the early morning sun beamed down on them. 'Is there anything more you can tell me about your brother?'

'Only what you probably already know.' Lou dabbed her eyes with a tissue. 'He loved Mum. Even if he lost the plot and did this himself, he would never have hurt her.'

Sarah shook her head. 'Your brother didn't do this. That much we're sure of.' Having obtained his medical records, officers knew it would have been physically impossible for Greg to get out of his wheelchair and kill his mother in such a horrific way before doing the same to himself. 'Did he have any old acquaintances he still kept in touch with? Any friends?'

Lou exhaled the sigh of a woman who'd been asked the same question many times before. 'I can see where you're coming from, but you're grasping at straws. Geoff was a virtual recluse. He didn't mix with anyone or have any enemies. If you're looking for someone to blame, you'll have to look elsewhere.'

'Not blaming, just enquiring.' Sarah closed her notebook.

'Experienced teams are working on the case, and specialist officers are being drafted in.'

'It won't bring them back, though, will it?' Fresh tears welled in Lou's eyes. 'Mum didn't pass peacefully in her sleep. She was butchered, along with my brother. What sort of monster would do that?'

'I don't know,' Sarah said, her features grim. 'But we won't rest until we catch them.' She meant it. She wouldn't be able to sleep until they were behind bars. She knew the pain of losing family. She could not fix the past, but she could stop it from happening again.

25

Sarah munched on a cereal bar as she worked through her checklist of outstanding things. She was thoroughly enjoying being busy, and the afternoon had flown. The Josef Pieper quote came to mind: 'Leisure is only possible when we are at one with ourselves.' According to him, people overworked as a means of escape. Was she working to bury reality? Whatever the case, she welcomed the list of tasks, from speaking to the residents in Slayton to watching hours of CCTV.

The investigation was moving quickly. The 'murder board' in the briefing room was filling up with persons of interest, potential leads and the victims' family history. The few relatives who kept in touch with Rosemary and her son had been interviewed and discounted. The public protection team had former offenders under scrutiny. There seemed little motivation for such a grotesque attack. The words *calling card or accident?* were written above the picture of the bloodied handprint. Sarah was prioritising her jobs carefully, delegating the ones she couldn't fulfil to the local Police Community Support Officers. Everyone had a part to play in investigating this case and Sarah was led by her gut. Scrunching up the cereal bar wrapper, she threw it in the bin.

'Boss, can I have a quick word?' She tapped a knuckle on DI McGuire's open door. He'd been so busy with the investigation, it was difficult to get five minutes alone with him.

'The door is open for a reason.' He smiled. 'Come in.'

He'd had a haircut, and his mop of brown hair had been transformed into a neat short-back-and-sides style. The top button of his shirt was open, his tie loosely bound in a way which would irk Gabby, a stickler for smart dress.

'I want to talk about Roger Newman.' Sarah held her folders as if they were some kind of protective force field. While they were

94

encouraged to be paperless, they had a way to go just yet. 'He's behind these mystery YouTube videos doing the rounds.'

'Ah, yes, Newman, the proverbial pain in the arse.' McGuire regarded her with a glint in his eye. He had an air of mischief, which could be unsettling in times like these. 'Take a pew.' He gestured to a chair. His office was warm and comfortable, a pile of neatly stacked paperwork to his left. To his right was a bottle of water, a collection of pens and a small pot-bellied Buddha statue.

Sarah activated the swivel chair to rise a couple of inches until she was meeting his eye. Her feet were almost dangling, but it felt good to be on his level for a change. 'I know you said we weren't to talk to the media, but—'

'No buts, Noble.' McGuire raised a finger. 'It's a rule set in stone.'

'Well, can we compromise on that rule?' Sarah inhaled a breath. 'It's just that I'd like to see what he's up to. He's always had an interest in Slayton. I want to see how deep that interest runs.'

'Newman hasn't been elevated to suspect status yet.' McGuire narrowed his eyes. 'Unless you've got something more on him?'

Sarah gripped her paperwork tightly on her lap. 'Not yet. But I'd like to sound him out.'

'Aye, but we must tread carefully. You know what happened with Wilkins. We don't want a repeat of that.'

Sarah knew of the Wilkins case, which McGuire's team had handled. A young woman was found murdered in her flat. Her landlord was an eccentric man who'd developed a crush on her. He was naturally a person of interest, but the press got hold of it and splashed him all over the front page. His life was made hell, and then the real killer, her ex-boyfriend, was revealed. Mr Wilkins ended up suing the force for damages and unsurprisingly, he won. Sarah crossed her legs. McGuire had a point.

'This Newman, he reminds me of Wilkins,' McGuire said thoughtfully. 'A bit of an oddball. I'm not even sure if we can call people oddballs anymore, but if the press got hold of police sniffing around, he could be front-page news. I've watched his videos. He knows the law and is a big advocate for free speech.'

Sarah nodded throughout.

'You think he'll entertain you?' McGuire asked.

'Well, you know what they say, it takes one to know one. I think he'll talk to me.'

'Aye, sure you could be right there.' McGuire steepled his fingers together.

Sarah raised her eyebrows at his brutal honesty. She'd walked herself into that one. Was that what he thought of her?

'Oh, don't you take offence.' McGuire smiled. 'You're a good spud. I wouldn't have had you on the team if I thought otherwise. But I don't want you talking to Newman just yet. The last thing we need is him bringing out another YouTube video exclusive.' The shrill sound of a police car siren filtered in from the car park outside.

Sarah knew better than to argue with her DI. Newman would be spoken to in time, just not by her. Her disappointment must have been etched on her face as McGuire's expression changed to concern.

'Come. Take a walk.' He grabbed his suit jacket from the back of his chair.

'But I've got to . . .' Sarah began, aware that time was ticking away.

'It won't take a minute. You look like you could do with the fresh air.'

He headed out of the office with Sarah trotting after him. Lean and long-limbed, he took one step for Sarah's two. A cold March breeze greeted them as they stood on the front steps of the station beneath the billowing police flag. McGuire seemed relaxed, his usual grin spread across his face. But Sarah was uneasy in the company of people she didn't know. It took her time to trust people and McGuire was an unknown quantity.

'Tell me about your hours,' McGuire said at last. 'You seem to come and go as you please. Are you still on restricted duties or has that come to an end?'

Somewhat taken aback, Sarah stared at the cement steps, grateful the traffic was quiet. If Maguire knew about her duties then he was aware of why she had been put on them. 'I'm due off restricted duties soon,' Sarah said, hoping he wouldn't tell her off for working extended hours before she had been officially cleared by occupational health.

'Riiight, right.' McGuire turned his gaze upon her, giving her a steely eye. 'What do yous want from your job?'

Sarah hadn't expected the question. When she first returned to work it had been under a cloud. She looked to him for clarity. 'Sorry, guv, but why do you want to know?'

A small crease rested on McGuire's forehead. 'Just trying to get the lie of the land with you, Noble. Do you want to be a statement taker or a detective? Because it feels like you're sitting on the fence. You're a wee bit unsure of yourself, but there's no grounding for that. I saw the work you did with your last big case and I was mighty impressed.' He smiled as he spoke, his words imbued with sincerity. 'You have potential, and I don't mean to be condescending. You might have an issue with someone a few years younger patting you on the back – am I right?' He dazzled her with a smile.

'Not at all,' Sarah replied instantly. But McGuire's intense gaze was better than any truth serum and Sarah cleared her throat. 'Well, maybe I was a bit unsure of you at the beginning, but not anymore.'

'Good!' he replied enthusiastically. 'How's about we officially clear you of restricted duties? You don't want your colleagues grumbling that you get to put your feet up when they don't, now do you? Because I think you can do more.'

Sarah accepted the compliment, but she still wasn't sure where he was coming from as she was only on loan to MIT. 'The only thing is' – she shoved her hands into her trouser suit pockets as a biting chill grew – 'my family have lived in Slayton for generations, and in a small town like this that counts for something. I'm more useful out taking statements and talking to the locals than being chained to my desk.' She shifted on her feet, conscious of the time. God knows how many phone calls and emails she had racked up. But she was in too deep to stop now. 'I'm not saying I'm better than my colleagues – quite the opposite – but I can relate to people on the street and I don't want to be too far removed from that.'

'Then we're in agreement, as that's what I want you to do.' McGuire's gaze turned to the sky and he pointed at a hawk hovering in the distance. 'Some officers are like that chappie up there. They circle around trying to get the best jobs to impress. They're sharp and ambitious and there's nothing wrong with that.' His gaze dropped to a group of pigeons on the pavement where they stood. 'Now take your humble pigeon. Always in the background. Part of the furniture, so to speak. We don't see them as a threat. But they're there, absorbing it all.' He leaned in to drive his point home. 'I want you to be more pigeon, Noble. What do you say, are you up for it?'

Sarah arched an eyebrow. She wasn't enamoured with being called a pigeon but she sensed there was a compliment in there somewhere. 'Sure,' she said warmly. 'Why not?' As they returned to the station, a question rose in her mind. McGuire would move on as soon as the investigation was dealt with, so why was he taking such an interest in her?

26

Elsie stared at the blank page, waiting for the words to come. She was halfway through writing the first draft of a new novel in her Forbidden Romance series. It was as hot as a jalapeño's coochie – and that was pretty darn hot! She dusted the biscuit crumbs off her top. She would tame her words in time. She didn't want to shock the pants off her future readers, after all. It was ironic, given she'd left one-star Amazon reviews for books only half as saucy as hers for years. *Potty-mouthed filth, porn-level writing, immoral trash.* All reviews she'd left for the well-thumbed books. Guilt bloomed at the irony. All the energy she'd put into bringing down the authors, and soon she would be one herself. 'Live and learn,' she sighed. At least she'd gone back and changed them all to five stars. She was enjoying this world a million miles from her own.

She'd lost hours of her time writing about the handsome Romany and his relationship with the guarded police detective. Elsie had toyed with other scenarios, but this one was crying out to be written and once she'd started typing, the words flew onto the page. She emitted a mischievous chuckle, toying with the ends of her hair as she wondered how Sarah would react. It was probably wise not to share it just yet. Perhaps she would be flattered. She was a sucker for a happy ending. There were so few of them in Slayton these days.

As a teen, she'd spent countless hours daydreaming of being saved. One of her favourite fantasies had been a *Wuthering Heights*-type love story, where she fell for a brooding Romany boy, much to her father's disgust. Elsie couldn't understand why her pa despised them so much. His face loomed large in her memory, his deep frown lines, the cleft in his chin. His overgrown grey sideburns. Papa Abrahams hated anyone who opposed his narrow-minded views.

She remembered the day the traveller children went missing.

Elsie was fifteen years old back then. She'd seen them in town a few times before. Thin, pale young 'uns, in clean but worn-out clothes. Sometimes they scavenged for biscuits at the local supermarket. Other times they collected their papa from the local pub. They were motherless, poor little critters. But there was no sympathy when they disappeared. Not that Elsie helped their plight. Her father tasked her with ripping down each 'missing' poster as quickly as it was put up. Christian was just a few months old back then, wrapped up warm in his pram. Beneath the cover of darkness, Elsie dutifully tore down each poster and shoved them into Christian's pram. It shamed her to think about it now, but she was a slave to her father's demands back then. If you disobeyed Papa Abraham you felt the weight of his belt on your back. *Those poor souls*, Elsie thought, remembering how the residents of Slayton had treated the Romanies as they went from house to house. When the knock rebounded against their own front door Elsie could barely stand to watch.

'Leave this place,' her father commanded, his craggy features stern. 'Your kind aren't welcome here.'

Elsie wished they had given him the beating he so richly deserved. He was by no means the only one who made the travellers feel unwelcome. Private meetings were held for townsfolk. Then word spread that the travellers were covering something up. Some said they were crying crocodile tears. According to local rumours, no child in Slayton was safe. But anyone could see that Mercy and Mikey's disappearance had hit the Romany community hard. Their faces revealed their devastation as they demanded to be heard. But the case was quickly forgotten by the public and the police.

Elsie felt shame for the part she had played by taking their posters down. She may have been helpless then, but she wasn't anymore. She shut down her laptop. There would be no more writing today. Not when there were people to call, enquiries to make. Somebody must know something. She knew how the rumour mill worked. They may not want to talk to the police, but they would speak to her.

27

Evening was closing in fast, turning Sarah's office window into a dull grey sheet dappled with rain. 'Here you go.' Richie rested a fresh mug of coffee on her desk. She blinked to relieve her eye strain. Their old Dell computers had been refurbished so many times they looked like they came from a different era, with big boxy processors which whirred if you opened too many tabs. The hot coffee tasted like heaven as it slid down her throat. 'Thanks, I needed that. How's it going?'

'I've been rushed off my feet all day,' Richie replied, taking an empty swivel chair. 'I've been going from pillar to post with ANPR checks and CCTV enquiries to check any suspicious cars in town . . . then there's the media enquiries and calls coming in. What about you?'

'Same,' Sarah replied with a sigh, weary from being on her feet all day. 'I was hoping the DI would let me interview Roger Newman but he's said no.'

'You're kidding!' Richie folded his arms, his sleeves straining over his biceps. 'Hasn't he seen his YouTube channel? The black-eyed children are all he can talk about. He's pulling in the viewers, too.'

Grateful for his support, Sarah nodded in the direction of Gav's desk. 'I know not everyone approves of spending time on it, but it can't harm to have a quick word.' Her colleagues were engrossed as they tapped speedily on their keyboards, but as busy as they were, they hadn't made any *real* headway. It made her both tired and uneasy, knowing a killer had been on the street where she lived.

'Newman is a media whore,' Richie said firmly. 'And Slayton is feeding his channel. Let me have a quick word with the boss.'

Richie was up before Sarah got a chance to reply. She sat, wondering if she should be offended or grateful. Either way, if he persuaded him to think differently it would be worth it. *Sod it*, she thought, rising from her desk to join them.

'Look at his latest video,' Richie said, his phone under McGuire's nose. They were standing by the water cooler and Richie was showing him a channel displaying videos of mysterious events. The thumbnails were ridiculous – Newman, wide-eyed and shocked, with pictures of UFOs and Bigfoot in the background. 'He's hit a million subscribers since coming to Slayton.'

'I've seen his channel,' McGuire replied. 'I can't understand why a middle-aged man is gallivanting around Slayton in the first place.'

'This is more than a hobby, boss.' Richie scrolled down. 'He's monetised his content, which means he's earning a fortune from these videos. And for someone like Roger Newman, it must be a dream come true.' He pointed at another video. 'The more views he gets the more income he receives. But people must watch it all the way to the end, which is why his videos are so sensationalist. The thumbnails draw people in, then his promises of shock revelations keep them watching.'

McGuire nodded. 'And the bigger the shock, the more people watch?'

'Yep,' Richie replied. 'He has a vested interest in keeping the rumours alive . . .'

'Which makes our job so much harder because people aren't thinking with a clear head.'

Sarah watched their interaction. Richie was a natural. She wished she had even a quarter of his confidence. But then Richie had been afforded a normal upbringing – she, on the other hand, had not. The dramas did not stop after she became an adult. She reminded herself that every day she achieved the illusion that she was a normal functioning person was a win. It wasn't that long ago that she was stashing tablets in her bedside drawer for the day she decided to take a permanent sleep. Now her thoughts were taken up with work, and what a godsend that was. She switched her focus to McGuire as he noticed she was there.

'Alright, Noble, you have my blessing. Speak to Newman in the morning. Keep it informal.' McGuire shoved his hands into his trouser pockets and his change jingled as he moved. Although cheerful, he was full of nervous energy. He didn't stay still for very long. 'In fact, do a mop-up in general. Revisit anyone who hasn't answered their door.' He didn't wait for her response before returning to Richie. 'Submit a sixty-one but keep it brief.' Sarah hated submitting intelligence. Protocol was strict and her email inbox was full of bounced submissions because she hadn't worded them right.

'Thanks, boss.' Sarah smiled at the minor victory. Richie returned to his desk but something told her to linger.

McGuire leaned in. 'Go alone. Richie will monopolise the conversation. Be discreet. Act like it's out of a personal interest rather than police business. Then report your findings directly to me. Tag yourself to the job as making neighbourhood enquiries so you don't get interrupted.'

'Will do.' Sarah checked the clock on the wall. It was time she was getting off home.

'Aye, well, get yourself off. There's nothing more we can do tonight.'

It was as if he'd read her mind. Calling on Newman at this late hour would only spook him.

'Don't you think it's disrespectful?' she continued, taking Richie's empty mug to wash it up before she went home. 'Making money out of other people's misery through YouTube.'

'Newman and his viewers don't mean any harm,' Richie said. 'There are lots of Facebook or Reddit groups where armchair detectives solve mysteries police don't have the resources for.'

Sarah understood where he was coming from but it still niggled, probably because she had been a victim of crime herself. 'But what about the people who treat killers like A-list celebrities? You're telling me they give a damn?'

Richie shrugged. 'Dark tourism is real. Like it or not, you can expect to see them in Slayton from now on.' He was speaking with authority. The strange and unusual was something he was passionate about.

But this was not what Sarah wanted to hear. It was bad enough, a killer walking the streets. Ghouls were not welcome here. The sooner they solved the crime, the sooner these people would go home.

28

Saturday, 7th March 2020

Sarah's stomach bubbled with nerves. She was getting used to socialising with her colleagues occasionally after work, and she met up with her friends Elsie and Maggie once a week. But now she was approaching a man who most likely wanted to eat his breakfast in peace. She had Maggie to thank for the tip-off. Given she worked at the Lakeside Hotel, she was first to know the comings and goings of anyone who stood out from the norm.

The sight of a small Yorkshire terrier caught her attention as its owner walked her on the hotel grounds. She recognised the dog, with its one black, one brown ear, but was sure it didn't belong to Maura Belham, the woman holding its tartan lead. She was Father Aloysius's live-in housekeeper, and they didn't own a dog as far as Sarah was aware. Perhaps she was doing its owner a good turn.

Sarah liked the hotel, with its rich furnishings and friendly staff. It was a big hit with Slayton locals, as well as visitors from out of town. Like Roger Newman. Sarah saw him the moment she entered. With his red frizzy hair and bulky stature, he was hard to miss. Gathering up her courage, she slipped into the booth and sat across from him. His fork froze mid-air, bacon dangling as he stared, one bushy eyebrow raised.

'Roger Newman, isn't it? Sorry to bother you . . .' Sarah began, 'but can we talk?'

Newman sat, shoulders hunched, and shovelled his food into his mouth. 'If you're a fan of the channel then talk to me online. I came here to eat in peace.' He spoke in a nasal tone, his words abrupt and to the point.

Not exactly the warmest of welcomes, but Sarah persevered. She took no pleasure in watching him eat, given his fried eggs were trailing halfway down his beard.

'I'm not a fan.' She interlaced her fingers. 'I'm here to ask you to stop.'

Newman finally raised his eyes to her, talking with his mouth full. 'You're a hater then. Either that or a local. Whatever the case, you've no right invading my privacy.'

'Ironic, isn't it?' Sarah snorted. 'That's what most of the residents of Slayton say about your videos.'

Swallowing the last of his food, Newman rested his fork on the table before wiping his beard with a linen napkin. He ran a tongue over his teeth, regarding her as he knocked back the remains of his tea. Sarah knew he was buying time, probably trying to think of something smart to say. Keyboard warriors like Newman thought they had it all figured out until they encountered a real-life person face to face. 'Who are you?' he finally said, with an ill-concealed burp. 'Press? Police? What's your angle?'

Sarah couldn't lie. But she didn't want him knowing exactly who she was. The last thing she needed was more videos about Blackhall Manor popping up. She glanced over her shoulder, her voice just loud enough to be heard over the bossa nova music filtering through hotel speakers. 'I'm police. But I'm here as a concerned resident of Slayton. The town has been through enough, and your gossip-mongering is sending people into panic mode.'

A sly smile rose to Newman's face. 'I'd say the infestation is doing that. I take it you're a non-believer?'

Sarah resisted the urge to roll her eyes. He didn't know her, nor did he know what she'd been through. Her mind was more open than most, but that wasn't why she was here today. She inhaled a deep breath as she composed her words. 'What I believe in has no relevance to this. You're hurting the town. Rein it in.'

'Or else?' Newman tilted his head to one side. 'Are you threatening me?'

Sarah's features tightened. McGuire's words echoed in her mind. The last thing they needed was a YouTube video casting aspersions on the police. She needed to watch her step. 'On the contrary. I'm looking out for you.'

'Oh yeah? How do you figure that?' Amusement danced in Newman's eyes as he mopped up his beans with a piece of toast.

Sarah responded with a sigh. 'I've nothing against your theories, and you have the right to free speech. But I'm asking you to be mindful when spreading some of the more . . . outrageous claims of spectral beings walking the streets of Slayton. There's a lot of pissed-off people around here.' She was about to say that she didn't want to see him get hurt, but that could also be taken as a threat. 'I can offer you safeguarding if it comes to it.'

Newman almost seemed disappointed by Sarah's sudden backtrack. 'I won't shy away from the truth.'

'I'm not asking you to. As long as it *is* the truth and not sensationalist gossip. What do you know about these black-eyed children? There's a dangerous murderer on the loose. I don't want you getting caught up with that.'

'Everything I know is in my videos. And I never give away my source.' Newman chewed rhythmically. 'Are you in charge of the investigation?'

'Hardly. I'm a DC. A worker bee. But I *am* heavily involved in the community. Feelings are running high. Try to take the locals into consideration before you upload your next video.' Sarah had a feeling his 'source' was the realms of his provocative imagination.

Newman delivered a thin smile, appearing anything but remorseful. 'I'm used to pissing people off. It's part and parcel of what I do.' He paused for thought. 'So I can add local police to the list of people who are riled by what I say?' He seemed to like the idea of this and a smile rested on his face.

'God, no.' Sarah laughed, playing things down. 'They're only interested in *serious* leads. But the longer I'm dealing with people about your claims, then the less time I'm spending investigating the case.'

'Then buzz off back to your hive, worker bee.' Sitting back in his chair, Newman folded his arms, his mouth downturned.

Sarah picked at the lint resting on her jacket sleeve. 'Just . . . look after yourself, Mr Newman.' She slid out of the booth, feeling more confident than when she'd first sat down. She may not have prised any information out of him, but she had picked up on a ripple of unease. Every word that passed his lips was guarded and thought through. Mr Newman may not know who the killer was, but Sarah would bet her wages that he had something to hide.

29

Sarah was thoughtful as she walked up the broken flagstones leading to Arnold's woodland cottage. The air was morning fresh and dewy, and she inhaled a deep breath to wake herself up. The sight of the Yorkshire terrier had prompted a return visit as she remembered where she'd seen it last. It was the same dizzy little dog she'd seen Arnold with before. So why was Father Aloysius's housekeeper walking it on the hotel grounds? Her footsteps slowed as she approached the cottage. The place was a woodland jungle swallowed up by spiky thorn bushes and overgrown weeds. She had been here before, on doorstep enquiries. The man inside was a recluse and never answered. But this was marked as an outstanding task and she wasn't leaving until he let her in. She rapped her knuckles against the grubby stained glass and caught fleeting movement from within.

'Right,' Sarah said, bending to the letterbox. As a police officer, she had no right to enter the property unless there was a serious concern for welfare. 'Mr Smith, I'm Sarah Noble, from Slayton police station. I'd like a quick word. Nothing to worry about.'

Another scuffle from within. A crash, followed by a groaning noise. *Give me strength*, Sarah thought, prising open the stiff letterbox. 'Arnold?' she called, making use of his first name. 'I know you're in there. Now are you going to leave me freezing my bits off on your doorstep, or are you going to let me in?' She sighed. 'I'm not leaving until you do.' She groaned as she straightened, her back emitting a cracking sound. She was getting a bit old for peek-a-boo. She glanced over her shoulder as the hairs stood sentry on the back of her neck. For a second, she could have sworn she heard whispering. The woods were eerily quiet this far out. Her imagination was running away with her. A shadow approached the door. She held her warrant card aloft as it opened.

107

Arnold was a small, stocky man with tufts of wiry white hair. His clothes had seen better days and his shirt was a stranger to an iron, but at least he was reasonably clean and dressed. Peering at her warrant card picture, he heaved a sigh. 'Come in if you must.'

A sweet, musty smell rose from the hall as he shuffled ahead of her, and she realised it was coming off his clothes which he'd probably worn damp. She doubted he possessed a dryer and he didn't appear the type to hang them outside. It was the opposite to Sarah, who overdosed her clothes with fabric conditioner and hung them outside to dry whatever the temperature. Next she was assaulted by the ticking of what sounded like a hundred clocks coming from the living room. She peeped in through the door as they signalled the hour in a cacophony of chimes.

Arnold swept a hand across his hair before beckoning her into the kitchen. There was no sign of the dog she had seen here before. A single cobwebbed bulb hung from the ceiling and Sarah glanced at the chequered floor and wonky cupboard doors. Every spare surface was covered in clutter and the sink was full of crockery which appeared to have been there for some time. 'I won't offer you tea because you're not staying,' he said stiffly. 'What do you want?'

Sarah cast an eye over the mouse droppings on the kitchen counter. The last thing she wanted was tea. 'What happened to your dog?' She could question him about the murders soon enough.

'I gave the thing away. Bloody nuisance, I'm well rid.' He flapped his arms in the air, becoming agitated. *Best get to the point*, Sarah thought. *Before he blows his top.*

'I see. I'm making doorstep enquiries, Mr Smith. A serious incident occurred—'

'I know,' Arnold interrupted, his mouth downturned. 'It's all over the news. I turn on the radio and it's there. It's on the local news too. I bought a paper and it's plastered all over the front page.'

'Then you know why I'm here . . .' Sarah continued, but Arnold wasn't finished grumbling.

'I leave this house twice a week to go to mass and buy groceries. They're talking about it in the checkout aisle. Even in the library . . .' He raised his finger in disgust. 'Did you hear me? In the library. The one place a man should be able to seek refuge. It's upsetting, that's what it is.'

'Did you know the victims?'

'No!' Arnold barked. 'I didn't. I know nothing about them, do you hear me? Nothing!' He wagged a finger in her direction. 'Write that down in your little black book.' He shook his head in disgust. 'And now you're knocking on my door, forcing me to talk about it. Well, I won't have it. I'm telling you now. Don't come knocking here again. Why can't a person get a bit of peace?'

His face flushed, he abruptly grabbed her roughly by the arm and yanked her towards the door. He was surprisingly strong for a shuffling old man. Sarah stiffened. She wasn't being manhandled today. 'Mr Smith,' she said in her best headmistress voice, 'get your hands off me or I'll have you done for assault of a police officer!'

His eyes widened and he released his grip and swiftly stepped away.

'If you want me to leave, you only have to ask.'

Arnold's face contorted in a mixture of emotions. Again, he swiped his hand over his head. 'I'm sorry, I . . . I don't know what came over me.' He shook his head regretfully. 'I should never have let you in.' He met her gaze, his face an apology. 'Can you go now? It's best if you do.'

'Just one last question. Has anyone threatened you? Do you need safeguarding? Because I can arrange it.'

He shook his head wearily. 'I just want you to leave me alone, please.' His words dissolved into a whine and Sarah could see he was getting upset again.

'Fine, then I'll go.' Sarah slid a card from her pocket and laid it on a dusty dresser table. 'If you change your mind then you can reach me on this number.' As she opened the front door, she welcomed the fresh air. She turned to speak but the door was slammed shut in her face. Arnold was disproportionately upset. Lots of people in Slayton had mental health issues, but there was more to it than that here. She cast her eye over the cottage as she eased her way through a gap in the brambles to the broken garden gate. It was disappearing into the vegetation, swallowed by the earth it was built upon. Did Arnold want to disappear along with it?

30

As Sarah sat in Maud's humble kitchen, she welcomed the opportunity to sit down. She'd knocked on so many doors, locals were calling her by her first name. Like many Lower Slayton residents Sarah had encountered this morning, Maud struggled to get by in a town forgotten by those with the power to change it. Drug use was becoming more prevalent, as was car theft and joyriding. At least once a night, Sarah was awoken by a stolen motor of some sort tearing down her street. This week she'd had some respite, now the street was closed, but it would soon be open to the tearaways again. Whatever force was driving them, they had little regard for the inhabitants of Slayton. It wasn't safe to cross the street when the joyriders were out. It saddened her to see the dark path so many of Slayton's kids were on.

Sarah suppressed a shudder in the cold kitchen as a draught rose from beneath the badly fitted back door. This was one of many bungalows on Slayton's Brewery Estate. It was named after the old brewery which once thrived on this land but was long since derelict and rotten. It loomed over the bungalows on the built-up estate near the playground and expansive parklands. Sarah had been called to visit Maud, who had been walking her poodle when she saw what she described as two 'black-eyed children' in the distance. It had been enough for her to summon the police and trot all the way home. Normally such reports would be attended by a Police Community Support Officer, if at all. But all calls reporting sightings of strange children were now referred to MIT.

'Frightened the living daylights out of me, they did.' With a shaking hand, Maud pulled a tissue from beneath the sleeve of her cardigan and blew her nose. 'I usually walk Trixie with my friend Enid, but she's come down with a cold. I thought I'd be alright if I left an hour early, but the evening drew in so quickly . . .'

'Would you like me to make you a cuppa?' Sarah said, hating to see the pensioner so upset. Tea was the answer to everything in Sarah's book, but Maud declined.

'I was walking along the common when I heard this moaning. At first I thought someone was hurt, but Trixie was barking so much that I couldn't make it out.' She lowered her head to stroke the skinny poodle resting at her feet. 'Then I saw them . . . two children dressed in dark clothes. Their faces were chalk white and their eyes were black hollows . . . just like on the video.'

'Wait, what?' Sarah's pen paused on her notepad. 'Did you say video?'

'Oh yes,' Maud said, 'I watch them on my iPad. Never thought I'd be next, though.'

'Next for what?'

'Next on their list. Haven't you heard? The black-eyed children follow you home and knock at your door.' She swallowed as she relayed the tale. 'It's said they whisper outside your windows. But you mustn't let them in or you're done for.'

'Mrs Leven . . .'

'Please call me Maud. I don't go in for this "Mrs" business, my husband has long since passed away.'

'Maud.' Sarah smiled at the woman before her. 'I consider myself to be open-minded. How could I not be, living in Slayton? But you mustn't pay any heed to those videos. Most of that stuff is made up.' Sarah fought the urge to tell her exactly what she thought of Mr Newman. Now she had met him, she didn't trust him an ounce.

'Tell that to Rosemary and her son,' Maud sniffed. 'You can't, can you? Because they're dead.' Sarah tried to reassure the woman as much as she could. Similar sightings were coming in over the police airwaves, as locals described pale-faced children dressed in black acting suspiciously on the outskirts of town. No real contact was made and no firm descriptions were given. 'They didn't approach you directly?' Sarah looked over her notes after taking Maud's account.

'Oh no, quite the opposite. They legged it when Trixie slipped her lead and gave chase.'

'Really?'

'It's the terrier in her,' Maud whispered, as if it were an embarrassment to her dog. 'One of the boys almost tripped up on their shoelaces.'

'Interesting,' Sarah said. As far as she was aware, ghosts had no need of such earthly things and they weren't prone to tripping up. 'What sort of shoes was he wearing?'

'Black trainers. Those ones with the bubbles in them,' Maud said. 'They both were. They took off into the woods and that was the last I saw of them.'

'I'm impressed,' Sarah said, stretching to pat the dog. 'Good girl, Trixie.'

'She's my shadow, that one. I don't know what I'd do without her.'

'Sounds like they were two scallywags up to no good. I haven't heard of ghosts wearing Nike Airs.' Sarah glanced around the kitchen. Each bolt was pulled on the wooden back door and her kitchen curtains were tightly closed.

'I suppose.' Maud sighed, calmer than she was when Sarah first arrived. 'But they gave me quite a fright.'

'I don't doubt it,' Sarah replied. She didn't blame Maud for calling the police, but she resented the time it was taking dealing with each report. It seemed the same two kids were frightening half the old dears in Lower Slayton. Antics like these were not unusual in Slayton and wouldn't be classified as genuine leads. They didn't bring the police any closer to capturing those responsible for the recent murders, but could act as a good smoke screen. After parting with some reassuring words, Sarah headed back to the station.

Roger Newman had a lot to answer for.

'Sarah!'

A voice beckoned from behind her as she crossed the station car park. It was Bernard, her DI. 'How's it going with MIT?' he said, slightly out of breath as he jogged over to join her. Bernard was unaccustomed to physical exertion, given the amount of time he spent behind his desk.

'Great, thanks, boss,' Sarah said, with a sneaking suspicion that Bernard had put in a good word for her.

'Champion. It'll do you the world of good. How's the case? Made any strides? I'm sure it won't be long until you solve it.'

Sarah laughed. 'I appreciate your faith in me, sir. But no, not yet.' She raised a hand to her face to shield her eyes from the fading sun. Today it was her turn to feel worried about him. 'How's Helen?'

Bernard shoved his hands into his pockets, giving a quick glance around the car park. 'You've not said anything, have you? Helen's a proud woman. She may not always be present, but she wouldn't want any fuss.'

Sarah noticed his pained expression and it saddened her. 'So are you, by all accounts,' she countered. 'A proud man, I mean. And no, I've not mentioned it. But if you need anything, you only have to ask.'

'Don't worry about me.' Bernard cleared his throat. 'She's on day release with the convalescent home, so when things get too difficult she'll move in full-time.' He gazed at Sarah wearily, as if it was the last thing he wanted. 'No leads in this case of yours then? No witnesses?'

His attempt at changing the subject was painfully obvious. 'I wouldn't know where to start.' She pointed at DI McGuire as he crossed the car park in his usual jaunty manner. 'He's the man to ask, not me.'

'Indeed,' Bernard replied. 'I must say it feels strange not to have ownership of a local case.' He cast his gaze towards McGuire but made no attempt to stop him.

'Can I ask . . .' Sarah said, hesitantly. 'What do you think of him? I can't seem to make him out. He's a bit . . .' she struggled for the right word, 'eccentric.'

'That he is.' Bernard's answer came without hesitation. 'But he's a good sort, ambitious, well educated. Got a photographic memory, you know.'

'I didn't know that. Must be useful when it comes to exams.' Sarah had memories of falling asleep over her Blackstone's manuals as she burned the candle at both ends. If there were drier, more long-winded passages of text to absorb, she hadn't encountered them yet. She'd coped by sticking copious Post-it notes all over her home. There were so many different offences to memorise it had made her head spin.

Bernard seemed wistful as he stared after McGuire. 'I envy him. A young man with his career ahead of him instead of behind. It would be nice to crack another big case before I say my final farewell.'

'You could always stay.'

'I don't know . . .' Bernard massaged the deepening lines on his forehead. 'I'm being squeezed from all sides.'

Sarah felt his frustration. It seemed her DI was torn between family and work.

'Ah well, don't speak too soon.' Sarah chuckled, in an effort to cheer him up. 'This is Slayton. We'll fit in another big case or two yet.'

'Heaven forbid!' Bernard smiled, before saying his goodbyes. Then he was off, whistling as he strode to his car. Sarah checked her watch. She was due to go off duty too but she wasn't quitting, not yet. Something told her the children were due a return visit to the park. And she wanted to be there when that happened. Such a covert operation would take time for McGuire to authorise – which was why she had no intention of telling him.

31

'Did you know the ocean is like a layer cake?' Elliott looked up at Jahmelia, who was sucking the lid of her pen. They were both sitting at the kitchen table, doing their homework as evening closed in. Mum was working again, but he didn't mind Jahmelia babysitting because she was his friend.

'I can't see it tasting too good.' Jahmelia smiled.

Sometimes Elliott had a hard time working out when people were joking or not. But Jahmelia was in secondary school so she must be smart enough to understand. 'It's got different layers,' he explained just the same. 'The top is the sunlight zone, then the twilight zone, then the dark zone and the abyss.' He turned the page of his drawing pad and showed her his sketch. Sometimes he had sunny days, but when he lay down to sleep, it felt like the abyss. But he didn't need to tell Jahmelia that. She'd touched the abyss too. Then there were deeper parts of the ocean known as trenches. They were black and scary, full of unknown creatures, and people didn't go there. Elliott knew what that was like too. Up until he met Miss Grogan, he thought he was the only one who did.

Jahmelia rested her pen on the table, the lid still wet from where she'd chewed it. That was icky. But he didn't mind because Jahmelia was his friend. 'Are you still going to be a marine biologist when you grow up?'

His eyes shone brightly as his favourite subject came up. 'No. I'm going to study giant tortoises on the Galapagos islands.' It made him feel warm in his tummy just to think about it.

'That's cool,' Jahmelia said, playing with the braids in her hair. Then she looked at him, her lips parted as if she wanted to say more. Elliott waited. Seconds passed.

'Are you OK, Elliott? I mean . . .' She nibbled on her bottom lip. 'Since everything . . . you know.'

He did know. They used to have a friend named Libby, but now she'd moved away. Bad things happened in Slayton and not everyone came out of it OK. The warm glow Elliott felt began to fade. He didn't like being asked questions. Especially not ones like these. But Jahmelia was waiting for an answer. He squirmed in his seat. 'I'm OK.' He slid his drawing book back around and turned a fresh page. He wanted to draw the children. The ones with the dark eyes who hung around his bed at night.

He began to sketch an outline.

'I'm glad you're OK.' Jahmelia smiled. 'Granny said all the spooky stories you hear about in Slayton are made-up poop.' She giggled at her use of the word. 'OK, she didn't say poop, but she's a police officer so she should know.'

Jahmelia's grandmother was Auntie Sarah's friend, Gabby. There were bad people in Slayton, but there were good people too. It was a town of dark and light. As Jahmelia turned back to her homework, Elliott continued with his sketch. He'd drawn the children before. Sometimes there were grown-ups. The woman with the hot chocolate. The man in the wheelchair. But today a new figure appeared on the page. Their features were blank because it hadn't happened yet. Today they were just an outline. They stood next to the children but soon they would be in the same place, staring with blacked-out eyes.

32

Hoodie up, Sarah trudged through the back alleys and shortcuts of Lower Slayton. In her black hoodie and jeans, Sarah had made every effort to blend in, although her presence at this hour of the night was unpaid and unauthorised. She reached for her phone as it vibrated in her pocket. It was Richie.

'Hey, Danger Mouse, are you still scouting the town?'

Sarah rolled her eyes. 'What if I am?' She had confided in Richie in case she needed backup. He was still at the station as far as she knew.

'Get yourself over to the Hare and Hounds. We've had a sighting of two black-eyed children looking in through their windows.'

'I'm not far from there.' Sarah quickened her pace down the muddy trail. 'Give me a description.'

'Two kids dressed in black hoodies, white faces, black eyes . . . Backup was on the way, but a fight's broken out in town so they may be a while.'

'On it,' Sarah said, jogging up the dark path.

'Be careful. I'll update the system to say you're off duty but attending. Any problems, call it in.'

But Sarah was busy listening to young voices from the other side of the hedge. 'Hang on. I've got eyes on them,' she whispered down the phone to Richie, her voice low. She leaned forward, looking for a gap. 'Two IC1 teenagers in hoodies. They've taken a bag from the hedge and they're changing their clothes. Can you update control and ask for a silent approach?' A police car arriving on blues and twos would scare them off. Sarah peered through the hedge, trying to distinguish their features. They were scrubbing their faces with what looked like wet wipes.

'Did you see that old guy's face?' The taller of the two chortled. 'He looked like he was gonna piss himself!'

'It was peng!' His companion laughed. 'Here, get that stuff off your face before the cops come sniffing round.'

'They won't find us here. Not yet.'

That's where you're wrong, Sarah thought, as she approached. She cursed herself as a twig snapped underfoot.

'Who are you?' The taller of the two turned. But Sarah recognised the second boy instantly. 'She's a cop!' His eyes widened as he grabbed his companion by the arm. 'Run!'

'Don't run!' Sarah called, giving chase. 'I hate running!' She made a mental note of the bag they had dumped behind the bushes as they gave flight through the parklands. 'Charlie Potter, you stop right now! I know where you live!' But she didn't know the bigger of the two, which was why she took after him when the boys went in different directions. It was a well-used teenage tactic. Split up and you've a fifty-fifty chance of getting caught. Luckily the bigger boy was the slower of the two, and Sarah was surprised to find herself gaining ground. A miracle had occurred. She had managed to find someone more unfit than her. 'Hey!' she shouted, a stitch burning in her side as she ran up the hill towards the houses that bordered the park.

She hadn't thought about what she was going to do when she caught up with him. She was alone in the wilds of Lower Slayton, where people would either turn a blind eye to a cop getting beaten up or stop to watch. At least she had brought her cuffs. 'Stop! I need to talk to you!' She panted as she gained ground. Her mind raced. Could she arrest him? What for? She didn't want to make a fool of herself. Was there a law against pranking? She lunged on top of him, bringing him thudding onto the soft, muddy grass.

'Get off me!' he squealed, as Sarah wrestled to keep control.

'I only want to talk to you!' she shouted. But the kid was in no mood for reasoning as he clenched his hands into fists.

'Get off me, psycho bitch!' he yelled, connecting with the side of her ribs. It was enough to deliver a sudden surge of pain, but not enough to knock her off.

'Right!' Sarah gasped, deftly clicking one rigid metal cuff onto his wrist. 'You're under arrest for assaulting a police officer.' Reeling off the caution, she grunted as she attempted to cuff his second wrist. One swinging metal cuff was a dangerous thing, and she'd been warned in training to be wary of it. Police cuffs weren't like the chain link ones people fooled around with from Ann Summers or fancy-dress shops. A swinging loose cuff was hard, sharp-edged metal; dangerous in the wrong hands – or wrist, in this case. As the boy squealed and fought, Sarah knew she would have to move fast. Grunting, she jabbed her thumb below his ear and burrowed it into his neck. It was a pressure point technique she'd learned which could make a grown man cry. He screamed in surprise, dropping his arms as she issued instructions to comply. Deftly snapping on the second cuff, Sarah caught her breath.

'Jesus! What was that?' the teenager cried, his eyes moist from the pain. 'It felt like a poker in my neck.'

'Non-compliance,' Sarah retorted, getting to her feet. 'Up, or I'll give you another one!' she instructed, taking him by the cuffs. 'You're lucky I didn't gas you. That would have given you something to cry about.' The flash of blue lights relayed backup was arriving and she walked him towards the road.

She hadn't expected to see Richie step out of the police car. Night had fallen hard and the wind was beginning to bite. 'What are you doing here?' she said, as Richie opened the passenger door to bundle the griping teenager in.

'You never hung up our call.' Richie closed the car door as their suspect was secured. 'I heard everything over the phone.'

'Oh!' Sarah said. 'I mean . . . I did that on purpose.'

'Sure you did.' Richie laughed. 'What did you do to him? He was squealing like a pig.'

A smug smile rose to Sarah's face. 'Pressure point to the neck. I was quite good at them in college. I can practise on you later if you'd like.'

'Nah, you're alright.' Richie backed away, a glint of new-found admiration in his eyes. Sarah spoke to the uniformed officer, who agreed to bring their prisoner to custody and present him to the sergeant for signing in. The teenager would be dealt with later, when witnesses were spoken to and any evidence recovered.

'Where are you going now?' Richie said, following as Sarah turned on her heel.

'They dumped a bag.' Sarah shoved her freezing hands into her jacket pockets. 'I'm going to seize that, then speak to Charlie. Find out what they've been up to.'

'You handled yourself quite well.' Richie grinned. 'I didn't know you had it in you.'

'There's plenty of things you don't know about me.' Sarah navigated the muddy hill with determination. Life had dealt her many cruelties, but she was finally turning things around. Work was the healing balm over her physical and mental scars. If she couldn't find her neighbour's murderers, she could at least interrogate the kids keeping the rumours of the black-eyed children alive.

33

Fifteen thousand. According to Sarah's watch, that was how many steps she had taken today. By the way things were going, she'd get another thousand under her belt before the day came to an end. Her walk to Charlie Potter's house would contribute to that. At least the lights were on, and his mum's car was on the drive. Tracey Potter was the local librarian and as an older single mum she worked hard to keep a roof over their heads. She also cared about the people who walked in through the doors. Her memory seemed capable of cataloguing everyone's choice of book. But Charlie was left to his own devices much of the time. Like many teenagers in Lower Slayton, he wasn't averse to a bit of shoplifting or spraying rude images on derelict buildings when boredom sank in. He was at that age where his life could take one of two directions, and Sarah hoped that early intervention would help. She'd only arrested his accomplice because he'd left her no choice, but she was loath to give Charlie a criminal record too. She knew more than anyone how your early years could influence the rest of your life.

Sarah glanced around Tracey's warm and homely kitchen. The kitchen was the hub of most British homes, and she was used to being ushered inside before the neighbours caught sight of her upon yet another Slayton doorstep. Tracey was an ample woman, with wavy red hair skimming her shoulders. 'I knew something was up,' she said, hands on her hips as she stood by the kettle. 'He ran upstairs like 'e was chased by the devil himself.' Her strong Northern accent filled the room.

'Not the devil.' Sarah smiled. 'Me.'

'Oh,' she said quietly. 'What has 'e done?' But Sarah didn't want to have to explain twice.

'Can we get him down here? I need to have a word.' She shifted in

121

her seat as her left side throbbed from the force of the earlier punch. It was not the first time she had been assaulted on duty. Had her attacker been carrying a knife, it could have been a whole lot worse.

A sheepish-looking Charlie joined them, looking furtively from his mother to Sarah and back again. His skin was bright pink from where he had scrubbed away the white face paint, but Sarah could still make out some faint blotches along the creases of his nose and ears. He shoved his hands into his tracksuit bottoms, which were baggy on his frame. On his feet were black Nike trainers – complete with bubbles in the soles. Sarah watched him closely. She had given him the benefit of the doubt by attending his home single-crewed, but people could be unpredictable when cornered. She had worked out an exit strategy and scanned the room for potential weapons which could be used against her should Charlie kick off. A knife block next to the sink. A stone paperweight on the dresser next to the door. Self-preservation was second nature. It had as much to do with her childhood as police training.

'We've got your friend in custody.'

Charlie responded with a double blink. The silence in the room was palpable as his mother gave him a daggered look.

'I didn't want to arrest him,' Sarah continued. 'But he gave me no choice. I'm hoping we can sort this out with a chat. That alright with you?'

Charlie nodded vehemently.

'Is someone going to tell me what happened?' Tracey folded her arms. Somewhere outside a dog barked, but Sarah's attention was on Charlie, who looked like he was about to dart out the back door.

'Can we sit?' Sarah gestured to the kitchen table. Charlie did as instructed, his knee bobbing beneath the table as he waited for Sarah to speak.

She looked from Tracey to Charlie. 'We've had reports of kids posing as black-eyed children in Slayton. They've created quite a fuss.'

'I read about that in the papers.' Tracey gave her son a withering look as Sarah's words sank in. 'No. Please tell me that wasn't you.'

''Fraid so,' Sarah replied, before Charlie could deny it. 'I caught him and his mate in the act.'

'He's not my mate,' Charlie blurted. 'Just someone I know from school.'

'Shush for a minute,' Tracey silenced her son. 'Why has Jamie been arrested?' she reasoned. 'Seems harsh for a prank?'

'Two suspicious-looking children were reported at the scene of the double murders.' Sarah watched Tracey visibly pale. 'Every second I spend chasing down reports of black-eyed children is less time spent on the investigation. And wasting police time is a serious offence. Besides . . .' She rubbed her side. 'I tried to reason with the other lad, which earned me a punch in the ribs.' Charlie's eyes widened at the mention of violence. Slipping her notebook out from her jacket, Sarah turned to him. 'I can talk to you about it here or in the station. What would you prefer?'

'Here.' Charlie's voice broke and he suddenly looked very young.

Sarah explained the process of a contemporary note interview. 'You're free to get legal advice,' she continued. 'You're not under arrest and you can stop whenever you like. But this is the best way of avoiding a trip to the station.' Of course, if Charlie admitted to being a double murderer, then an arrest would naturally follow, but Sarah thought that unlikely.

'He'll do it,' Tracey said firmly.

'Good.' Sarah proceeded with the caution and describing how she had come upon him that night. 'What were you doing? Tell me as much as you can, from start to finish.'

Charlie exhaled. 'I was on detention with Jamie at school when he asked if I wanted some extra cash. He said we'd get a tenner each for every prank we played.'

Sarah nodded, scribbling down his reply.

'He said all we had to do was dress up in some dark clothes, whiten our faces and wear black contact lenses. It took a while to get the hang of them but I managed to get them in.'

So that's how they blackened their eyes, Sarah thought, listening intently. 'Go on.'

'At first, we hung out in the park, but then Jamie said we had to go to the pub, where more people would see us. I said no way, it was too chancy. But he said I was fast and I'd be able to get away.' The trophies taking pride of place on the dresser behind him were testament to that.

'No argument there,' Sarah said. 'You were like a bullet going over that hill. But you should put your talents to better use than trying to outrun the police.'

'I wanted the money to buy a game, that's all.' Charlie shrugged, picking at his fingernails. 'I was going to stop once I had enough.'

'Is that the zombie game you asked me for?' Tracey interrupted. 'Flamin' hell, Charlie. What were you thinking?' But recrimination could come later. Sarah needed to know more.

'Who paid you?' There were quite a few sightings around Slayton, and she couldn't see how anyone would benefit from such pranks.

'Dunno. Jamie wouldn't say.'

'Are you sure?' Sarah didn't believe him. 'Because this goes beyond pranks. Whoever paid you could have their own reasons for keeping the stories going.' She watched Charlie swallow hard. 'Do you understand how serious this is? If anyone's pressuring you . . .'

'I don't know any more, honest!' Charlie blurted, his chin giving a little wobble as it all became too much. 'I'd tell you if I did.' He looked to his mother, who slid an arm over his shoulder and gave it a squeeze.

'It's OK,' she said, as he sniffled. She looked to Sarah. 'I believe him. Charlie has had his moments, but he'd never be involved in anything like that. I knew Mrs Simmons. She came into the library once a week. The woman had a heart of gold.'

'I knew her too.' Charlie took a clean tissue as Sarah offered it. 'She always said hello to me when I did the paper round.' He paused to blow his nose. 'I wouldn't do anything to hurt her. I thought we were just playing pranks.'

But Sarah couldn't let him off the hook that easily. She had to drive her message home. 'What's funny to you could be terrifying for someone else. What if someone had a heart attack? You're old enough to know that actions have consequences.'

Charlie's remorseful expression relayed that the message had sunk in. He could have responded with defiance, but instead he was in tears, turning to his mother for comfort. There was hope for him yet.

'You can make a difference in the world, Charlie. The police cadets are a great way to start, you know. Someone as fit as you would make a great copper one day.'

'Really?' Charlie said, watery-eyed.

Sarah nodded. Boys like Charlie were written off by the system far too young.

'It's not too late. Knuckle down at school, you've got plenty of time. It's a lot better to be the one doing the chasing than the idiot running away.' It warmed her to see his face brighten as she gave him a spark of hope. As she hugged her son, Tracey silently mouthed her thanks.

Sarah walked to her car, stifling a yawn. It had been a long day and Charlie had been in way over his head. But who was behind these pranks? And what did they have to gain? Was the killer diverting police attention to take the heat from them? Sarah hoped they were having more luck with his friend Jamie in custody. It was a thin lead, but a lead just the same. She only hoped her colleagues would agree.

34

Elliott stared at the softly glowing stars on his ceiling. On good nights they helped him to sleep. But tonight was not a good night, and the night whispers were near. He was trying not to be afraid. This wasn't like before, when a vision of the Midnight Man made him wet the bed. Mercy and Mikey were lost. But Mercy was mad at the grown-ups who put her there. Common sense told Elliott not to get caught up with that.

Yesterday his favourite teacher, Miss Grogan, had taught him about per-spec-tive. During playtime, she'd found him sitting on his own in the corridor and asked if he was OK. Miss Grogan was old, even older than his friend Sarah, but like Sarah, she always knew when things weren't right. Her eyes had been as blue as ice as she asked after his mummy, and how his daddy was too. Then she said a funny thing. She said that while everyone lived in the same world, some people saw more than others, and that he wasn't to worry or feel so alone. That when he got older it wouldn't seem so scary and he wasn't the only one. Elliott had sucked his bottom lip because he wasn't allowed to talk about it and he was scared the words might tumble out.

'I was like you once,' she'd said. 'I saw and heard things that I couldn't explain. But then I realised that if I stayed strong, they couldn't hurt me any more than scary programmes on TV.' She smiled, tapping the side of her nose. 'I can teach you how to quieten the voices, if you want me to.' Elliott was about to ask how but the bell rang, making him jump.

'I'd like that, Miss,' he managed to blurt, before she left for class. Maybe one day she could show him how to make the whispers go away.

He relaxed in his bed now, allowing her words to coast over him.

But it was no use. The air was turning cold. He shuddered beneath his duvet. Mercy and her brother were here. Mercy's voice was dry and brittle. They smelled of the woodlands. Of rotting moss and worm-infested earth.

'You must help us.' Her words were insistent as Elliott pressed his hands against his ears.

'You can't hurt me,' he whispered. 'Go away.'

'You *must* listen. *Please.*'

Elliott had no choice. He was probably the only person who had heard her speak since she had died. Apart from one or two others, maybe. The thought rose in his mind as she closed in. Only then did he realise that Mercy and Mikey were there when the old lady and her son died.

'They wouldn't listen,' Mercy said, reading his mind.

Is that what happens to people who don't listen? Elliott's breath quickened as fear sliced through him. He couldn't move. He could barely draw air into his lungs as Mercy appeared at the side of his bed. Her brother was at her side, his long dark lashes framing empty eyes.

Elliott's breath fogged as she stepped into him. The hairs stood on the back of his neck as he was brought back to Mercy's time. He could see Blackhall Manor, but the roof wasn't broken and covered in moss like it was now. He saw Slayton, which looked like the pictures which hung on the school walls. But this was alive. He was seeing it through Mercy's eyes. She brought him through the woods to her caravan, where the air smelled like the stinky cigarettes his mother smoked in secret. Elliott had stayed in a caravan with Mummy when they went on holiday once. But it was nothing like this. Mercy's caravan was cold, with yellow-stained ceilings and curtains hanging off the rail. Elliott wasn't just watching. He was given an insight into Mercy's life too. It felt like when his mum watched the soaps on TV. Suddenly, he knew all about Mercy, her brothers, and how tough things had been. He knew that Mercy's other brother, Noah, usually slept on the caravan sofa bed, but tonight he was somewhere else. Elliott could hear Mercy's father's snoring from the other side of the wall. Since her mother died, there was no heat in the small tin box Mercy called home.

Mercy planned to escape before her father woke up. Noah was not there to stop her tonight, just as he had done before. Elliott could feel her heart pounding fast as she checked the wind-up watch on her wrist. It was a present from her Granny Olive, and that's where she was going now. But she had to leave before the sun came up so she could sneak onto the morning train. Elliott watched as she reached for her backpack, which contained sugar sandwiches, a book and Granny Olive's address. Olive didn't like Mercy's daddy, because he wouldn't let her visit them after their mother got sick and died. Mercy tiptoed around the small space, knowing that if her daddy caught her, he would skin her alive. She pulled her socks to her knees and dragged her clothes on over her nightdress. A slice of sun broke through the window. Time was running out.

'I want to come,' Mikey whispered, rubbing his eyes.

'Come on, then.' Mercy threw him his clothes.

All at once, Elliott knew that Noah was in hospital because of a burst appendix. This time, Elliott could read Mercy's thoughts rather than the other way around.

'What about you?' She turned to her brother, Samson. His eyes were wide as he shook his head. 'Then say you didn't hear us go,' she whispered. 'I'll send for you.'

Elliott could feel Mikey's small warm hand in Mercy's as she gripped it tight. He felt the cold chill of the night as they crept out of the caravan and into the woods. A full moon lit their way down the forest path. 'Granny Olive will be so happy to see us.' Mikey smiled hopefully and Mercy wondered if she was doing the right thing.

Then rain came in icy sheets and Elliott could feel it soak through Mercy's clothes as it dripped from the branches overhead. She gripped Mikey's hand tighter as they walked to the muddy field where the builders had been. Elliott saw the machinery, the high chain link fences with signs that read KEEP OUT in big red letters. The rows of unfinished buildings looked like the Lego houses in his room. Mercy squeezed through a gap in the fence. She knew where she was going. She had been here before. 'In here.' She guided Mikey into a tall brick building with windows but no door. It was a house she would walk into but never walk out of.

Elliott didn't remember falling asleep. He was awoken by his alarm at seven thirty, his head foggy as he tried to collect his thoughts. Piece by piece, Mercy's story crept in, ending when she took shelter from the storm. What had happened? He stretched his arms as he yawned, trying to make sense of something that had happened before he was born. Should he tell Auntie Sarah? Or should he be like Miss Grogan and keep the door on his nightmares closed?

35

Arnold's bed creaked in protest as he turned over to face the wall. Sleep would not come, and he felt claustrophobic within the tomb of heavy blankets. At least the cottage was quieter now he'd got rid of that yappy dog. A part of him was loath to admit that he missed the stupid little thing. But he missed his wife more. What was the point in his existence, when the person he wanted to be with most in the world was dead? Perhaps Father Aloysius was right, and there was a heavenly paradise waiting for him on the other side. Lately, thoughts of suicide came as naturally as the dark, its thick, heavy presence doing little to ease his troubled mind. But fear held him back, and there was no heaven for sinners who took the easy way out.

He threw back his blankets, mumbling as he slipped on his shoes. He hadn't bothered changing into his pyjamas, because sleep rarely came. Perhaps he would be able to nod off in his chair. He sloped into his living room, greeted by the ticking of too many clocks to count. As he switched on the light, it was as if he was seeing the place for the first time. Stacks of newspapers and books were piled in every corner. Empty cardboard boxes were shoved into each other like matryoshka dolls. The floral wallpaper he'd once picked out with his wife was tattered and stained. As for the carpet . . . he could barely make it out for all the dog hairs, crumbs and litter.

His gaze roamed to where the picture of Jesus hung on the wall, the image of the Saviour obscured by the doily he'd thrown over it previously. He shuffled towards the picture, raising a hand to remove it, when a scratching noise clawed against the window outside. Arnold froze, hand mid-air. It was one of the bramble branches, that was all. But then he heard it, faint at first but growing louder. The whispers were back. He stood, raking in shallow breaths as the children's whispers grew, moving around outside the house.

'Please, mister. Please let us in.'

They were at the door now, speaking properly for the first time. Three faint knocks signalled their presence. Arnold couldn't speak. His mouth was bone dry. Shuffling towards the wall, he flicked the light off. But this wasn't some copper knocking. It was the children. They had come for him. A rattle erupted from the back door. The air carried an edge, and he sensed shadows moving around him. Then another knock, this time at the front door again.

'Let us in.'

It was the voice of a little girl, growing more insistent. Arnold whimpered, engulfed in a wave of dread. They had come for him and they weren't leaving until he answered. He entered the gloom of the hallway and found himself approaching the door. His mind searched for a rational explanation. Perhaps it was teenagers playing pranks? He knew that people in town looked at him funny; some even said he was mad. It wasn't normal after all, was it, going to bed fully clothed . . . And when was the last time he'd brushed his teeth, or showered? Maybe he was losing his marbles, and all of this was in his head.

'Alright then!' he shouted, years of frustration coming to the fore. But his hopes of children playing pranks evaporated the second he opened the door. Cold bit into his flesh as the air curled around him, and the smell of rotting flesh made him stagger back.

'What? No . . . you're not real.' His words were strangled as he retreated into the hall, sliding against the wall for support. His lungs seemed devoid of air as he stared into the faces of the little boy and girl. 'You're . . . not . . . real . . .' he uttered again, as they came towards him.

This couldn't be. But he had opened the door. He had already let them in. Warmth spread through his trousers and the smell of urine competed with the stagnant air. They were upon him now, their black unseeing eyes casting judgement. Arnold retreated into the living room, the ticking of his clocks impossibly loud.

'I'm sorry!' he cried, falling back against the sofa. But as the figures loomed over him, he knew it was too late.

36

Sunday, 8th March 2020

'Noble!' McGuire shouted in Sarah's direction as she entered the station corridor. Urgency coursed through his movements, and the irritation she felt at the use of her surname dissipated. 'Come with me,' he said, gesturing at her to go back outside. She sighed, hoping he wasn't treating her to another pigeon analogy. Her pace quickened as she followed him out to the station car park.

'Morning, boss,' she said, still wondering why he was dragging her back outside when she was yet to make Gabby her hallowed morning cup of coffee.

McGuire almost lost his long, striped scarf as he crossed the station car park. She wondered if he was a *Doctor Who* fan. But this was not the time to ask as he pressed the keyring's remote activation to find the marked police car.

'Has something come in?' she said instead, before sliding into the passenger side. She kicked aside litter in the footwell before turning up the heat.

'You could say that.' McGuire fumbled with the indicators and wipers as he worked out which was which. 'Who owns Arnold's property? It's on your land, isn't it?'

'I think it's a rental, owned by Irving Industries.' Sarah's face soured at the mention of the name. Now she had accepted the offer on Blackhall Manor, the sale was going through. She pulled her seat forward as she focused her thoughts. 'I own three quarters of Blackhall Woods, but there's a couple of rental properties on the outskirts owned by Irving Industries when they bought the rest of the land. Why? Is that where we're going?'

'Yep.' McGuire reversed out of the space. 'Strap in.'

As they sped out of the car park, Sarah held onto her seat belt. McGuire was driving like his house was on fire. He flicked on the lights and sirens and the traffic parted before them. Her spirits plummeted as the latest update from control came through on the car radio before McGuire had a chance to update her. Arnold, the loner in the woods who practically threw her out of his home, had been found dead.

'Oh no.' Sarah absorbed the news. 'Not another murder.'

'Aye.' McGuire's eyes were fixed on the road. 'A grim one at that. His eyes have been gouged out.'

'No,' Sarah said quietly. 'That poor man.' He was a prickly little ball of anger, but she couldn't help feeling sorry for him.

McGuire listened intently as an officer updated that he had gone code three-two.

'They've made an arrest?' Sarah's pulse quickened. 'Who?' Her mind raced for possible suspects, but she was not prepared for what McGuire said next.

'That traveller fellah from the campsite. He was found at the scene. They're bringing him in.' He indicated left before taking the busy junction with ease. Sarah's grip tightened around her seat belt, her face fixed in concentration as she tried to hide her shock. Not Noah. It couldn't be. Was this what had brought him back to Slayton? Was he capable of such butchery?

'What do you know about Arnold?' McGuire interrupted her thoughts. They were coming out of the town now, past the shops and businesses. The roadside trees passed in a blur of green as they sped to the cottage in the woods. She thought of the last murder scene and the smells that still lingered in her memory. Was she ready for this? But McGuire was waiting for a response.

'He's been in that cottage for so many years that he might have bought it outright.' The place had been in such a state, she couldn't imagine any landlord being happy with the amount of clutter filling each room. She thought of Arnold, stiff and agitated as he demanded she leave. She knew a little bit about him, but not enough to explain his recent behaviour. 'He moved to Ireland when his wife was ill, then came back after she died. Keeps himself to himself . . . or at least he did.' Elsie had filled her in on those details. What her friend didn't know about the neighbourhood wasn't worth asking about.

'You know a fair amount, given he's a recluse.' McGuire seemed to read her mind. They were jolted in their seats as the car bumped along the narrow road. McGuire flicked off the blue lights and siren. There was no need for them here.

'I have a friend who keeps me up to date on the comings and goings of people in Slayton – whether I want to know or not.' Sarah hung onto her seat belt. Elsie seemed determined to help with the case. She would have a field day with this one. 'I can't believe Noah is involved.'

'Noah is it, now?' McGuire looked at Sarah. 'You're on first-name terms, then?'

Sarah wanted to say that unlike him, she wasn't fond of using surnames but she curtailed the response. 'I'm struggling with it, if I'm honest. If he'd set out to kill Arnold then surely he wouldn't camp on his doorstep.'

'Aye, but that's the thing.' McGuire gave her a knowing look. 'If all murderers covered their tracks then our prisons would be empty and we'd be out of a job.'

Sarah recalled the way Noah had cared for his grandmother, and his devotion towards his dog. She couldn't comprehend him leaving them like that. 'What have we got against him, apart from him being at the scene?'

'That's what interviews are for,' McGuire said resolutely. 'Something was clearly troubling Arnold. His place is in a state, from what I've heard.'

Sarah inwardly groaned as McGuire's lack of understanding shone through. There were plenty of hoarders in Slayton. They weren't *all* involved in a murder plot.

McGuire slowed as the woodside lane narrowed, and the lights of the car came on automatically as they were plunged into a strange morning twilight. 'Good work catching those two scallies last night. We should be able to stamp out these rumours now we've caught the person behind it.'

'Those kids were being paid,' Sarah said. As much as Jamie annoyed her, he didn't deserve to be criminalised.

'Ah, you don't know, do you?' McGuire glanced over as the car bumped along the potholed road. Soon they would have to park up and make the rest of the way on foot. 'The late turn interviewed him. He coughed the lot. Said Roger Newman was behind the whole thing.'

'Newman?' Sarah said. 'Is that the—'

'The YouTube guy,' McGuire interrupted. 'Fecking eejit.'

Sarah's eyebrows rose. 'You're not saying he murdered those poor people for views?'

'No, not at all. We got him in early doors. He has an alibi, and doesn't match the print on the wall.' McGuire steered with one hand on the gearstick. 'He hired the kids to boost his YouTube channel. He'd no way of knowing that people would end up dead.'

'But Charlie said they didn't call on Mrs Simmons.' Sarah wished he would slow down as she was jolted out of her seat for the third time. She could feel her fillings virtually rattling in her head.

'Of course they're gonna deny it. They're in way over their heads. Don't you worry about Newman. We'll take care of him.' But it didn't sit easy with Sarah. If Charlie and Jamie weren't the ones, then who knocked on Rosemary's door? A thought brought a familiar sense of dread. What was the real reason behind Noah's visit to Slayton? Had he unearthed information regarding his siblings' whereabouts? Was Arnold somehow involved?

37

Elsie scanned the shelves of her local library, grateful for their Sunday opening hours. It was a welcoming place, with two floors and lots of cosy nooks to sit and read undisturbed. She loved the smell of old books, the soft hush of whispered voices and the low whirr of computers and photocopiers in use. It was her sanctuary, and since regaining her independence, she'd spent countless happy hours there.

Christian had rung to say he wouldn't be home this weekend because a colleague had asked him out on a date. Her name was Lucy, and their friendship had bloomed over the last few weeks. As Elsie perused the romance section, she floated in a bubble of happiness for her son. There was a time when she'd thought that he would never leave home, let alone come out of his shell long enough to find a partner. Elsie had never been in love, not with a real-life person anyway. The daughter of a Presbyterian minister, she emigrated from the US to England where her father set up a branch of the Presbyterian church. They were a God-fearing family, but behind closed doors her father's treatment of his family was hell. Elsie was glad he was dead. He had skewed any chance she had of a normal, loving relationship in her adult life.

'You've got lovely skin, has anyone ever told you that?' Simon Irving's words loomed large in her memory. At fifteen years old, she had never received a single compliment from the opposite sex. When Irving paid her attention she'd been as happy as a clam at high tide, too naive to see that she was being played.

'No,' she found the courage to reply, her throat a dry passage for any further words.

'It's so soft . . .' He'd pressed the palm of his hand against her cheek which burned beneath his touch. His blue eyes twinkled as he smiled at the obvious effect he was having on her. 'You're different to other girls around here. I like your accent – it's hot.'

Irving had spoken to her a couple of times, out of sight of other people. Winked at her as she walked home from school, waved at her in the shop. At first, she'd turned to look behind her, unable to believe she had caught the attention of the most sought-after boy in Slayton. 'Come to the outdoor cinema with me,' he'd whispered into her ear as he caught her on the way out of the local newsagent's one night. The feel of his breath on her neck had made her weak at the knees. 'They're showing *Jurassic Park*. I'll pick you up at the bottom of your road at nine.'

She'd lied to her parents and told them Sarah and Maggie were taking her out. But she wasn't even friends with Sarah and Maggie. Back then, they wouldn't look twice at someone like her. Fantasising about being Irving's girlfriend, she had worn her best home-made dress, using a little Vaseline to smooth her lips. She had even fashioned ringlets in her hair. That night she left the house and got into Irving's car. But they didn't go to the cinema, not straight away.

He parked in the desolate country park, kissed her full on the lips and told her to get into the back seat. His kiss had been welcome. A gesture of his love. With nobody to talk to and little knowledge of relationships, Elsie presumed that was how things worked. 'You want to be my girlfriend, don't you?' Irving had said, coaxing her to lie back. 'Because I love you, Elsie. I always have.'

His words cast away any lingering doubts as she closed her eyes. It had all been so quick. She consoled herself that she was his girlfriend. This was what people in love did. He was the one person who could save her from her miserable life at home. But when they got to the outdoor cinema afterwards, Irving's words were cold. 'Get out.' He opened the door. 'We're done here. I don't want to see you again.'

'But . . . I'm your girlfriend.' Her face pale with shock, she watched his friends gather round.

Irving's face creased in incredulity. 'You really believed that, didn't you?' His friends joined in with his laughter, slapping him on the back. She heard them saying something about cherries and winning a bet. Tears pricked Elsie's eyes as her humiliation and shame grew. His final words rang in her ears with cruelty.

'Ugly girls are the most grateful.'

Closing her eyes, Elsie brought herself back to the present day. She stared at the library book in her hand. On the cover was a man in a cowboy hat and plaid shirt, cradling a flame-haired woman with love in his eyes. She wrote better. In her stories, the men were brooding but kind and devoted, and sex was an adventurous act of love. Women were strong, and came in all shapes and sizes. Inspired by her heroines, she had even found the courage to send the first three chapters of one of her manuscripts off. It was a spicy home-grown romance, in her pen name of Caroline Brookes, with thinly veiled characters based on people she knew in real life. And there was none of that potty-mouthed filth that some romance authors debased themselves with.

Elsie finalised her book choices and rested them on her lap as she sat in her mobility scooter. The librarian, Tracey, smiled as Elsie approached her desk. She was called Marcie, and was having a romance with a hunky doctor in Elsie's latest book.

'Hey, Elsie, I didn't see you come in. How's it going?'

'Good, thanks,' Elsie replied. Tracey had worked in the library for as long as she could remember and made it her business to know everyone by name. The two of them shared a bond, as they were both single mums. 'Christian's got himself a date, bless his tender heart. So it's just me and my books tonight.'

'Good on him!' Tracey grinned. She took the hardbacks from Elsie's hands, her smile fading as she spoke in a low voice. 'I can't believe I'm saying this, but Charlie brought the police to my door last night.'

'Oh no,' Elsie said, dismayed. 'He's always been such a sweet boy.'

Tracey shook her head. 'Honestly, I don't know him these days.' She stamped each book in turn, her concerns set deep in her face.

'Nothing too serious, I hope.' Elsie was itching to know more.

'Just pranks. He and his friend have been dressing up as black-eyed children and spooking half the residents of Lower Slayton. I could wring his neck, honestly I could.'

Elsie was well aware of the mischief local youth got up to. While the younger kids played knock down ginger, the teenagers were stealing cars. She did her best to appear shocked at this latest revelation. 'What did the police do? I hope he wasn't arrested.'

Tracey shook her head. 'It was Sarah Noble. Instead of telling him off, she said he could have what it takes to join the police.'

'Get away,' Elsie said. She wouldn't mention that she and Sarah were friends, not when Tracey was confiding in her. It was just like Sarah to encourage instead of admonishing the young tearaway. If it was possible to be both strong and soft at the same time, then Sarah had it nailed.

'It worked, too.' Tracey handed over each book in turn. 'He's been looking into it. Says he's going to become a police cadet when he leaves school.'

'The power of a few encouraging words.' Elsie smiled.

'I know. I wish he had a father figure in his life. I spend so much time juggling work and home, I never think to sit down and say stuff like that to him.'

'Don't be so hard on yourself.' Elsie knew how tough single parenting could be. 'And fathers are overrated.' She knew that too. Carefully, she placed her books into the basket on her scooter. 'We both know how hard it is to bring up a boy on your own. He's finding his feet. He'll come good in the end.'

'I hope so,' Tracey replied. 'He could have been arrested. That would have ruined any chances he had.'

'Well, if Christian can turn things around then so can you and your boy. I'll pray for you tonight. It can't hurt to have the Lord on your side.' She delivered a wink.

'Thanks,' Tracey said graciously. 'I guess it can't.'

'So what do you make of all this black-eyed children business?' Elsie said. 'D'you reckon it's hokum?' She rubbed the stiffness from her right knee as she talked. She had been on her feet for the last hour, but it only really hurt when she sat down.

The librarian shrugged. 'Who knows, in Slayton? If weird stuff is going to happen anywhere, it's going to be here. I just hope they catch whoever did it soon.' She nodded an acknowledgement to a pensioner as she walked past, but Elsie wasn't ready to let things lie just yet.

'Did you know Rosemary and her son?'

'Only in passing. They didn't come here much but I hear they went to church. Apparently they were in quite a state when they were found dead,' she added, in a low voice.

'Really? How so?' This was news to Elsie. When it came to the gritty details, Sarah's lips were tighter than a camel's butt in a sandstorm.

'Apparently one of the neighbours saw a police officer throwing up outside. Not one of those probationers either, it was Derek Duffy. He's been in the job for years. It must have been bad to get to him like that.'

Elsie nodded. Come to think of it, Sarah *had* been as white as a sheet when she broke the news. She itched with curiosity. Tracey wasn't the type to be loose-lipped, but Elsie could tell that she needed to talk to someone. She was clearly shook up from the night before. If Elsie happened to be there at the right time, was that so wrong?

'So it wasn't your Charlie and his friend calling on Rosemary that night, then?'

Tracey shook her head. 'He was at home that night, two of his friends were round. I ordered pizza for them all.'

Elsie believed her. Charlie wasn't a bad kid. He wouldn't have been mixed up in that. 'Don't ya think it's weird, how those kids called to her home? She didn't have grandchildren, did she? Her son . . . he didn't hang out with kids . . . if you get my meaning.' Elsie gave her a knowing look. An inappropriate relationship could be enough cause to spur payback.

'I did wonder the same thing,' Tracey replied, looking uncomfortable. 'But he's been a recluse since his accident. Stopped socialising. Barely spoke two words when he was in town.'

'Hmm.' Elsie was thoughtful as she rested her hands on the handlebars. 'I guess we all want answers, so we know none of us are next.'

'Isn't that the truth,' the librarian replied.

Elsie started up her scooter. She wouldn't say any more about it. Walls had ears in Slayton, and sometimes bad things happened to blabbermouths.

38

Gerard's heart stalled at the sight of his wife's car parked outside his rented cottage. He had only been gone a short while, and the woodland walk had done little to clear his troubled mind. He pushed through the open front door and inhaled the light fragrance of Ruth's perfume that lingered in the hall. It felt like a rose had bloomed in the dark, dank woods. How had his life come to this? His heart lifted even as he saw her in the cramped living room, standing before the fireplace. She was wearing a black pencil skirt and cashmere jumper, impeccable as always. She didn't belong here.

'Hello, Gerard,' she said, her chin tilted upwards. 'You left the back door unlocked.' She was trying to appear aloof but the tips of her fingers were white as she held her designer bag tight.

Their relationship had never involved big emotions or gestures. Weeks would pass without a kiss or hug. But they relied upon each other to keep the family together in a fast-paced, chaotic world. But now he was part of that chaos, and he did not want to bring it down on her. Their children may be adults, but Ruth deserved more.

'Ruth,' he said eventually, 'what are you doing here?' He searched her face for clues. 'Are the boys OK?'

'The boys are fine. I was just concerned about you.' Ruth glanced around the cottage as the atmosphere between them thawed. 'I heard about the murders. It's all over the news. Are you OK?'

Gerard delivered a tight nod, but he was as far as you could get from OK.

'Look at this place.' Ruth stepped back, looking him up and down. 'It's worse than I thought. You look terrible. I want you home.'

Gerard ran a hand through his hair, feeling a familiar tug in the gut. He loved his wife, and he hated causing her this pain, but he couldn't leave now. 'I can't—' he began to say, but Ruth cut him off.

'I'll book you into a private clinic. *Gerard*, I know something isn't right, and this place . . . it's not safe to stay here. Come home. Please.' She swept an arm around the dilapidated cottage. 'You can't tell me you prefer this.'

The worry on her face almost broke Gerard's heart. He hadn't realised quite how much she cared until now. 'I can't bring this to your door.' His stomach churned at the thought. 'It's not a doctor I need. It's the police.'

Ruth guided him towards the worn leather sofa that had seen better days. 'Sit.' She brushed the sofa cushion before joining him. 'Tell me everything.' Gerard knew his wife. She wasn't leaving until he did. The clock on the wall ticked away the seconds as she awaited his response.

'I think I've done something awful.' He shook his head, unable to look at her. How could he tell her he'd turned into a monster? That the man she had married, had brought up a family with, had murdered two helpless people in cold blood? The words backed up in his throat.

'Whatever it is, we'll face it together.' Ruth wore the steely look that he loved her for. If only it were that easy. But he was no stranger to the legal world. It was his profession, and he knew exactly how these things went. The police were bound to have harvested his DNA from the murder scene. The only reason they hadn't come knocking was because he wasn't on their system – yet. As soon as they took his fingerprints he would be pegged as guilty for the crime. Innocent men didn't run away. Innocent men didn't boil-wash their bloodied clothes and dispose of evidence.

He stared at his shaking hands, still seeing the blood that had stained them. 'I've been having blackouts.' He was unable to look up. 'It started months ago, with the manor.' She knew about his obsession with Slayton and Blackhall Manor. He didn't need to reiterate that. 'And when I got here . . . I had the strongest sense that I knew this place, and that it knew me.' Gerard thought he was the only person suffering up until now. But judging by the expression on Ruth's face, all was not well in her world either.

'I thought if you came here, you'd get to the root of what was bothering you, but from what I can see, it's made things a million times worse.'

'Oh, Ruth.' He took his wife's hand. Her skin was warm and comforting – a comfort he needed right now. 'You've no idea . . .'

'Then tell me.'

'The blackouts have been worse since I came here. It's like the flick of a switch. I open my eyes and I have such a dreadful feeling that I've done things . . . terrible things I would *never* do in my right mind.' He watched her face crease as she tried to put the pieces together.

She pulled her hand away. 'Are you saying you've been unfaithful? Is that what this is about?'

Gerard was shocked to see tears glistening in Ruth's eyes. 'I know we've grown apart. I hold my hands up to that. But I need you, I didn't realise how much until you left. I want my . . .' She choked a sob. The sudden display of emotion took him by surprise. 'I want my husband back.'

Gerard couldn't feel any worse than he did now. Ruth was never getting her husband back, and his heart ached for her. He had taken her for granted and would give anything to be able to make it up to her. But it was too late. He had committed a crime and he had to pay. Her presence clarified things. It was time to stop hiding.

He shook his head. 'You don't understand. I've not been unfaithful. I've hurt people. At least, I think the part of me that functions during my blackouts has.' Distressed, he gesticulated with his hands. If only he could make her understand. But how could he expect Ruth to come to terms with things that he couldn't fathom himself? His old life was slipping away and tears rose to his eyes as he grieved its loss. There was no going back now.

Ruth rested her hand on his back. 'What do you mean? What people? Say something. You're frightening me.' Her complexion grew pallid, her sea-green eyes boring into him.

Gerard rose, his gaze fixed on the window as he prepared to tell her what he was. A thought sent chills throughout his body. What if he hurt *her*? What if she wasn't safe around him? He was flooded with a sense of urgency as he tried to confess. At least then she would leave him. The safety of his family was all he could hope for.

'It's about the murders.' He touched the windowpane. The glass was cool beneath his fingertips. He needed to ground himself. Everything felt so surreal. 'It was me, Ruth. I killed them. Which is why you need to get away from here. I'm scared of what I might do next.' He had thought he might experience some relief saying it all out loud, but the words felt alien on his tongue. How could they possibly be true?

He turned to face her, expecting to see horror in her eyes. But a sudden shrill of shocked laughter escaped his wife's lips. 'Don't be silly!' she exclaimed, rising from the sofa. 'You couldn't hurt a fly.'

'But it's not *me*.' Gerard set his jaw firm. 'It's another part of me that comes alive when I have my blackouts.' He relayed the story of his clothes in the wash and the blood swirling down the shower drain. 'It had to be me.' He watched the colour leave Ruth's face.

'I don't believe it. I won't.'

'But it happened,' Gerard said. 'And I can't let someone else take the blame. I need to be locked away before I hurt anyone else.'

'You need help.' Ruth didn't waver. 'And we're going to get it, but I'm bringing you home today.'

She wasn't listening. What she was suggesting was ridiculous.

'Can't you see?' Gerard turned to face her. 'What if I hurt the boys? What if I hurt you or the people around us?'

'You would never do that,' Ruth scoffed.

'And what about Rosemary Simmons? Or her son, in a wheelchair? They weren't just murdered. They were butchered, Ruth. Whoever did it was deranged. I'm going to the police, and that's it.'

'Then I'm coming with you.' Ruth picked her handbag up off the floor. Gerard weakened. The presence of a supportive wife could only help. She raised a hand in the air as he took a breath to argue. 'They'll have to give you access to a doctor. And I'm hiring the best legal advice money can buy. You don't know what's going on beneath the surface of this creepy place. We'll go to the station together, but not a word until you've spoken to my lawyer first. Agreed?'

'OK. Agreed.' Just like that, Ruth had taken control and he was so damn grateful for it. The dam of tears welling in his eyes finally broke. He sobbed in her arms, shoulders heaving as he released the tension and fear of the past few weeks. He may be a monster, but at least he wasn't alone.

39

Noah sat in the boxy interview room, his long legs sprawled beneath the table. He hated police stations. The feeling of confinement hit him the second he was led through the door. He glanced at the female detective sitting across from him. Her long dark hair shadowed her face as she scribbled on her writing pad. He had been arrested before. This was nothing new. He hated being in this room, breathing in stale air. But he had been fully cooperative when uniformed officers arrested him in Arnold's home. He had no choice. Police were twitchy around travellers. As a teenager he'd had his fair share of encounters with the law and came off the worse for it. Today, he'd calmly answered the custody sergeant's list of questions about his no fixed abode address, his ethnicity, his meal preferences, his religious beliefs, his mental health status and his next of kin. He removed the laces from his boots and emptied his pockets, which thankfully didn't contain his Swiss army knife. The long booking-in procedure was something he had reconciled himself to, as well as his fingerprints and photograph being placed on the system for everyone to see.

At least Olive knew the state of play. The custody sergeant was decent enough, organising his phone call. It had taken his grandmother forever to answer her mobile and she had sighed wearily before telling him to get back soon. But Noah wasn't sure when 'soon' would be. In cases like these, pressure was on for the coppers to find someone to blame. A traveller man who'd turned up like a bad penny was as good a target as anyone. He settled into the uncomfortable plastic chair and went over things again in his mind. What did they have on him apart from him being there? There was no weapon, no blood on his clothes. His thoughts clouded over. But there was motive. He needed to step carefully.

*

A disposable cup of custody tea was placed before him as a male officer entered the room. He introduced himself as DC Richardson while offering him a smile. His stony-faced colleague was DC Yvonne Townsend. Noah said nothing, listening patiently as the officer talked of his right to have legal advice and ensured he understood what he had been arrested for. Noah trusted lawyers as much as he trusted the police.

'I know *what* I was arrested for but I don't understand why,' Noah interrupted.

'We'll discuss that shortly,' Richardson said, carrying on with the introductory spiel before he could get to the meat of things. He looked tired, no doubt from the investigation, but all Noah felt was mistrust. His heart tripped in his chest as he imagined being imprisoned for the rest of his days. Staring at a ceiling instead of the sky and waking up to the same four walls. He could not allow that to happen. His soul belonged to the outdoors. If he had to live a life in confinement then he would rather not live at all. Thoughts of being away from animals, from the wind and the smell of rain was too much for him to bear. He ran a hand through his hair.

His thoughts were making him agitated. As the question of his presence at the scene was finally broached, Noah forced himself to relax in his chair. He took a deep breath, counted to three and exhaled. *Someone was watching me. They knew I'd been visiting the old man every day. That I had a grudge against him. So they killed him and waited until I turned up again. That's when they called the police. They're the person you need to question, not me. This is a set-up.* These were the words Noah wanted to say, but he did not trust the people before him. They would find a way of twisting anything he said.

'I went for a walk,' he said, instead. 'It was just gone nine. I was heading into town for milk and a newspaper when I came across the cottage. The place was falling apart, so I called in to ask if the owner wanted any work done.' Surely the copper before him would fall for the traveller stereotype he was portraying. It did not set him in a flattering light, but neither did it cast him as a murderer.

'Go on,' Richardson said. Noah looked at the woman beside him, her pen scratching notes on her pad. Her facial muscles twitched as they locked eyes. She didn't believe a word. Her nose wrinkled. Nor did she appreciate the smell of the outdoors. He paused to clear his throat.

'There was no answer at the front so I tried the back door. It was open. I had a bad feeling about it so I called out. I thought maybe someone was hurt.' He sighed. 'Living in that neck of the woods, it might be that nobody would see you for days. So I went inside. That's when I saw the man, dead on the sofa. I was leaving to call for help when the police landed down on top of me.' Noah remembered the scene as he entered the house. He had gone in there for one thing – to find out what happened to his siblings so many years ago. 'You won't find any part of me on that man. Looked like he'd been dead a while.' He recalled the colour of his blood, congealed like jelly in dark red pools.

'And where were you before that?' the officer said, without missing a beat. His sleeves were rolled up to his elbows, his tie loose and askew, as if he'd been tugging on it. Noah looked him straight in the eye.

'In my grandmother's caravan. She'll testify to that. She has no love for the police, mind. She hasn't had the best dealings with them.' His eyes narrowed as he glared at the woman across the table. She didn't need to speak. Her disbelief couldn't be any more clear on her face than if she'd written it in pen.

'Why did you come to Slayton?' Richardson asked, another in a long line of questions. An hour had passed and they were no further on.

'It's no crime to travel. That's what we do.' Noah crossed and uncrossed his legs. He felt like he was seizing up, sitting at the table, unable to move around. He raised his hands over his head to stretch and the woman before him flinched. 'Can I stand?' he said, to ease his growing discontent.

'I'd rather you didn't,' Richardson said. 'Are you here visiting anyone in particular? Has the timing of your stay got anything to do with your brother and sister, Mercy and Mikey?' He looked at his notes. 'Who disappeared on the second of March, 1995.'

Noah jabbed the air with his finger as his temper rose. 'You don't get to mention their names. Not when your lot did nothing to find them.' His eyes darted towards the female officer shooting him daggers. 'You make me sick. So quick to point the finger at me while my brother's and sister's remains lie God knows where.' It felt good to finally get it off his chest. 'Twenty-five years, and I've had nothing from the police. Where were the helicopters when my little brother and sister disappeared? Where were the town meetings? The press releases? The appeals?' He was referring to the recent disappearance of Angelica Irving – a blue-eyed, blonde-haired little rich kid, whose disappearance had made national news. 'So don't say their names aloud. Not unless it's to tell me where they are.'

He wanted to tell them of Arnold's involvement. Of the rumours he had heard. But it would only serve to incriminate him and he couldn't risk that.

'I was sorry to hear about your brother and sister,' Richardson replied. 'I wasn't here when they went missing, but we are all aware—'

'Save your breath.' Noah waved his concerns away. 'I've heard it all before. I'm not answering any more questions. Either charge me or let me go.' But the detective persisted with his questioning, going over his account in detail. Noah answered 'No comment' every time.

He didn't feel sorry for Arnold – the man had got what was coming to him. He only wished he'd been able to get answers before he died.

<h1 style="text-align:center">40</h1>

'Are you alright, Noble?' DI McGuire peered over the top of his surgical mask. Arnold's home was swarming with crime scene investigators carrying out their duties as a matter of urgency. A team of officers had searched the surrounding undergrowth. If Arnold's eyes had been discarded, it was likely the local wildlife could have had them away. Sarah balanced on a step plate, dressed head to toe in forensics gear, trying to resist the unbearable urge to scratch her nose. They weren't the only ones wearing masks. Sarah noticed them becoming more prevalent in the community. The government was under mounting pressure as coronavirus figures rose. There was no time to think about that now.

'I'm fine, boss,' she replied, focusing her thoughts on the task ahead. But her pulse had picked up pace since entering Arnold's living room and was showing no signs of slowing down. Arnold's body was still in situ, sprawled on the sofa, face down. As with Rosemary and her son, his eyes had been removed. She imagined attending officers moving his head to check for a pulse. Had their stomachs lurched as they saw the gaping holes where his eyes should have been? Her glance fell to the floral-patterned sofa. It may have been pink and green once, but today it was soaked with the old man's blood. Like the rest of the house, the living room was evidence of his hoarding, with newspapers, old shoes, coats and piles of tattered books taking up much of the space. The incessant ticking of his multitude of clocks was getting under her skin. She wondered if she would ever become hardened to such grisly scenes. She hoped never to see anything like this again, but in her job you never knew what you were going to see. A religious picture hung on the wall over the sofa. Sarah stared at the doily hanging over the glass. Given the state of disarray, it didn't look that out of place.

Just navigating Arnold's home was a challenge, as she had discovered the last time she was here. She stepped around the room, being careful not to touch the grime-ridden ornaments. How did CSI work out old stains from new ones? She watched officers move quietly but diligently around the room. The ring of McGuire's phone stole her attention and she was happy to follow him out, listening to the lilt of his Northern Irish accent as he negotiated the overgrown garden path. Sarah pulled off her mask when she was clear of the house and took a deep, soothing breath. McGuire was stepping out of his overshoes, his phone cradled between neck and ear.

'He's confessed to the whole thing?' he spoke down the phone before throwing her the car keys. Sarah's spirits plummeted as they took the woodland path to their car. She couldn't equate Noah with such carnage. But then life experience had taught her that people could surprise you in the worst possible ways. Had he murdered Arnold as part of some vigilante revenge? What about Rosemary and her son? Where did they come in?

The air felt charged as Sarah returned to the briefing room. Her concerns for Noah had lessened now McGuire had filled her in. The murder board had been updated with maps, sightings, locations and crime scene photos. It didn't feature details of the man who had just confessed to all three homicides, but that would come. The evidence was building as the team came together and Sarah was proud to be a small cog in the investigative machine. Her gaze fell on the mugshot pinned below the suspect list. Noah's eyes appeared deadened, the healthy blush that coloured his features evaporated. Only now did she notice the worry lines creasing his face. Twenty-five years of searching for his brother and sister and it had come to this.

She took her seat as the unscheduled briefing was called. A ripple of chatter grew in the room as the rest of the team took their seats. Sarah smiled at Richie as he approached.

'Our suspects are like buses,' he whispered. 'Wait around for ages and then two turn up at once.'

'He's really confessed?' Sarah could barely believe the news.

'Kind of,' Richie said, rising as McGuire beckoned for him to speak. The room grew loud with chatter. The mood was buoyant; after days of mounting pressure a confession was a major result. But how could you 'kind of' confess to murder? She shifted in her seat as Gabby took Richie's place.

'I may not be McGuire's biggest fan' – Gabby leaned into Sarah – 'but give him his due, he gets results.' Sarah nodded in agreement. It was a shame Arnold had had to die before the suspect gave himself up.

'I know him,' she whispered to Gabby in confusion, as Richie spoke of their latest suspect, Gerard Baker. 'He's the solicitor who put a stop to my demolition. This doesn't make sense.'

'A solicitor?' Gabby's forehead knotted in a frown. 'How the hell is he connected to this?'

Sarah couldn't answer. For once, she was lost for words.

Her colleague's chatter was quickly silenced as McGuire spoke to the room. 'Baker's confession is thin, but it's backed up with forensic evidence. His handprint matches the one found on Rosemary Simmons' wall.' Sarah's stomach churned as she struggled to concentrate. It seemed they had their killer. But where was the motivation? Had Gerard Baker come here because of her? Was she responsible for drawing him in?

41

Sarah shook the rain from her jacket as she stood in Elsie's hall. She was welcomed by three of her cats as they miaowed at her ankles and curled their tails around her legs. Sarah could justify her evening visit. Elsie had called to say that she'd uncovered a lead. In true Elsie style, she'd invited Maggie over too, no doubt enjoying the drama which was about to unfold.

'Hello, pusses.' Sarah bent to stroke each one in turn. 'It's only me!' she called out to Elsie, who had entrusted her with a key which saved her climbing off the bed in her living room to answer the door.

Elsie's home was a lot cosier now that it was redecorated. Gone were the rickety furniture and old-fashioned pictures lining the walls. In were a colourful sofa, squishy chairs and Elsie's new double bed. But one thing had not changed – her plethora of cats. Sarah sanitised her hands before plopping a bag of grapes on the table next to the bed.

Elsie was not fit enough to sleep upstairs just yet, but it was a goal. Her living room was toasty warm, and Sarah resisted the urge to open the window as the heat got the better of her.

Elsie peeked into the bag of grapes. 'Please tell me you've come from the arms of a new lover. I need inspiration. I'm stuck on chapter three.'

Sarah snorted a laugh as she glanced at the writing pad on Elsie's bed. 'Don't look at me. My love life is dead in the water.'

'Gee, a fine help you are.' She rolled a grape around her tongue before biting down.

Sarah sat on the edge of the sofa. At the station, her colleagues were building up the case against Gerard Baker to bring to the CPS.

But it seemed Elsie was in no hurry to get to the point as she gave Sarah the once-over. 'I heard about those boys you chased down. What a pair of scamps.'

Sarah crossed her legs. Nothing escaped her friend. 'How do you know about that?'

Elsie plucked another grape from the bag. 'Charlie's mom works in the library. She was grateful you didn't arrest him. She said his friend gave you a bit of a hard time.'

'Nothing I couldn't handle.' The bruise on Sarah's side had turned a dappled shade of yellow. She hadn't pushed for police assault. If someone jumped her bones in the middle of a field, she would have lashed out too.

Sarah petted a tortoiseshell cat as it clambered onto her lap. They may have had a confession, but Sarah wasn't yet convinced they had the right man. A satisfied smile spread across Elsie's face as she began to divulge the reason for her call.

'Rosemary Simmons was a bit of a hermit. Her son shopped online and she used the mobile hairdresser every few months. She went to the library once every three weeks, but that was pretty much it.'

'How do you know all that?' Sarah said.

'We used the same hairdresser, and I put some feelers out in town. I swear I should be writing detective novels. Only problem is, they'd spend more time having bunk-ups than solving any darn crimes.'

Sarah chuckled. She was one of Elsie's beta readers now and her books were good. Her ability to live in a dream world had kept her going through the toughest of times.

'But there was someone else Rosemary visited,' Elsie continued. 'Because I saw them with my own eyes. Even in the house of the Lord, nothing passes me by.'

'The house of the Lord?' Sarah echoed her words as the cat on her lap purred. 'I didn't know you went to church.' Elsie had converted to Catholicism after her parents died, but as far as Sarah knew she did her praying at home.

'Well then, let me tell ya . . .' Elsie's face brightened, just as it always did before she told a story of some sort. 'Jesus himself came to me in a dream. He said, "Elsie, if you're able to ride that darn scooter to the library then you can sure as heck make it to church!"' Sarah bit back a laugh at the conviction in her voice. Elsie never failed to brighten her day.

'Y'all know what I did?'

'You got yourself to church?' Sarah grinned.

'Darn tootin' I did!' Elsie said, with pride. 'That's where I saw Rosemary. She was never out of that confessional box.' She leaned forward, her words conspiratorial. 'Would a woman like Rosemary Simmons need forgiveness every week?'

'A fondness for a confessional doesn't make her a bad person,' Sarah interjected.

'Sure. But folks round here say Rosemary only started going after her son moved in with her. Isn't *that* queer?'

Sarah mulled it over. 'You could have a point.'

'Uh-huh,' Elsie replied. 'I should have mentioned it earlier but sometimes my thoughts stew like a fine apple pie.' She gave Sarah a knowing look. 'Now this is where things get juicy. Father Aloysius changed his name when he joined the priesthood. Does his best to distance himself from his family. Not that I blame him, bunch of snakes in the grass.' Elsie grimaced as she shifted on her bed.

'What? Who?'

'The Irvings, of course. Father Aloysius is Simon Irving's brother.'

'No. That can't be right.' Sarah frowned. 'I grew up in Slayton. I would have noticed.'

Elsie shook her head. 'Father Aloysius, or Teddy as he was called, was sent off to a swanky boarding school. It's said his father was experimenting. He sent one son off to boarding school and kept the other one at home to see which one did the best.'

'Who was the success, then?' Sarah mused. 'The ruthless son who lived for money or the one who gave his life to God?'

'Depends on your viewpoint, I suppose. Give me the Lord our Saviour any day.' Elsie briefly crossed herself as she gazed at the novelty cat clock on the wall, its eyes darting left and right in time with its pendulum tail. 'Maggie's late.'

'She'll be here soon.' Sarah brushed cat hairs off her trouser legs as her furry companion jumped down.

'Is she still bringing Elliott?'

Sarah tilted her head to one side. 'You don't like him, do you?' She had noticed her friend's reticence at the mention of Elliott before. Being a single mother, Maggie didn't always have childcare to hand.

'That kid gives me the heebie-jeebies.' Elsie shuddered. 'He's so quiet, you know. But when he looks at you, it's like he can see right into your soul.'

'He's a sweet little boy once you get to know him.' Sarah rose as the doorbell rang. 'Be nice.' Elsie's own son Christian was hardly the chatty type. Sarah was confident she'd bring her friends together in time.

Maggie appeared hesitant as Sarah allowed her in. 'Did we have to meet here?' she whispered, as Elliott shrugged off his raincoat. 'All these cats give me the creeps.' Sarah couldn't help but smile. Her friends were more alike than they knew.

'How are you today?' Sarah turned to the little boy, who was holding his iPad with both hands. A shy smile warmed his face. His eyes were brown today. Some days they were darker, reflecting his mood.

Sarah showed them into the living room. With Elsie's son Christian away, the house was quiet, apart from the occasional mew of Elsie's six cats.

'We were talking about the case,' Elsie said with some satisfaction, after Sarah had made drinks for them all.

Sarah's glance fell to Elliott, who was playing on his iPad, headphones on. 'Elsie was telling me that Rosemary's priest, Father Aloysius, is Simon Irving's brother.'

'Really? That should give you something to get your teeth into,' Maggie said, giving Elsie's cats a cautious eye.

'I saw on the news that you've got someone in custody,' Elsie exclaimed. 'Is it the traveller? I heard he'd been arrested. All that business with poor old Arnold Smith . . .' She lifted her cup as her cat almost upended it on her lap. 'Kizzy! Skedaddle!' She returned her attention to Sarah. 'At least you've caught him now, before he can hurt anyone else.'

'But that's it,' Sarah said. 'Noah has been bailed, to sign on at the police station every day.' It was not an uncommon practice for those with no fixed abode, and a good way of keeping tabs on him. As for the news release – their team were under pressure to get quick results. A piece about their most recent arrest should buy them a little more time.

'*Noah* is it, now?' Maggie delivered a wry smile. She was the second person to remark on Sarah's use of his name.

'Well, that's his name.' Two spots of pink stained Sarah's cheeks. She liked Noah. Despite his gruff exterior, he seemed a kind man. 'Someone else has confessed.' She could share the information, it would be public knowledge soon. 'And his handprint matches the one left at the murder scene.' Sarah followed Elsie's gaze as she looked behind her. She hadn't seen Elliott get up from his chair, much less heard him approach. His gaze was steady and unwavering, his stance rigid, his face ghostly pale.

'The children. They want to go home.' His words fell like a stone.

'Oh my Lord . . .' Elsie whispered, one hand resting on her chest.

'Elliott . . .' Maggie began, but Sarah gave her a pleading look. If Elliott was compelled to overcome his shyness, there was good reason for it. Her face pinched, Maggie relayed a reluctant nod.

'What children?' Sarah said, taking Elliott's hand in her own. His fingers were limp, his skin cold to the touch. His pupils were two dark pools of dread. All at once, the cats ran from the room.

'They're in a box.' As Elliott spoke, Sarah had a thought. She slid her phone from her pocket. She'd saved pictures of Noah's missing siblings. This was against police procedure and completely against the grain. But she was doing it anyway.

'Mercy.' Elliott pointed to the photo Sarah had taken of an old newspaper clipping. 'Mikey.' He pointed to the gaunt little boy beside her.

'He's right.' Sarah looked to her friends. 'Those are their names.'

'Where are they, darling?' She turned back to Elliott, a wave of emotion rising inside her. Elliott's gaze moved around the room. Slowly, his finger rose.

'Mother of pearl,' Elsie whispered dramatically, only to be shushed by Maggie with a glare. Sarah followed the direction of Elliott's finger as it finally pointed to a picture of Jesus on the wall.

'They're with the Lord,' Elsie said sadly.

'Are you OK?' Sarah said to Elliott. 'Do you want a hug?' She opened her arms and embraced him, feeling him sigh with relief in her arms. 'It's OK.' Sarah rubbed his back. 'I'll find them. I'll bring them home.'

Elsie wasn't the only person in Slayton with that picture. She had seen the exact same one in somebody else's home.

<h1 style="text-align:center">42</h1>

There was a time when Sarah could barely bring herself to speak to her sergeant, let alone knock on her door, but she had been unable to sleep – this couldn't wait until dawn. Gabby did not suffer fools gladly, and Sarah had found herself on the receiving end of a tongue-lashing more than once. But she was the only person she trusted enough to confide in tonight. Gabby didn't believe in the supernatural, although living in Slayton would surely serve to broaden her mind. But the woman couldn't resist a lead and Sarah had given her results in the past.

Sarah could have called Richie, but she needed the security of a senior officer who would have her back if things went awry. DI McGuire was uncharted waters, and as much as Gabby intimidated her, the woman had earned her trust. She only hoped that she was not making an utter fool of herself. She was slowly gaining her sergeant's respect. If she cocked this up it would bring her back to square one.

Gabby nodded to the officer on scene guard as he added her details to the log. It would take officers time to pick through Arnold's abode and it was not ready to be released just yet. Which was just as well, because if Sarah's gut was right, answers would be found here.

'I hope you know what you're doing, Noble, dragging me out of my bed to come to this godforsaken place at this hour of the night,' Gabby grumbled as she pulled on the plastic overshoes. Something told Sarah that Gabby was not the outdoor type. She had already slipped twice in the walk from the car to the cottage.

'Sorry, Sarge.' Sarah did her best to sound repentant. 'But I've an awful feeling we've missed something.'

She knew Gabby hadn't been sleeping, despite her protests. She had sounded as sharp as a tack when she answered her phone after just one ring. The stepping plate creaked beneath Sarah's weight as they entered the dimly lit cottage, the room still looking like an abattoir.

'Well?' Gabby rasped. 'What are you looking for?'

Sarah tugged on her PVC gloves with a satisfying ping. 'That picture,' Sarah said, pointing to the religious image of Jesus Christ hanging on the wall. 'He'd covered it with a doily. He must have been plagued with guilt.'

'So?' Gabby said, standing next to her as she examined it. 'Isn't that part and parcel of being a Catholic?'

Given the doily had been removed, Sarah felt confident enough to lift the heavy wooden-framed picture from the wall. 'Give me a hand with this,' she said, in such a confident manner that Gabby complied. Sarah had hoped for a note, or maybe even a map stuck to the back of the frame. But there was nothing of the sort. There didn't need to be. The answer was staring them in the face. The large religious picture was covering a safe in the wall.

'Well, I'll be—' Gabby uttered on a low breath. 'How did CSI miss that?'

'They would have found it eventually,' Sarah replied, trying not to sneeze as dust floated in the air. 'There's a lot of stuff to get through.'

Sliding her camera from her pocket, Gabby took some photos. They should not disturb the scene. This was best left with CSI. They stood, staring, both wondering what secrets it contained. 'I don't suppose it's open,' Gabby said, breaking the silence at last.

'I feel like I'm in a movie.' Sarah smiled, her pulse picking up pace at the thought of finding out. 'What do you think we'll find?'

'Nothing if you don't get a move on,' Gabby instructed. But the safe door was shut tight. 'How old was he again?' Gabby said, trying to remember his date of birth.

'Sixty. He was born on Christmas Day. I remember because I'd thought he was much older than that.' Gabby clicked the dial to the four numbers of his date of birth. But the safe refused to budge.

'OK, we should call this in.' Gabby sighed. 'Leave it to the specialists.'

'We should . . .' Sarah reasoned. 'But that would take time. God only knows what's behind that door.'

'Alright, then.' Gabby's eyes twinkled in the darkness. 'Let me make a call.'

Within minutes, they had obtained Arnold's wife's date of birth. Sarah bit on her bottom lip as she turned the safe dial and was met with a satisfying click. Excitement was intermingled with dread as she opened the safe door.

<h1 style="text-align:center">43</h1>

Shhhh. The sound came from the darkness as the child stepped forward and pressed their finger against mottled blue lips. Gerard's eyelids flitted open in the darkness as he jerked awake. His limbs, which had been floppy and rested, were now as tight as a bow. Were the whispers that had awoken him real or part of a dream? Feeling detached from reality, he took in his surroundings and remembered he was in a custody cell. His bed was a thin blue plastic layer of foam, the toilet a cold and lidless stainless steel. His movements were recorded under the watchful eye of CCTV, his body pixelated when he urinated. The custody sergeant had explained everything, given this was Gerard's first arrest. Perhaps he had sensed his fear. His actions may have been noble, but it didn't make him any less scared. His surroundings were alien but at least he couldn't hurt anyone here. A series of moans echoed down the corridor as his drunken neighbour wailed. Was this his life now? He tugged the thin custody blanket around his shoulders as he sat up on the uncomfortable strip of foam.

There was a prologue to his life, and it frightened him to think about it. This was about more than his frequent blackouts. He could see it now. 'No,' he whispered, holding his head in his hands as if it were an unexploded bomb. He wasn't ready. He didn't want to know. A tsunami of emotions threatened to break him. Saying goodbye to Ruth had been hard enough. They had drifted over the years, both so wrapped up in work that they had little time for each other. But now their love was renewed and he physically ached for her. He had brought this upon them and now she had to live with the stigma of a husband in prison. He would encourage her to divorce him in time, but right now she was all he had.

The doctor had examined him briefly, deeming him fit for interview. Frustrated detectives had pushed for answers, showing him pictures of the grisly murder scene. The sight of their empty eye sockets had made him recoil. Gerard had hit a stone wall. The revelation that his DNA had been at the first murder scene winded him. At the back of his mind, he'd hoped that he was wrong. He didn't feel capable of such grotesque acts. Yet he remembered the first time he came to . . . the taste of someone else's blood on his tongue. He had relayed his experiences in detail, against his solicitor's advice. Officers had descended on his rented cottage, seizing his clothes and shoes. He exhaled a long breath as a disquieting feeling grew. What sort of animal was he? The truth was, he didn't want to know. His mind was protecting him for a reason. But what had compelled him to come here? It was about more than Blackhall Manor. Even now, the whispers followed him. He had given himself up. He'd done the right thing. Why were they still here?

He pulled the blanket tighter around his shoulders as childish voices rose in the air. *Go.* He heard a young girl's insistent voice. *Go now!* But what did they want from him?

44

Monday, 9th March 2020

Sherlock stretched in contentment on the sofa as soft music played from the speaker in Sarah's living room.

'This has really shaken you, hasn't it?' Gabby was sitting across from her, legs crossed in a wide armchair.

'I'd be lying if I said it hadn't.' Sarah cradled her mug. 'But you don't need to babysit me.'

'I'm hardly babysitting,' Gabby retorted. 'But I won't rest until I get to the root of your source.'

Sarah didn't answer. This was a serious investigation and the last thing she wanted was to implicate a seven-year-old boy. Elliott deserved to be kept out of things. He'd been through enough.

'I thought we'd find a letter,' she said eventually. 'Or something that points the finger at the killer. I never thought we'd find bones.' The charred remains which were wrapped in dirt-stained cloth told a sombre story. Somebody had burned them before burying them in the ground. The blackened crumbles of mud still clinging to the bones told Sarah they came from one place – Blackhall Woods. Nowhere else in Slayton had the same rich, dark earth. Sarah's eyes grew moist as realisation hit. 'They belong to the children. Everything revolves around them.'

'But the black-eyed children were a hoax.' Gabby watched her intently.

'Not *those* children. Noah's siblings. He's been searching for them for twenty-five years.' She stiffened as a thought entered her mind. 'I should go there. Somebody needs to tell them.'

'Not yet. You heard McGuire.' Gabby's red nails flashed as she raised a hand. 'Not until we know more.' Their DI had been pleased with their discovery but urged caution for now.

'But there were two sets of bones, and they weren't adults.' The forensic examiner had given some early deliberations and now all they could do was wait.

'One more day won't make any difference to Noah and his family.' She paused, turning to look at Sarah with an expression of consternation she had come to know well. 'Just how did you know where to look?'

Gabby was talking about Sarah's knowledge of Arnold's safe. 'Just a hunch,' she explained. 'And the doily hanging over the picture of Jesus. It felt . . . significant.' She hoped that would satisfy Gabby, who had gained results from Sarah's insights in the past. But now it was one o'clock in the morning and Gabby was making no effort to leave.

'I'm not going until you tell me who your informant is,' Gabby said, as if reading her thoughts. 'If I have to sleep on the sofa with the cat, I will.'

'Can't we just put this down to copper's intuition?' Sarah said hopefully.

But Gabby shook her head. 'McGuire will want to know your source.'

'I can't.' Sarah sipped her coffee. 'Because how do I tell him . . .' She hesitated, winding her fingers tighter around her cup.

'Go on,' her sergeant encouraged.

'How do I tell him that it came from a seven-year-old boy?' A beat passed between them.

'Elliott.' Gabby knew of him. He had helped them in the past.

Sarah didn't deny it. 'I don't want him involved. Him, or his mother.'

'Then stick to your guns.' Gabby rested her cup on the coffee table before her. 'We've been here before. If anyone pushes just tell them the picture played on your mind, and the fact that Arnold had covered it up.' She stood, masking a yawn with the back of her hand. 'At least I'll get to sleep in my own bed tonight.'

But sleep was far off for Sarah as she contemplated her source. How had Elliott known about Mercy and Mikey, much less been able to guide her to where their remains had been laid? But had he, though? The sensible side of her psyche argued the toss. He'd pointed to a religious picture and spoke about children 'in a box'. But *she* had made the link to Arnold's home. She saw her sergeant out, keeping her conflicted thoughts to herself. In a few hours she would be back in the office. Who knew what the day would hold?

45

'There's a bad man in Slayton. His blood is warm but his thoughts are black. You *have* to tell the woman about the bad man.' Elliott woke with a start, scooting up on his elbows as he stared around his room. Mercy's voice seemed to come from inside him, the words sounding like a piano played out of key. It was so long since Mercy died that she couldn't quite remember how to talk in his world. He felt them stronger than before. So strong that he had stood up before Maggie, Sarah and Elsie and spoken. He hadn't wanted to do it, but he wasn't able to stop. He hadn't understood why he'd pointed at the picture of Jesus, but Sarah did.

Now Mercy and her brother were leaving, but thoughts of another 'bad man' in Slayton made Elliott's tummy feel sick. He yelped as his door creaked open and drew his teddy to his chest. But it was not Mercy or Mikey standing there, it was Mummy. She was dressed in her pyjamas, which meant she had come from her bed.

'Did you call?' She squinted in the dim light, rubbing her arms.

Elliott shook his head.

'It's freezing in here.' She laid a hand on his radiator. Elliott knew it would be warm. It wouldn't matter if they lit a fire in the centre of the room. When the whispers came, they turned the air to ice. Maggie couldn't hear them, but she felt something just the same. 'Do you want to sleep in my room or are you OK here?'

'I'm OK.' Elliott was meant to be a big boy. If the whispers found him in Elsie's house, then they would find him in his mother's room. Maggie pulled his duvet up and fixed his pillows. He bounced along with the springs as she sat on his bed.

'Sarah called. She said that I was to tell you that everything is OK now. You don't need to worry about the children anymore.' Maggie's face was as sad as a rainy day. She hated talking about the things that made him different to other kids.

'OK.' He snuggled down into his pillow, pushing thoughts of the bad man away. He would talk to Miss Grogan. She would help him make the whispers stop. He opened his arms as his mother took him in an embrace.

'One day, we're going to move out of this place.' She drew away and smoothed over his hair. 'We'll live in a nice house and you'll have good dreams. I promise.' Elliott brightened at the thought.

'Will we? Promise?'

Maggie smiled, her eyes shiny with tears. 'Yes. I promise. With all my heart.'

The words made Elliott feel warm inside. 'I love you, Mummy,' he said, settling down to sleep. There would be no more whispers tonight.

46

It was with some surprise that Sarah learned that Gerard was being considered for bail. While his confession held weight, he was not considered a flight risk and given his impeccable record, he could be released into his wife's care. While the Crown Prosecution Service was happy with the DNA link, police were advised to proceed with further investigation to ensure a watertight case for both sets of murders. There was no arguing with the DNA which put him at the scene. Police had descended on his rented cottage in search of evidence, but there was nothing there to tie him to Arnold's murder apart from the same MO. If police wanted to charge Gerard with all three murders, and feel certain of a conviction in court, then more digging was needed and that would take time.

'People are talking about you,' Richie said, handing Sarah her morning cup of coffee. She'd done well to get to work so early, given her late finish last night.

'Nice to know I've got a fan club.' She masked a yawn with the back of her hand.

'They're wondering who your secret contact is.' Richie leaned across his desk, staring her down with his big brown eyes. 'You're not holding out on me, are you?'

Sarah rolled her eyes. His tactics of persuasion may have worked on younger female officers but they were having no effect on her. 'There's no secrecy about it, just plain old-fashioned policing. It pays to go with your gut.'

'Hmm.' Richie watched her over the top of his mug. As she grew older, Sarah found that pleasing everyone was impossible, but pissing them off was a piece of cake. She would have to tread lightly where Elliott was concerned. The same went for Elsie and Maggie. If McGuire knew she was discussing the case with outsiders he would bring holy hell down on her. She was pretty sure when he advised her to 'be more pigeon' he didn't mean carrier.

It was something she bore in mind when she approached Gerard's wife, who had asked to speak to a female officer. 'I'm afraid I can't discuss your husband's case.' Sarah directed her to a chair. 'But if you want to speak to him over the phone, he'll be able to tell you himself.' Sarah had brought her through to a witness interview room situated in the heart of the station. It offered privacy and was more comfortable than the draughty rooms just off reception. In her silk blouse and black trousers Ruth Baker appeared a complete professional. But there was also something wholesome about her presence, and given she wasn't in the area when the murders occurred, she was not considered a witness for the case. Sarah had her undivided attention as she explained the protocol. 'You've already given officers a statement, so I'm not sure what more I can do, other than tell you Gerard is comfortable, fed and cared for. He has access to a phone and should be free to call you later today.'

'That's not why I'm here,' Ruth said. 'Although I'm glad he's well. I've been thinking about the . . . situation.' She began to wring her hands, which had been resting on her lap. 'As I said to the officers, none of this makes any sense.'

'I understand,' Sarah said with some sympathy. 'And remember, he's not been charged with anything yet.'

'But it's likely,' Ruth said, 'given his handprint matches the one found at the cottage where those poor people . . .' A sigh escaped her lips as she struggled to finish. 'He told me. He wants to get to the bottom of this as much as you do.' Her eyes were wide and sincere as she looked at Sarah. 'But I know my husband. He's not physically capable of hurting another soul. There's something you need to know.'

Sarah felt for the woman before her and was willing to listen. When it came to working a case, she kept an open mind. You never knew which piece of information might prove the linchpin.

'If you've got anything to share that's relevant to the case then you can add it to your statement and it will go on the file.'

Ruth's lips thinned. 'I don't want to add to my statement. I want you to take what I'm telling you and do something about it.' Her words carried an edge. 'Sorry,' she said. 'It's so frustrating. It's like he's resigned himself to spending the rest of his life in prison. But something drew him here. A memory, perhaps? A sense of unfinished business? Then he got tangled up in the murders and he's blocked it all out.'

Sarah frowned as she tried to decipher the words. 'Gerard said he'd never been here before all this business began.'

'Delve deeper. My husband needs a psychiatrist, not a prison cell.'

'He's been spoken to by the force medical examiner.' Sarah scratched her temple. 'He's not reported any traumas that I know of.' But the custody process was like a conveyor belt and his examination would not have taken long.

'He wouldn't. He's not ready to face up to it. But there's something you don't know. I should have figured it out earlier on. Gerard's fascination with Slayton. His feeling of déjà vu. He's been here before. It all adds up.'

Sarah's phone buzzed with an incoming text. It was Richie.

Update. Get to the briefing room.

'Sorry.' Sarah pocketed her phone. 'I'm needed in briefing. Can you spell it out for me?' She didn't mean to be abrupt but precious seconds were ticking by.

'My husband was adopted. He refuses to talk about it but I'm sure it's connected to this.'

Another text buzzed on Sarah's phone. Richie was getting impatient.

Are you coming? You won't believe this.

<h1 style="text-align:center">47</h1>

Robbed of his senses, Noah kneeled in dark silence. 'Bless me, Father, for I have sinned.' His words were directed towards the dim figure on the other side. 'It has been one year since my last confession.'

Father Aloysius spoke in a low droning voice, repeating holy words he had recited a thousand times. Noah made out the glint of the priest's auburn hair as he tipped an ear towards the open shutter. He was probably thinking that there must be a terrible sin for Noah to return after a whole year. The truth was, Noah had not stepped inside a church since his siblings had disappeared. He and God were on bad terms. It had taken every ounce of self-control to force himself into the confessional. It was bad enough that he'd lost his mother at such a young age. Now he was sitting in the darkness with a cynical heart, his knees aching against the wood as he tried to remember what to say. In the old days, his parents stopped off at Slayton because it was predominantly a Catholic town. His mother used to describe them as 'many stars scattered in the sight of God', when people asked what faith Romany people followed as a whole. There was no rule when it came to faith, but his mother was Catholic through and through. He remembered being prodded into the wooden confessional box along with his siblings as she prayed for their souls. One at a time they entered to be suitably chastised. Noah had learned to recycle his sins so he always had something to say.

But he didn't come here today to be forgiven by a God he'd stopped talking to. Neither was he here to be patronised by a priest who was a far bigger sinner than he was. His visit was a worm on the hook. Over the last few days his community had been alive with speculation. It seemed he wasn't alone after all, at least, not in the traveller community. Word had spread of his recent arrest and his Romany brothers and sisters were outraged, after everything his family had been through. His grandmother Olive was fondly thought of in many communities, both in England and far beyond. His network finally found answers in a little Irish town outside Ballinasloe – the place where Arnold had lived with his wife as she saw out the remaining months of her life. According to the rumour mill, Arnold was drunk at her wake and became loose-lipped. In such a close-knit community, nobody was in any hurry to go to the police. Only now had Noah's Romany brethren been able to unlock the shameful secrets of his past. But how much was speculation and how much was fact? Noah took a breath when it was his turn to speak.

'I'm not here about my sins, Father, but someone else's. I know who took my brother and sister twenty-five years ago.' His words were free-falling in the darkness, his hands clenched into fists. He could not stop now. 'Their names were Mikey and Mercy. We were staying in Blackhall Woods when they disappeared.' He recalled his father's face when he came to pick him up from hospital. His bloodshot eyes and the shake in his hands as he explained how they had gone. Noah inhaled the scent of the church: incense, wilted flowers and damp. 'At first we thought they'd run away. Mercy's backpack was missing, and she'd taken food. It seemed they'd planned to go to my grandmother's place.' Each word pierced Noah's heart. 'But somebody stopped them. They never left Slayton that night.'

'Then let us pray for their souls . . .' Father Aloysius began.

'Tomorrow I tell everything.' Noah gripped the wooden lip of the confessional. 'Who took them, why and how. Tomorrow I go to the press.' He released the wooden shelf as it threatened to break beneath his grasp.

'Then why . . .'

'I need forgiveness, Father. Forgiveness for not being there. I was their big brother. I didn't keep them safe.' Frustration rose as his emotions got the better of him.

'Suffer little children to come unto me.' The priest spoke solemnly. 'They will sit by the side of the Lord.'

'But I never said they were dead.' In the darkness, Noah's words were knife-sharp. 'Did I?' He knew everyone assumed as such but it stung to hear the words.

'Let us pray.' The priest didn't falter. Noah's temple began to pound as his blood pulsed through his veins. Soon he would have justice. It would not be long now.

48

'I've put the good towels out!' Elliott said cheerily, bounding down the stairs. He'd finished his homework early so he could spend time with their guest.

'Good boy,' Maggie said, washing her hands in the sink. The air smelled of the citrus-scented cleaning fluid Maggie used to clean her paintbrushes. She had just finished her latest picture, a woman with her hand on her sun hat as she stared out at Slayton's lake. Elliott's eyes danced around their clean and tidy kitchen. Miss Grogan was coming to visit, and he couldn't have been happier than if Auntie Sarah had turned up at their door. She had told him of the visit, long before she'd rung his mother to check it was OK. He knew it was nothing to worry about. Elliott was ahead of all the other kids in class. So far ahead, that sometimes Miss Grogan let him read his library books while the rest of them caught up. He had learned just about every tortoise fact there was to know, so sometimes he'd sit and draw them in their natural habitat. There were lots of different species of tortoise, but his favourites were the giants who lived in the Galapagos. His heart gave a little flutter as the doorbell rang. Miss Grogan was different to the other teachers. She knew Slayton. And he could tell even without her saying that she had been to the deepest level, like him – the abyss.

Within minutes she was seated at the kitchen table, a cup of coffee in hand. 'I hope I'm not intruding on your evening,' she said. 'I just thought that as you missed the parent-teacher evening, it would be nice to catch up.'

'I'm so sorry about that.' Maggie sighed, running a hand over her hair. 'I was working and they wouldn't let me change my shift.'

'Please, don't apologise,' Miss Grogan replied. 'You've done a marvellous job raising Elliott. I don't know how you manage work, home . . .' She cast an eye over the freshly painted picture. 'And painting, too! Elliott told me you were an artist. You're gifted.'

Elliott smiled. His teacher had a way of making people feel better about themselves.

Miss Grogan looked at him and winked, and Elliott's heart gave another flutter as it felt like a 'thank you'.

'Oh, that's just a hobby,' Maggie said. 'Although sales *have* picked up. It's hard, finding time with work and . . .' She looked to Elliott, faltering. 'Not that I would change a thing . . .' Elliott wished his mother didn't feel so bad about everything. A shaft of sunlight beamed through the kitchen window, highlighting his mother's art. Sometimes it felt like her pictures were alive.

'Well, I know you're a busy woman so I'll get to the point of my visit.' His teacher rested her cup of coffee on the table. 'Elliott is doing brilliantly in school. He's a high achiever, way ahead of the rest of his class.'

'Oh,' Maggie exhaled in relief. 'I'm so glad to hear it. I was worried his marks had slipped.'

'Not at all.' Miss Grogan looked to Elliott and back at Maggie again. 'Although it would be forgiven, given the past few months.' The room fell silent, as it did when the topic of his father was discussed. Elliott looked at his hands, feeling his mother's discomfort grow.

'Why don't you go into the living room, Elliott? So Miss Grogan and I can talk.' But straightening in her chair, Miss Grogan raised her hand.

'Do you mind very much if he doesn't?' She smiled and tilted her head to one side, just the way Maggie's mother used to do when she was alive. 'Elliott wants to talk things over, but he's scared it will upset you.' She paused. Elliott had never told Miss Grogan this. She just seemed to know. 'I know he's young, but his life experiences have shaped him. You can count the number of people that Elliott trusts with one hand.' She gave him a reassuring smile. 'Which makes me very lucky to be in that circle of trust.' Elliott shot his mother a furtive glance. He felt a little squirmy, but Miss Grogan was right, he wanted Maggie to know how he felt.

'I know he's had counselling, but it's hard for him to trust strangers who don't understand what he goes through. Some people call them night terrors, but we both know they're much more than that.'

And there it was. Out in the open. Elliott nibbled his bottom lip as he watched his mother's face darken.

'With all respect,' she said, a prickle in her words, 'the counsellors are trained child psychologists, while you're a primary school teacher. I know you're coming from a good place, but are you qualified to analyse my son?'

Elliott shifted in his chair. Sometimes Maggie was rude when she was scared. He met Miss Grogan's gaze. She was smiling. Patient. She patted his mother's hand. 'My dear, please don't take offence. I know you want to protect your son. So do I. But if it helps, one of my degrees is in child psychotherapy. All I'm asking is that we give Elliott the opportunity to discuss how he's feeling without fear of upsetting us.'

Maggie sighed. 'It's just hard, after what happened with his father. Did Elliott tell you we're getting a divorce?'

'He did,' Miss Grogan said. Although Elliott didn't remember saying it out loud. 'But this is about more than his relationship with his father, learning how to cope with it, and everything else.'

Elliott sensed that Miss Grogan had come here to talk about his nightmares, but given Maggie's reaction she had pushed that to one side.

'What do you suggest we do?' Maggie replied.

'I'd like to be there for Elliott, help him with some child-friendly coping strategies when it comes to blocking out scary thoughts. Does that sound OK with you?'

'Anything that helps Elliott is fine with me.'

'Good. Because he's an amazing little boy.' She stopped for a moment. 'Slayton is a great place to live, with a tight-knit community. But it's had its fair share of . . . unusual events. Elliott can't help but pick up on that. But if we work together we can silence the whispers in his mind.'

Maggie opened her mouth to speak then closed it again. Elliott realised his mother didn't know what to say. 'It's OK.' He smiled. 'Miss Grogan is my friend.'

His teacher rose from her seat. 'I won't intrude on your evening anymore. If you ever need to chat, you know where I am.'

'Thank you,' Maggie replied, showing her out. But his mother's face was stiff as she led Elliott back to the table and asked him to sit.

'What have you told Miss Grogan?'

Elliott shrugged.

'Because you need to be careful, Elliott. What you have. It's special. But not everyone understands. If you need to talk about it, you come to me. OK?'

Elliott nodded. His mother was scared. Scared of the whispers. Scared of what people thought. Scared of the bullies who tormented him in school. But what she didn't understand was that Miss Grogan was just like him.

'Mummy?' he said, because she liked it when he called her that.

'Yes, sweetie?' She curled his hair around his ear.

'Don't drink wine tonight.' He looked to the canvas on the easel. 'I like that.' It was a bright and happy picture. He wanted things to stay that way.

'You don't like it when I drink?' Maggie said softly. Elliott shook his head.

'It makes you sad.'

'Well then, I'll drink milk tonight.' Then she kissed him on the forehead and gave him her brightest smile.

49

Sarah zipped up her coat as she left the comfort of her parked car. She knew she was making extra work for herself, but not long ago everything was falling apart quicker than she could put it back together. After her husband died, she wavered between giving up and seeing how much more she could take. Now, as she trudged through the brooding forest, she was grateful for the job which gave her the strength to carry on. Her glance flicked upwards. You were never alone in Blackhall Woods, and she didn't want to wonder what nocturnal wildlife was shaking droplets of rain from the tree branches. In such an unwelcome place, it was a battle not to turn on her heel and run. At least it wouldn't be hers for much longer. The sale of Blackhall Manor and its woodlands was going through. Irving had persisted with his demands to buy the manor – even upping his offer from before. With a warm sense of satisfaction, Sarah imagined his anger at being turned down. The torch on her iPhone illuminated only a couple of feet before her, but the journey from her car to Noah's caravan was short. At least she'd had the sense to pull on her boots to negotiate the slippery earth. She'd barely had time to feed Sherlock before getting changed and heading back out. The sooner she reached Noah's caravan, the faster she'd make it home. The last few hours had been a whirlwind of briefings, phone calls, paperwork and tying up loose ends. She was bone-weary but determined to do whatever she could.

Tonight, she wasn't working under orders. Her colleagues had accepted Gerard's confession, although motive had not been established yet. A full background check was being carried out on Gerard and his family, and the Crown Prosecution Service had advised officers to make the case watertight. Sarah wasn't sure what to believe. Gerard's wife came across as genuine, but surely no woman would want to accept being married to a man capable of such brutality.

She approached the caravan tentatively, expecting Noah's dog to alert him of her approach. But there was nothing, apart from a dim light inside. Sarah glanced around the camp, which was tidy but bare. Noah's outdoor sleeping quarters had been removed and the washing-line taken in. Were they getting ready to leave? But Noah had been bailed. Had the evidence against him been stronger, he would be sitting in a cell. After what Sarah heard today, more questions needed to be asked. Gerard Baker may be their main suspect but other leads were still being chased. Father Aloysius had provided a statement stating he hadn't spoken to the victims recently. But it didn't rest well with Sarah. Something was off. She turned off her iPhone light as she approached the caravan door.

'Hello?' she said, knocking hard. Her nerves jangled at the thought of their meeting. As much as she liked Noah, she didn't know him all that well. The narrow caravan door opened and Noah's face fell as he saw her waiting on the step.

'Can I have a quick word?' she said, peeking into the caravan. But there was no sign of his grandmother, much less his rescue dog, Storm. 'What's going on?' She sensed more to the situation. 'You're not leaving town, are you? Because I can't let you do that.'

As Noah glared at her, she became aware of her own vulnerability, in the woods with no backup to hand. A flock of restless birds shot from the trees in a cacophony of caws. The air cooled as evening closed in. Why hadn't she told anyone where she was? She was putting too much faith in her instincts. What if Noah couldn't be trusted after all? She smoothed her rain-damp hair, trying to read his troubled thoughts.

'I'm not going anywhere,' Noah's mouth thinned into a hard line. 'But you are. You can't be here. You need to leave.' He stood, arms folded, in jeans and a plaid shirt. But Sarah was fed up with being bossed around.

'I'm not going anywhere either!' she retorted. 'It's my land and . . .'

'Have it your own way.' His gaze darted around the woodlands. 'Either go or come in and shut the door.'

Sarah stepped inside, because the urgency in his voice dictated that something serious was going on. 'Where's Olive, and Storm? What's happening?'

'They're somewhere safe.' Noah peeked through the net curtains, checking every window before pulling the curtains closed. 'You only have yourself to blame, getting involved in this.'

'In what?' A spike of annoyance grew as she took a seat. 'I'm not a mind reader, what's going on?'

Noah sat across from her, hands on his thighs as if ready to spring up at any second. 'I suppose it's too late now. You've probably blown the lot.' Finally, he met her gaze. 'I've been doing some asking around. Seems Rosemary went to church the night before she died, as did Arnold.'

'There's no law against it,' Sarah said, averting her gaze. If he met her eye, he'd see that she already knew where this was heading – because she had her suspicions about Father Aloysius too.

'Maybe not, but I reckon Father Aloysius was the last person to see them alive.'

Sarah nodded in agreement, although she was loath to say anything. The last thing she wanted was for Noah to get himself in deeper than he already was. She thought about Arnold's dog, and how the priest had denied seeing him. The Irving family were slippery sorts and were well connected. Which was why she had yet to report her suspicions to her DI.

'I went to confession,' Noah carried on. 'Told the priest I knew everything. I said I was going to the press tomorrow after I broke the news to Olive tonight.' Noah's eyes narrowed. 'I'm on the right track, aren't I? He's involved. I think Arnold was ready to confess before he died.'

Sarah nibbled her bottom lip as Noah relayed details of his bluff. She could neither deny nor agree with the statement, given he had been bailed for the offences himself.

'I'm not going to prison to keep that bastard's secret.' He shook his head grimly. 'I know what he did.'

'We've already got a confession,' Sarah blurted. 'You're pretty much off the hook.' A bloom of guilt rose. If McGuire could see her now . . .

'From the outsider? Yeah, I heard,' Noah replied. 'But someone is running scared, and they're not getting away with it. Not anymore.'

'Getting away with what?' Sarah asked. Without a caution, anything he told her now wouldn't count as evidence, but she needed to know.

'They killed my brother and sister and between them, they covered it up. All these years, they've kept their silence. And now, when they were ready to talk, the ringleader finished them off.'

You're almost right, Sarah thought. But there was a link in the chain that Noah wasn't aware of – Simon Irving. 'You went to confession using yourself as bait to draw him out?'

Noah nodded. 'Olive wanted to do it, but I couldn't have that. I packed her and Storm away. They're at a camp twenty miles up the road.'

Sarah's heart beat a little faster as the situation became clear. 'And you're going to sit here waiting for the killer to strike?'

'I'm ready for him.' Noah's fists clenched. 'Or I was, until you showed up. You're putting yourself in danger by being here. I can't be responsible if anything happens to you.'

'So that's the plan?' Sarah shook her head, incredulous. 'You hang tight and wait for some psycho killer to try to slash your throat?'

'That's pretty much it.'

Sarah thought through the scenario. At least he hadn't come to the conclusion that she was involved. Turning up alone like this had been a bad move on her part. She imagined what would happen if the killer did appear. Noah would lose his head, end up in prison. His actions wouldn't bring his siblings back. 'I can't let you do that.' Sarah gathered her composure. She was in way over her head.

Noah gave her a shifty look. 'Which is why I want you to go.'

But Sarah wasn't walking away from this. 'I'm calling this in.' She slipped her phone from her pocket. She couldn't be party to whatever madness Noah had planned.

'Sorry—' Noah's hand clamped down over hers as he took her mobile phone. 'You're not. But if you lot were doing your jobs I wouldn't have to resort to this.'

'You're out of order, Noah. Give that back, right now!' Sarah tried to sound stern but a small part of her understood where he was coming from. He had set the trap. It was too late for him to back out now. She opened the palm of her hand. 'Don't dig yourself deeper into this hole. We *are* doing our jobs. There's a lot more to this than you know.' That was an understatement. She thought about the revelation that came out of briefing. Gerard wasn't an outsider – he was Noah's brother, who had been placed for adoption twenty-five years ago. His flashbacks and compulsions were remnants of a childhood not ready to let go. Noah would discover the truth soon enough. An image of her sergeant's disapproving face flashed into her mind. Right now, the best thing Sarah could do was defuse a situation that had the potential to go horribly wrong.

'I'm not stopping you from leaving.' Noah shoved the phone deep into his jeans pocket. Sarah didn't want to get physical with him. The last thing she wanted was to be wrestling for her phone if an intruder arrived. If she left now, by the time she got to the nearest phone she could be too late.

She crossed her arms. 'I'm not going anywhere until you give me my mobile.'

Her mind raced forward to work. If anything came of this she would explain she'd been left with little choice. Given what Noah had said, Blackhall Woods wasn't the safest place for her to be walking alone. They sat in silence, listening for the slightest movement but for a long time there was nothing but the hoot of an owl in a nearby tree. Noah was tensed, ready to jump at any second and defend them both. He had tried several times to convince her to leave, but she was having none of it. At the very least, she had a duty to protect him. And she was under no illusions: the killer was dangerous and did not leave a trail. Sarah worked out her theories. DI McGuire had explored the fact that Geoffrey and Arnold had one thing in common when Mikey and Mercy disappeared – they were working for Simon Irving on a new development situated a mile from the woods. Now officers were looking into the building site, which comprised sixteen detached four-bedroom houses. Evidence suggested that Mercy and Mikey had run away. Mercy had taken her backpack and her favourite book. It was raining hard that night. Had they taken shelter from the storm in one of Irving's new builds? The more Sarah thought about it, the more it rang true.

Irving was a man who was used to getting his own way. Sarah had already deemed him a psychopath, his philanthropic efforts a way of bringing in the adoration which was his lifeblood. He would do whatever it took to ensure his image wasn't tarnished, and the lives of Noah and his mother would mean little to him. Had his brother warned him that Rosemary and Arnold had confessed? How far would he go to cover it up?

The atmosphere was thick and Sarah took a breath to speak. Noah raised a hand to quieten her before pointing to the window. He silently pressed a finger to his lips. He rose to his full height and opened the cupboard next to the door. Sarah had seen him glance at it a couple of times. As he pulled out his weapon, she was relieved that it wasn't a gun. Her heart picked up an extra beat as he rested the hammer by his side.

'If you have to use that, it had better be in self-defence,' she whispered, as he waited at the door. He signalled at her to be quiet as they heard movement outside. Another heavy snap of twigs underfoot.

The killer was here.

50

Sarah tensed at the sense of evil brushing past. It was not the first time she'd been in an enclosed space, heart hammering, as she wondered if it was her turn next. There was movement on the other side of the caravan, and she fought the urge to peek through the window out into the woods beyond. 'It could be an animal,' she spoke in a hoarse whisper. 'A deer, or a badger?'

'Shush!' Noah commanded, as he stood, poised for attack.

Sarah shook her head tightly as he raised the hammer. She couldn't become embroiled in this. At the very least, she could lose her job. At the worst, they could both end up in prison. By the way Noah was holding that hammer he wasn't messing around. Her senses heightened by adrenalin, she detected a faint sloshing sound as footsteps approached the caravan. Noah stood, frozen like a statue of a Greek god, wielding the hammer mid-air. Sarah's mind ticked over. Why weren't they coming in? Why would the killer risk implicating themselves when a suspect was in custody about to take the flack?

She sucked in a cold breath before darting towards the window and pulling back the curtain a fraction of an inch. There *was* a figure in the darkness but they weren't coming in. Then it hit her just how stupid she'd been. Sometimes her lack of service shone like a beacon and this was a prime example. This wouldn't be like the other murders; they would make it look like an accident. She sniffed the air as the sound of sloshing intensified. 'Petrol,' she whispered, catching the pungent odour. They had drenched the caravan with petrol and now they were going to set it alight. This time it would appear unrelated to the previous murders. A crime against a minority group. Such things weren't unknown, as disgruntled townsfolk rallied against them. Noah had smelled it too. Wide-eyed, she met his gaze. 'It's an arson attack. Get out!'

Noah fumbled with the door as heat shimmered against the windows. 'Open it, for God's sake!' Sarah shouted. Smoke billowed beneath the door as the fire took hold.

'It's jammed!' Noah shouted over the racket, swinging his hammer as he rained down blows on the door. As Sarah pushed a window open, the door splintered beneath Noah's brute force. Grabbing Sarah by the arm, he pushed her outside. The flames thundered around them, heat rising fast. It was a relief to feel solid ground. The caravan crackled and splintered, sending bright orange sparks into the sky as the fire took hold.

'Noah!' She called for him as he rooted around the caravan. But not before she caught sight of a figure in the distance, their features lit by the flames. As the arsonist turned and hurried away, the shock of their identity made bile rise in her throat.

Sarah rubbed her smoke-stung eyes, exhaling in relief as Noah escaped the caravan with a small bag of belongings in hand. The fire extinguisher under his arm did little to hold back the flames. Sarah glared at the padlock hanging from the broken door. This was attempted murder.

'My phone!' She raised her voice over the roar of the flames. 'I need to call this in!'

'Stand back.' Noah guided her away after returning her phone. 'The gas canister might blow.' Sarah choked a cough as the smell of burning upholstery and rubber filled the air. She dialled the emergency services, informing them of the blaze. But she didn't say who'd lit it. Not yet.

'Who's done this?' Noah's face was white with fury as he flung his bag of belongings to the ground.

'Stay here,' she said, determined to take control. 'Guide the emergency services in. The last thing we need is the woods catching alight.' Flames had already engulfed the caravan, but Noah would not leave the woodland. Methodically, he sprayed the surrounding ground with the fire extinguisher. Given where Sarah was going next, she could not afford for him to tag along. Clutching her phone to her ear, she waited for Gabby to answer. This needed to be handled with care.

51

Her throat scratchy from coughing, Sarah jogged to her car, taking a little-known shortcut. Gabby had agreed to meet her alone. Her breath was heavy, but Sarah would catch the arsonist because the person she was chasing was unfit. With Gabby blocking the road ahead and Sarah not far behind, they would stop him en route. Sweat dampened her armpits as she pulled her car keys from her jacket pocket. She could smell the smoke on her clothes; she had been lucky to escape with her life. Her red Mini Cooper was parked in a clearing in the woods. She hoped Noah would stay put. His method of justice would spell trouble for them all – particularly given who she was chasing.

'Trust me,' she'd said, when Gabby demanded the identity of their arsonist. 'This is sensitive. We've got to keep this between us until we know how to handle it.' It was only then, when she uttered his home address, that Gabby asked her if she was sure. 'One hundred per cent,' Sarah had replied with conviction. 'If we catch him before he goes home, he should still have the accelerant on his clothes.' With any luck, Blackhall Wood's black soil would be ingrained into his car tyres too.

'I'm bringing backup,' Gabby insisted, as Sarah raced to meet her, the call on speakerphone. 'I've kept it off the main airwaves, at least until we know what's going on.'

As Sarah peered through her windscreen, she didn't blame her sergeant for being cautious. She was looking out for both of them. She dimmed her headlights as she caught up with the arsonist's car. 'I see you,' she said, as Gabby approached the junction, but she was not quick enough to cut off the man in front. Sarah put her foot down until she was directly behind him.

'He's almost home,' Gabby relayed over speakerphone. 'We'll get him when he parks up.' The blue flashing lights of the police car were turned off. There was no need for a high-speed chase here, not on Slayton's narrow woodland roads.

She pulled into the gravel drive, her pulse picking up speed as she rehearsed her words. The large drive easily accommodated the marked car carrying Gabby and her colleague. It was imperative that they speak to the suspect now.

Sarah's heart was heavy as she watched Bernard exit his car. She wished it had been anybody in the world except him. She was no stranger to betrayal, but the sight of her DI setting the caravan alight had shocked her to the core. Her breath quickening, she and Gabby approached in a pincer movement as Bernard worked his face into a smile. He was dressed in full black, and he pulled off his leather gloves, shoving them deep into his jacket as they approached.

'So that was you behind me. What are you doing here? Everything alright?' His tone was a strange, forced jolliness, his eyes dancing to each of them in turn. Sarah could smell the petrol emanating from his clothes, and in the distance, the sirens of the firefighters driving to the blaze. She was facing the worst outcome for this case. Her heart felt as black as the caravan DI Lee had just torched.

'Sir.' Gabby's tone was quiet and respectful as she approached her DI. She nodded to the uniformed colleague and he peeped in through the window of Bernard's 4×4.

'There's a petrol drum on the back seat.' If they had come just minutes later he would have surely disposed of it. Gabby moved quickly.

'I'm sorry to do this, sir, but I'm arresting you on suspicion of arson.' She continued to recite the caution. Other offences could come later when they had built the case against him. Because Sarah knew there was so much more to this than setting Noah's caravan alight.

'What are you on about?' Bernard appeared both insulted and incredulous as his voice became gruff. 'You can't arrest me, I'm your superior officer.'

'Nobody is *superior* in our team,' Gabby replied in a dead tone. 'Experienced, yes, but not superior.' She shook her head. 'I really didn't want this to be you. But you can either come gracefully or I can relay this over the main airwaves where everyone will hear.' Gabby was upping the ante because Bernard's body language had changed. The soft-spoken man who walked with his shoulders slouched was now standing at his full height. His muscles were tensed and his expression thunderous. Sarah felt sick at the sight.

'I'm sure there's a reasonable explanation.' Sarah hid her shock with a slight smile. 'The sooner we get it sorted, the quicker we can get you back home.'

But Bernard stood, feet planted solidly on the ground. 'Then I need to go inside, speak to Helen. I need to change into my suit.'

'No,' Gabby said firmly. 'You don't and you won't.' There was a distant flash of blue lights as more backup approached. Gabby seemed surprised.

'I called another unit on point-to-point . . .' The young male officer behind them spoke up. 'So you can take this car and we'll travel back with the boss.'

Good thinking, Sarah thought. He had read the situation well. The direct call to nearby officers wasn't about the use of cars. It was in case their DI kicked off. Bernard's muscles untensed as he realised he was outnumbered. Like the flick of a switch, his expression changed again, and he laughed awkwardly.

'You're right, Sarah, this is a big mistake and someone's head is going to roll.' He gave her a knowing look. 'I just hope it's not yours, eh? I've always looked after you. But there's nothing I can do for you now.'

Sarah did not miss the threat behind the smile.

'Sorry, boss.' Taking his cuffs from their holster the male officer clicked them onto Bernard's thick wrists. 'Procedure.' But it was more than procedure; this was career-ending. Bernard wouldn't only lose his job, he'd lose his pension too. How would his family cope?

Gabby's boots scrunched in the gravel as she updated their colleagues of a suspect in custody. He would be processed at another police station and his family would be notified. There was nothing more Sarah could say. Bernard was passed to the stocky attending officers. This would spread around the station like wildfire. The sense of betrayal was palpable.

'We'll check on Helen,' said Sarah as Bernard got into the back of the police car. But the man stared straight ahead, no doubt trying to figure out how to get himself out of this mess. Gabby was speaking into her radio, organising seizure of his car. There was enough evidence to prove arson, but what about the murders? Bernard was a seasoned police detective; she couldn't see him leaving any trails behind. Getting caught had been sloppy enough. Her gaze wandered to his home.

'We should check in on his wife,' Sarah said.

'He can call from custody. We don't owe him anything.' Gabby's features were grim.

But Sarah wasn't doing this for Bernard. 'Trust me,' she said. 'It's the right thing to do.'

52

Sarah felt a sense of loss as she watched the police car drive away. Gabby was by her side, the two of them reeling from the revelation. Bernard's home was in darkness. How would they break the news when they could barely believe it themselves? DI Lee had been a father figure to them all. He couldn't have known that Sarah was in the caravan, but the sight of the padlocked door left her in no doubt of his plans. Father Aloysius was a link in the chain, but how many people were involved in this cover-up?

'Get in.' Gabby pointed at the marked car.

'I thought we were going to let his wife know?'

'In a minute. First, get in.'

It was a command, not a suggestion, and Sarah slid into the passenger seat. The windscreen was dappled with rain, making Bernard's home a blur.

'Tell me everything.' The timbre of her voice suggested that right now, Gabby was her sergeant, not her friend. Sarah had done nothing wrong. Nothing she couldn't justify, anyway. She cleared her throat before filling her sergeant in on her visit to Noah and the fire. It felt surreal, sitting on Bernard's drive while he was being taken into custody. They had a long night ahead of them, and detailed statements would be needed from them both.

'Are you in cahoots with Noah?' Gabby's expression was stern. 'And before you reply, take a deep breath and remember who you are.'

Sarah prickled at Gabby's warning. She knew exactly who she was. Being a police officer was the heart of everything she did. 'I was checking up on him, that's all.' She zipped up her hoodie as the night air bit. 'I didn't tell him about the case, or the updates in briefing.'

But Gabby did not appear convinced. 'I'd like to know more about your decision-making, Noble. You must have gone straight from work to his place, but nobody tasked you with that.'

'Not quite.' Sarah's cheeks began to burn. 'I went home and fed Sherlock first.'

Gabby stared at the blur of Bernard's home. She seemed in no hurry to shatter their world. 'Be honest with me, Sarah, because I can't protect you unless I know the truth.'

'Honestly, I went there to sound him out.' Sarah was grateful her sergeant had her back, even if she was furious with her. 'I wanted to see if he knew anything about Father Aloysius.'

'Why?' Gabby's frown grew. 'That's all in hand.' The priest may have provided a statement saying he'd had no recent contact with Arnold, but it was the sight of Arnold's little dog that suggested otherwise. A quick phone call to the priest's housekeeper told Sarah all she needed to know. She had updated her findings on the police intelligence system but there was no rush to double-check if the priest was telling the truth, given a suspect had already confessed.

She watched her sergeant's face change as she relayed everything she had learned. 'I wasn't the only one who noticed. Noah was watching Arnold too. He knew the priest was the last person to see him alive.'

'The pair of you were sitting ducks waiting for the killer to arrive?' Gabby rolled her eyes. 'I despair over you, I really do.'

'No, not at all,' Sarah hastily added. 'I'd just got there when it kicked off.' But in her mind's eye she could see Noah standing at the caravan door, hammer raised. She could so easily have ended up in prison. She could have . . .

'Your face says otherwise,' Gabby interrupted her thoughts. 'But that's the story you need to stick to if you don't want to end up under investigation.'

Sarah delivered a weak smile. Her sergeant was sticking her neck on the line by having a quiet word. 'This is the plan,' Gabby continued. 'Bernard doesn't know you were suspicious of the priest, does he?'

'No, and there's no record of it anywhere.'

'Good. Then we won't spook Father Aloysius. Given he's Irving's brother, we may have bigger fish to fry. We'll update Bernard's family, then go back to the station, speak to McGuire and take it from there. God . . . I can't believe old Saint Bernard's involved in all this.'

'He padlocked the door.' Sarah's heart fluttered at the thought. Each time she moved the acrid stench of smoke rose from her clothes. 'Noah and his mum weren't meant to get out of this alive. If he's capable of that, then . . .' She couldn't bring herself to finish the sentence. Was Bernard responsible for the previous murders? She knew he'd grown up in his family's slaughterhouse business. He was no stranger to blood. He was also Simon Irving's friend. Was he doing Irving's bidding, or was he at the heart of it all? She looked up at the grand house. Too grand for a police officer to be able to afford?

One step at a time, she reminded herself.

'His wife has dementia,' Sarah hastily added. 'We need to handle her with care.'

Then they were out of the car, walking up the generous gravelled driveway to Bernard's home. A light came on in one of the rooms. It was gone ten but at least someone was up. The front door opened as Sarah lifted a brass knocker shaped like a lion's head.

'Oh!' A young woman with chestnut hair started at their presence on her doorstep. 'Who are you?' Her hair was falling out of her ponytail and there was baby sick on her dressing gown. She looked every inch the stressed mum. As Gabby introduced them both, the woman told them her name was Sam and that she was Bernard's daughter, home from Australia. 'Are you looking for Dad? He went to bed early, but I've just checked and he's not there.'

Gabby and Sarah exchanged a glance. Had he concocted an alibi before he left to start the fire?

'That's why we're here,' Gabby replied. 'Your dad is at the station, helping us with our enquiries.'

'Can we come in?' Sarah added, shifting from foot to foot. Bernard's daughter led them into a warm and cosy living room. Helen was sitting, staring at the wall. Her dressing gown was tied around her, her white hair askew. The dying embers of a fire danced in the hearth. Sarah absorbed the pictures of Bernard in uniform during various times in his career. Photos of his children and grandchildren took up every inch of shelf space.

'Hello, Helen,' Sarah said with a smile. But no response came.

'Mum was asking after Dad.' Sam toyed with the belt of her dressing gown. 'They sleep in separate rooms because Dad snores like a chainsaw.' She afforded them a smile. 'Has he been called into work?'

'Not quite,' Gabby replied, her features grim.

'Hello, Helen,' Sarah tried again. She was desperate to connect with the woman who had been married to Bernard from a young age. Any second now, Gabby would usher them both out. She bent to the woman before her, making eye contact. 'I'm Sarah, I met you in the supermarket the other day.'

'Are you from social care?' Helen's expression tightened. 'Because I told you lot already. Naff off!'

'I'm not a social worker.' Sarah smiled. 'I work with your husband.'

Her daughter stepped in, resting a protective hand on her mother's shoulder. 'Mum's quite direct these days, aren't you, Mum?' She gave her a sad smile.

Sarah nodded knowingly. 'My grandad had Alzheimer's.' Sarah had seen it all. The bouts of confusion, frustration, uncharacteristic swearing, lashing out, then sadness, blankness and finally the empty peace that followed as he became more dependent on specialist care.

Sam sighed as Helen brushed her hand away. 'Dad has found it very hard. My brother is based in Scotland and my sister lives in London. I've flown over with the kids from Australia for a few weeks to help with her care. Mind you, the way things are looking with this virus, we could all be stuck at home soon.'

Sarah nodded, surprised. It seemed that Bernard's children were scattered, with none of them living nearby. They were not the close family he had portrayed.

Sam looked at her mother with sympathy. 'Mum needs specialist care, but the place she goes to for day care is so expensive . . .' She shook her head. 'I don't know how he's going to manage it full-time.' She walked to the window and pulled back the curtain. 'Where did you say Dad was again?'

'Those poor children . . .' Helen spoke into her hand as if a part of her was trying to stem her words. 'Poor, poor children . . . I heard them whisper . . . outside, in the dark. They come when everyone's asleep.'

'It's OK, Mum,' Sam returned to her mother. 'Annie's upstairs, asleep. There's nothing to worry about.' A wail rose above them, the baby's cries echoing on the monitor. 'I spoke too soon.' Sam sighed. 'Can you stay with Mum for a minute? I need to sort her out.'

'Helen,' Sarah said, turning to face her as her daughter went upstairs, 'when we say Bernard's at the police station, I mean that he's been arrested.' From the corner of her eye, she caught Gabby's warning glare. But the last thing Bernard had said was to tell his wife. Words she had made a note of in her police pocket notebook. While the testimony of a woman with Helen's condition may not be admissible in court, Sarah needed to find out what she knew. She allowed the words to sink in, gauging the woman's reaction. 'I think you know what this is about. I think you've known for a long time. Tell me about the children.'

Sarah glanced pointedly at a picture of Bernard and Simon Irving. She felt Gabby's presence, taut and concerned. She was alluding to something that they knew very little about.

Sounds of Bernard's daughter soothing her child came over the baby monitor. They did not have long. Helen shook her head in irritation, having an internal monologue with herself. 'Those poor bairns,' she said, her voice frail. 'Poor, poor bairns.' She stared at the photographs of a younger version of her husband. The one she was thinking of now. 'Out there in the cold. He should have taken them home. But it was too late . . . too late.' Her eyes pricked with tears. The baby monitor fell quiet.

'Mrs Lee,' Gabby said, her voice low and soothing. 'Bernard's gone to the police station to talk about an arson offence. I'm sorry if there's been some confusion.' She glared at Sarah before returning her attention to Helen. 'We didn't mean to upset you.'

She rose to leave just as Bernard's daughter entered the room. 'Your dad will be allowed a phone call. I'm sure he'll be in touch soon.'

'What do you mean, a phone call?' Sam said, jiggling her baby in her arms. 'I thought he was at work. What's going on?'

'Your father is helping us with our enquiries. I'm afraid that's all we can tell you.' Gabby slid a card from her pocket. 'Here's my office number. He'll have access to a phone soon.'

Sam stood, open-mouthed, her hands full with a grizzly baby. Sarah followed her sergeant as she let herself out. As soon as they were out of earshot, Gabby rounded on Sarah.

'What the hell do you think you're playing at, questioning a vulnerable woman? You know none of that would stand up in court.'

'Sorry.' Sarah shoved her hands into her pockets. 'I didn't think you'd mind.' They walked down the drive, the moon high in the sky.

'Why do you do this job, Sarah? Who do you expect to help?' As she fiddled for her car keys, Gabby didn't wait for an answer. 'The old, the vulnerable? People who can't speak up for themselves? Do you think Helen would have told you anything about her husband if she was in her right mind?'

'She might have . . .' Sarah withered beneath her sergeant's gaze. 'Well, OK then, maybe not.'

'Helen has as much right to compassion as anyone we deal with. An officer will speak to her soon. But it will be controlled and recorded in the proper way.' Gabby exhaled a short breath. 'You infuriate me sometimes. You display flashes of real insight among acts of total idiocy.'

Silence fell between them and Sarah noticed that Bernard's car was gone – no doubt already seized as evidence. 'I'll meet you back at the station.' Gabby jingled her keys, pressing the fob to activate the central locking system. Sarah had fallen out of favour with her sergeant, but as she approached her red Mini, Helen's words echoed in her mind. She hadn't been talking about her grandchild. She was talking about Mercy and Mikey, in the cold, forever wandering. Who else knew of their fate?

53

Tuesday, 10th March 2020

There was a sense of defeat in Father Aloysius's stance as he pulled his chair back from the interview table and took a seat. Sarah found it odd to have such a figure of virtue across the table from her. He was still wearing his dog collar and black shirt, a slight paunch hanging over his belt as he sat. He ran a hand over his thinning hair, his eyes flicking up to the camera in the corner of the room. Richie had set up the digital recording equipment and Sarah settled down next to him, grateful for his presence. Her stomach felt like it was taking flight, fuelled half by nerves, half by excitement at the confession she hoped was to come. So much for keeping their suspicions low-key. Father Aloysius had come to the station first thing this morning, on a voluntary basis, to 'get things off his chest'.

'I knew this day would come,' he said, after Sarah had gone through the preliminaries. 'And it comes at a very high cost.' The priest's hands were trembling as he rested them on the table, one cupped over the other. The skin was pink, his nails manicured – so unlike Noah's weathered, calloused skin. A silver ring graced his middle finger, and Sarah noted the Tag Heuer designer watch on his left wrist. Quite extravagant for a Catholic priest.

'Then tell me,' Sarah responded. 'What do you know about the murders of Rosemary Simmons, Geoffrey Simmons and Arnold Smith?' The open question was pre-planned for maximum effectiveness. Despite Gabby tearing a strip off her, McGuire had been impressed by her taking the initiative and visiting Noah. Her curious mind had earned her control of the interview.

'I want to say something on record first. Sarah, your name is, isn't it?'

'It is, Father.' Sarah flushed. She had been brought up Catholic and calling a priest 'Father' was second nature to her. But by doing so, she had put herself on the back foot. She was meant to be the one in charge. *Fiddlesticks.* This was something McGuire would pick her up on later. But the priest was too wrapped up in his own problems to notice her inner turmoil. He took a deep breath.

'Well, Sarah, I am severely bound by the seal of confession to keep my penitent's sins in secrecy.' He leaned forward, driving his point home. 'There are no exceptions to the sacramental seal.' He nodded towards Richie's coffee going cold on the desk. 'If you told me in confession that you had poisoned your colleague's drink, not only would I be unable to warn him, I couldn't even spill the cup of coffee to stop him drinking it. Breaking the seal of confession would risk expulsion from the priesthood as well as eternal punishment in the afterlife.' He explained with the patience of someone well practised in dealing with the public. 'But I have kept their secrets for too long. I must do what's right for the parish now, even if it's at odds with the Catholic Church.'

He tugged at the neck of his shirt, resting the thin strip of white material on the table. Without his dog collar, he was just like them. The significance of his act sharpened the atmosphere. He was going to tell all, even if it meant giving up his vocation.

'Then tell us,' Sarah said, with as much sympathy as she could muster. She had not forgotten that Simon Irving was his brother. He had to be involved.

The priest gave three slow nods of the head. 'Arnold Smith came to me two decades ago. I knew who he was when he spoke of my brother's housing development a mile outside Blackhall Woods.'

Alongside her, Richie scribbled on his notepad with short strokes. Head down, he was listening intently, allowing the priest to speak.

'Arnold told me about two traveller children who had taken shelter from the rain. It was his job to secure the building site that night, but he'd fallen far short of that. The houses had steps from one floor to another but no bannisters at that stage.' He paused for thought. 'They'd had some problems with kids breaking in. Geoffrey was inspecting the building with Arnold and the local police constabulary when he found the children upstairs. They only meant to frighten them. No one was meant to get hurt.' The words fell like stones in the small room. 'Spooked, the children ran and lost their footing on the landing. There was no barrier to save them. They died instantly.' He shuddered. 'It was a terrible accident.'

Sarah felt a wave of sadness as the scene replayed in her mind.

'Go on,' she encouraged, waiting to hear of Simon Irving's involvement. He had to be the one behind this. Sarah had nicknamed him 'Teflon', as despite all his dodgy dealings, nothing stuck. Until now. His days of being above the law were coming to an end. She watched as unshed tears glistened in the priest's eyes.

'Arnold said their little bodies were at an angle after they fell, and the . . .' He paused for a shuddering breath. 'The colour had left their skin. There was no saving them. The police officer said nothing more could be done for the children, so it was best to bury them.'

Richie's scribbling came to a sudden halt. Neither of them believed a word.

'Who was the police officer?' Sarah interrupted.

'Sorry, didn't I say? It was Bernard Lee. He was in uniform back then. But not that night. Arnold said he was off duty and turned up as a favour to them both.'

Sarah's eyes narrowed. 'So you're saying that Bernard Lee, a uniformed police officer, told Geoffrey Simmons and Arnold Smith to bury the bodies of two children who died an accidental death?' It sounded utterly ridiculous to Sarah as she relayed it back. And where was Simon Irving in all of this?

The priest wouldn't meet her eye. He was staring at his dog collar as if his life depended on it. But its removal was merely theatre, to demonstrate how serious he was. 'That's what Arnold said, and I have no reason to disbelieve him. Geoffrey gave a similar account in confession years down the line. He said he and Bernard were friends. Bernard advised him to bury the bodies and Arnold went along with it because they didn't want to delay the build. Neither did they want to tangle with the travellers camping in the woods.' His hands were clasped tightly on the table, his knuckles white.

Sarah could hold back her question no longer. 'What about your brother, Simon? What part did he have to play?'

Father Aloysius looked at her blankly. 'Simon? He wasn't there.'

Sarah's mouth fell open in disbelief. It felt like all the air had been sucked out of the room. 'But he had to be involved. It was his development. He had the most to lose.' She glanced at Richie for confirmation, her stomach churning at the thought of Irving wriggling off the hook.

'My brother had nothing to do with this. Whatever plan they concocted was between the three of them.' But his eyes told another story and his words were flat.

'Then why did Bernard Lee set fire to Noah's caravan after he confessed that he was going to the press?' She jabbed the table with her finger. 'I think you went straight to your brother, Simon Irving. He put a hit out on Noah, just as he did with Arnold, Rosemary and her son. He couldn't afford for the truth to get out.'

'My dear . . .' The priest smiled, as if trying to placate a child. 'That's far too fanciful to be true.' He leaned back in his chair, his arms folded over his chest.

'Then why come here?' Sarah's annoyance rose as the interview took an unexpected turn.

'For the good of my parish. I didn't want anyone else to get hurt.' But while his voice may have been condescending, his body language said otherwise. His arms were tightly crossed, sweat beading his forehead in a room which was stuffy but not warm.

'You're lying. Tell us the truth!' As Sarah's voice rose, Richie placed a guiding hand on her arm.

'Sarah,' the priest said softly, 'I've given up everything to come here, voluntarily I may add.' He looked up at the ceiling thoughtfully. 'Come to think of it, I remember my brother saying that Arnold and Geoffrey were acting strangely.'

Sarah retorted with a snort. As if he'd suddenly remember a throwaway comment from decades ago.

'Why would Bernard advise them to bury the bodies?' Richie finally spoke. 'Help us to understand.' He rested his pen on the table next to his A4 pad.

'There was another confession.' The priest's nostrils flared as he drew in a long breath. 'I wasn't going to divulge it but . . .' His words faded as he took stock. 'I've come this far. I warn you, though, you won't want to hear it, much less accept what I have to say.'

'Our feelings don't come into it,' Sarah said, despite her earlier outburst. 'We're here to gather evidence.'

'Very well, then.' Father Aloysius sat back in his chair, arms clamped to his sides as he clasped his hands over his stomach, but not before Sarah caught sight of the sweat stains under his arms. 'Arnold came to see me shortly before he died,' he continued. 'He was agitated. He even gave me his dog. The church was closed but I offered him confession and he was grateful for it.'

Sarah imagined Arnold launching his dog upon the priest before accepting one more confession. The dog was with his housekeeper. That much was true. She watched Father Aloysius recall what happened that day. 'Arnold said Bernard had been blackmailing him and Geoffrey for years. But Arnold couldn't keep up the payments. His wife's illness had left him penniless. He was struggling to exist.'

Sarah recalled the state of his cottage and his frugal lifestyle. But could her old DI commit blackmail? It was true that the fees for his wife's luxury care home were astronomical. A care home owned by Irving Industries. She listened as the priest relayed his story, wondering how much of it was rehearsed.

'Arnold was scared to go to the police. He didn't think he'd be believed. He was also scared of the travellers and what they would do to him.'

'And you just listened? You didn't advise him on what to do?'

'It wasn't my job to question it, only to hear his confession. It tortured him for years.' His gaze flicked up at the camera. 'I only hope he has finally found peace.'

In the bland interview room, Sarah's stomach sank with disappointment as Richie continued with questions of his own. Had Bernard, not Irving, been orchestrating things all along? Was she too blind to see? She would not find the answers she wanted here.

54

Wednesday, 11th March 2020

Elliott didn't mind that Elsie looked at him funny or was sometimes scared when he spoke. He was happy his mother had a new friend. He had made a new friend too. As he sat at Elsie's table, he tried to do his maths homework, but his mind was back at school. Today he'd found out his favourite teacher was just like him. She could see the other world too. He had gone to her during lunchtime when he was supposed to be in the playground. Miss Grogan was at her desk, staring at the door as if she was expecting his visit all along. He told her he wanted to make the bad feelings go away. He didn't want to see the other side anymore.

'Are you sure?' she'd said, her blue eyes like icy fingers reaching into his mind.

'Yes,' he'd said. 'I don't want to hear the whispers. They make me sad.'

'Ah.' She nodded in understanding. 'And they make your mummy sad too?'

Elliott nodded, convinced that Miss Grogan must be magic. She didn't just know about the stuff she taught him in school. She knew everything.

'Well then, I can help you quieten them,' she said, her eyes crinkling at the corners as she spoke. And she did. She explained how sometimes you were born with gifts you didn't want. How he wasn't to feel guilty about pushing them away for now. She said there was nothing wrong with being different, as long as he was happy. But sometimes, the people that whispered thought only of themselves. They were *pushy* and *in-sis-tent* and it was OK to want a life of his own. Then she'd showed him how to make his mind what she called im-penna-trouble. She talked about dungeons and walls, about castles and moats, drawbridges and portcullises. He understood all of it because they were studying medieval times in school. By the end of breaktime his mind was his castle, and he controlled who he let in. Miss Grogan said it didn't matter what ideas you used, as long as you turned your thoughts around. She said that his mind was a magnet, and he had to switch it the other way so that it *repelled* the whispering children instead of drawing them in.

He liked that Miss Grogan explained every word so he understood what it meant. He learned a lot of new words that way. She said it would take practice to get it right, but he'd already been able to get rid of the bad feeling in his tummy when Mikey and Mercy were near. He thought of their still, lavender faces, of the dark caves where once there were eyes. They came to him, like moths in the darkness, seeing his light. Miss Grogan said his soul burned very bright. But each time they visited, they touched him with their anger. Bad feelings clung in the other world. When you died all of a sudden, hate made you strong. But their mummy was waiting. She would make them good again.

He glanced over at Maggie. She was sitting next to Sarah on a squishy armchair trying to push away a big black cat from her lap. Mummy didn't like cats. She almost suffocated as a baby because a cat slept on her face when she was in her pram. Most people can't remember that far back, but a small part of his mother remembered it very well.

'Tell him to git.' Elsie chuckled as she watched Maggie wrestle with the over-affectionate feline. Elsie was sitting against the headboard of her bed. Her face wasn't as round as when they first met, and she didn't huff and puff quite as much either. But the room smelled of the hot chocolate she had drunk before they got there. Then there were the cake crumbs on her sheets, and the crisp wrapper under her bed. She was trying, but she wasn't there yet.

He looked to his mother, so skinny in comparison. Maybe now things were better, Maggie would eat food instead of drinking red wine every night before bed. He slipped on his headphones, knowing that the grown-ups wanted to chat. Sarah was fidgeting, her legs crossed, foot bobbing as Elsie talked. Sometimes Elliott turned off the sound on his game so he could listen in. Sarah knew about the terrible thing that had happened to Mercy and Mikey. He could see it in the lines on her face when she walked into the room. She could look after things now.

'The plot thickens,' Sarah said, her gaze creeping to Elliott. Head down, he stared at his copybooks.

'Oh goody.' Elsie rubbed her hands together, her mattress bouncing as she shifted on her bed. 'You have an update?'

Sarah looked from Maggie to Elsie. 'A witness has come forward. They've implicated Arnold, Geoffrey and a third person in covering up Mikey and Mercy's deaths.' She sighed. Elliott could feel her sadness in waves. Whoever that person was, it made Sarah feel bad. He tried to chase the thought but it was gone.

'I can't tell you who he is yet,' Sarah carried on. 'You'll find out soon enough.'

'Oh Lordy.' Elsie rested her palm on her chest. 'Did they kill those poor sweet souls? Is Simon Irving involved?'

Elliott stared at his copybook even harder now, his fist tightly holding his pen. Mercy and Mikey *had* passed to the other side, but he didn't know who put them there.

'It looks like it was an accident.' Sarah's voice was low. 'We've no evidence against Irving but I know he's involved.' Elliott tensed as her energy changed. He didn't like to see his friend so angry and upset.

'Are you sure?' Maggie said. 'There's no love lost between you two.'

Before Sarah could speak, Elsie butted in. 'Be careful. Irving's dangerous. Folks who push against his wheel get crushed.'

'Don't I know it.' Sarah caught Elliott's eye. 'But this subject isn't suited for little ears.'

Elliott slipped off his headphones, giving Sarah the faintest of smiles. He had one last message to pass on. He watched Elsie pull her blanket to her chest as he took a breath to speak.

'It's OK, Auntie Sarah. Mercy and Mikey are with their mummy now.' He hadn't known for sure until he uttered the words. Sometimes the knowing came from deep inside him. He just had to let it out. This time there was no cold air settling around him as he spoke.

No sense of sinking into the darkness like before. But there was a warning. Auntie Sarah wasn't safe. 'But the bad man . . .' He looked to Sarah, feeling a sudden prickle of despair. 'He's still out there.' He didn't want to see it. Couldn't face another dark thought. He lifted his mental drawbridge and lowered the portcullis as defence. One, two, three breaths and everything was safe and warm again. He returned to his homework and sat. It was just a sudden warning for Sarah to let things rest. Because the bad man Mercy told him about was still in Slayton, and Elliott didn't want Sarah to get hurt.

55

Sarah shook off the cold as she stepped into her warm hallway, grateful she had set the heating timer to kick in. Even now, every day felt like winter, and she slid off her muddy shoes and deposited them next to the front door. Elliott's warning had spooked her, but after what he'd been through this last year it was hardly any wonder that he saw 'bad men' everywhere. 'Sherlock,' she called brightly, hearing a faint miaow from the kitchen at the end of the hall. She frowned at the sight of the closed door. She normally gave him the run of the house while she was at work. Had she locked him in the kitchen on the way out? She walked down the hall in her stocking feet. She wasn't worried, not until she opened the door and saw the man sitting at her kitchen table with Sherlock clamped tightly to his chest. For a second, Sarah couldn't breathe. Couldn't vocalise the words building up in her throat. How. Dare. He.

Fists clenched, Sarah demanded Irving release her cat. She stood, watching from the doorway as the man she hated most in the world gently deposited Sherlock onto the kitchen tiles. Instead of jumping through the cat flap, Sherlock ran to her. Miaowing his unease, he curled around the back of her legs as Sarah stood, rooted to the floor. Calmly, Irving brushed the ginger cat hairs from his black trousers, a thin smile resting on his face. A motorbike helmet sat on the table, as shiny as a black billiard ball. She'd never seen him in casual wear before and his leather jacket and black chinos seemed out of place.

'What . . . what the hell are you doing?' Sarah pushed her fringe off her face, self-conscious as his gaze bore into her. There was no sign of forced entry, but hers was a rental property that Irving Industries owned. If he wanted the key to her home, then he could find a way. His presence tonight proved that.

'There's no need to be afraid.' He stood, flashing a set of unnaturally

"

white teeth. 'I'm just paying a visit. You left your back door insecure. You should be more careful, after what happened to your neighbours.' His words carried a chill but his smile relayed that he was enjoying the encounter. There was another side to the successful businessman and philanthropist. He was a misogynist, who got a kick from intimidating women when he didn't get his own way.

Sarah entered her kitchen, her body shaking from a fury that simmered beneath the surface. 'I'm not afraid of you. Get out, before I arrest you for breaking in.' She cursed the tremble on her breath. She was alone, with no radio or baton. Irving would overpower her in a flash. She could leave. Her mobile phone was in her pocket. A sensible person would go back the way they came and call for help. But Sarah would not give him the satisfaction of running scared from her own home. Rain slapped against the window as darkness closed in.

Slowly, she inched towards the knife in the sink from last night. The small, sharp object still had crumbs of blue-veined cheese stuck to its blade. She didn't want to up the ante, but her body was moving without any conscious decision from her. Irving showed no signs of backing off as he approached with slow deliberate steps.

'I'm warning you.' Sarah spoke with as much confidence as she could muster. 'I'll call for backup.'

Ignoring Sherlock's low growls, Irving groaned in mock disappointment as he drew near. 'Really? When you're so close to the truth? This is your one and only chance to find out. Don't you want to know?' His dark eyes twinkled. He had her. Because right now, she wanted to know more than anything in the world. But she wasn't blind to his manipulation as he dangled the truth under her nose.

'Why are you here?' She moved towards the knife, her heart racing behind her ribcage. Irving was the picture of composure as Sherlock jumped up on the kitchen counter and hissed.

'Because our families have history. You and only you deserve the truth.'

Sarah laughed at his theatrics. But it was brittle laughter. There was a look in his eyes that unnerved her. A man detached from reality. The look of someone who had done this before. She had always thought Irving got others to do his dirty work, but now she wasn't so sure. But he wouldn't hurt her, a police detective. He couldn't.

'You're acting as if I won't arrest you the second you confess.' But while she may have had the power to arrest him, she lacked the physical strength to force him to comply.

'Arrest me for what? You'd be laughed out of the station.' Irving spread his arms wide. 'I was never here. And nobody would believe that I'd step into the gutter with someone as common as you.'

Sarah frowned. What did he mean by that? The man was talking in riddles. As his gaze roamed over her body, her stomach clenched.

'But the thing is . . .' His voice lowered as he closed the gap between them. 'Even pedigree dogs roll in shit when they're let off the lead.' He was close, far too close now, and he leaned in, the stench of whisky and cigarettes on his breath.

Sarah swatted his hand as he tried to touch her face. Irving laughed. 'Ask your friend fat Elsie if you don't believe me. She and I go way back.' Sarah knew all about Elsie and how he'd used her for his entertainment when she was a vulnerable young girl.

His face was darkening now, and something deep inside warned Sarah not to provoke him. This was another side of Simon Irving that she didn't want to know. The side of him that wasn't always in control.

'It's the thrill of the hunt,' he continued, bearing down on her. 'The rush I get from watching you lot run around, chasing your tails. Because you know who killed Rosemary, Geoffrey and Arnold, don't you, Sarah?' His voice was so low it was gravelly, all humour evaporating from his face. 'You know, but you don't have proof. And you never will. Because I'm keeping an *eye* on you.' He winked as he enunciated the word. Its meaning was not lost on her. The fact the victims' eyes were removed had never been publicised. Her cat miaowed loudly behind her, visibly distressed.

Irving was feeding off her shocked expression, watching the rise and fall of her chest as her breathing accelerated underneath his gaze. Her fingers edged along the kitchen counter as Irving leaned in to whisper in her ear. 'How far would you go for the truth?' As his hand slid over her breast, Sarah gripped the knife. But Irving grabbed her by the wrist with such force that she cried out in pain.

'Don't get ahead of yourself,' Irving growled, raising her arm in the air. 'I cut my teeth on people like you.' He was pushing himself against her and Sarah could feel his excitement build. As he squeezed with a vice-like grip, Sarah was forced to drop the knife.

'You won't get away with this.' Sarah hated the shake in her voice as she fought to assert herself. 'I won't let you.'

The kitchen walls seemed to close in on them as Irving kicked the knife away. It skittered into the corner, hitting the back door with a clang. Seconds passed between them, Irving's breath heavy on her face. He seemed to be assessing his options. She was considering raising her knee and driving it between his legs when he suddenly stepped away.

'See this?' He slid his phone from his pocket and brought up his Ring camera app. 'Footage of me, at home right now, enjoying a drink with my wife. She's nothing without me, and there's nothing she won't do to protect our happy home.' He looked from the phone to Sarah. 'As for you . . . well, your mental health has been an issue in the past, hasn't it?'

'What? How?' Sarah's words evaporated as she watched the live footage. The man on the camera had his back turned to her. Dressed in navy trousers and white shirt, he was the same build as Irving, with the same colour hair. But there was something off-kilter about his wife's movements as she interacted with him. The man behind the camera was a decoy. Was this how he had got away with so much, always having an alibi backed up by physical proof?

'It would have been so much easier if you'd sold us Blackhall Manor and the woodlands when we asked.' Irving slid his phone into his pocket. 'Who knows what we would have found buried on that land? But now you've opened up a festering can of worms.' He stared, unblinking, his features conveying the malice behind his words. 'You owe me.' He prodded her hard in the chest. 'And you won't be the first.' *Is he talking about Bernard?* Sarah thought.

'Everyone has their price, even the boys in blue.' He confirmed her suspicions.

'No.' Sarah grimaced. 'I'll *never* answer to you.'

'Then think about Elsie, so reliant on her treatment at the obesity clinic that I fund.' A smile curled on his lips. 'Then there's Maggie. It would be a shame if anything happened to that kid of hers. The world is a dangerous place. Accidents happen. It's how Geoffrey ended up in a wheelchair.' Sarah felt sickened. The workplace incident was no accident after all.

'If you've hurt them . . .'

'Now why would I hurt my own tenants?' Irving smiled, reaching into his jacket pocket. The object in his hand glittered as it caught the light. Sarah's stomach churned. It was a medal for bravery. The one Elliott kept next to his bed at night. He had been in their home. 'Give me that!' Sarah flared, stamping on his foot with her heel and grabbing the medal from his hand. 'You little bitch!' Irving spat, drawing back his fist. But his movements were halted as his phone beeped loudly with a text. Sarah panted, shoving the medal into her pocket. It belonged to Elliott. It was worth the risk.

'Shame.' Irving gave her a venomous smile. 'I have to go. Just when I was enjoying myself.'

Sarah's anger mounted as he turned to leave. 'If you so much as look at Elliott sideways, I'll have you locked up!'

He slid his helmet from the table, staring her down as he fixed the strap beneath his chin. 'If you want your friends to sleep safe in their beds then you'll keep that . . .' he pushed his finger hard against her lips, 'shut. That is, unless you *want* me to come back.' A grin lifted his features beneath his helmet. 'Then again, we might both enjoy that.'

Sarah's mind spiralled. If she called the police now, he would be gone by the time they arrived. It would be her word against his, and even if she could prove his threats, he would get off with nothing more than a caution because his record was impeccable. She would have put her loved ones at risk for nothing. This man had friends in powerful places and could come and go as he pleased. She picked up her cat and held him close, her mind racing as she followed Irving out. He had to be stopped.

'Come to my house again and I'll have you arrested, do you hear me!' But her words were empty, and by the look on Irving's face, he knew it too.

'Goodbye, Sarah. And don't forget . . . you belong to me now.'

Like the onset of a vicious migraine, Sarah's head was buzzing as anger and hatred rose. A motorbike revved from across the road. Someone was picking him up. But there was another sound too.

'Simon Irving!' Sarah's voice pierced the night as the familiar noise grew louder. He was stepping off the pavement now, ready to cross the road for his ride home. 'Simon Irving broke into my home!' He paused halfway across the road, distracted by her screams. 'Simon Irving!' She screamed again, clutching her cat as she shouted his name at the top of her lungs. As he was dressed in black, she could barely make out his form. The streetlamp above them was broken. A curtain twitched across the road. Then the roar of the joyrider's car approached, just as they did every night around this time. But Simon hadn't heard it; he was too focused on her, screaming like she'd lost it at her own front door. The buzzing in Sarah's ears grew louder. It was happening and she couldn't stop it, even if she wanted to.

By the time Irving heard the stolen Ford Focus come round the bend it was too late. A flash of headlights. A squeal of brakes. The teenage driver's face, slack with shock. Life seemed to move in slow motion as the joyriders mowed into the figure in black. A sudden crash of metal against body and bone. Then a dull thud as Irving rolled over the roof of the car and landed on the potholed road. After a horrible pause there was another screech of tyres as the motorbike that had been waiting for Irving took off. The smell of burning rubber filled the air as the Ford Focus was floored. Sarah watched its occupants, pale and wide-eyed, staring out in the night as the car screamed away. Then they were gone and it was just Irving, Sarah and Sherlock, who was nestled in her grip. Puddles of rainwater seeped through her socks as she walked down the garden path, her eyes never leaving his twisted body on the side of the road.

56

There was nothing more joyous to Gerard in this moment than the sound of his wife's soft snores in the hotel bed they shared. Tonight, they'd behaved like a couple of lovesick teenagers, renewing their commitment to each other with their bodies instead of words. And now he lay, breathing in her perfume as if he'd just come up for air. For the last six months, he felt like he'd been living in a cave. He wasn't a murderer. His family had nothing to fear. He turned his gaze to the window which provided a glorious view of Slayton's lake. It shimmered beneath the moonlight, inducing a sigh as Gerard reflected on the past.

He could only describe it as a quickening as dormant memories came to life. The fog clouding his mind was finally clearing and it was all thanks to Ruth. While most wives would have turned their backs on such erratic behaviour, she had informed the police of his adoption, doggedly seeking answers for the predicament he found himself in. Dissociative amnesia, she called it, a term plucked from the numerous psychotherapy books she had consulted. She couldn't directly diagnose him, but judging by his recent psychiatric assessment, it fit. He would not get better overnight, but the diagnosis was a start. He never imagined his past would hold the key to a brighter future for them both. He wasn't a killer. He really wasn't. But it was taking time to sink in. The incident he'd witnessed as a child was the centrifuge which separated him from the little boy named Samson who watched his siblings die.

The anniversary of their disappearance was buried in his subconscious, triggering his blackouts as his past grew more insistent each day. The whispers he'd heard were Mercy's, an echo of a traumatic childhood incident. He recalled his obsession with Blackhall Manor and his sudden need to save the building. His focus on the manor had lessened from the day he arrived; it had just been a means of getting him there.

The mind is a wondrous thing, he thought. And now his memories flooded the corridors of his brain. He would embrace his traveller heritage and be reunited with Noah and Olive at Mercy and Mikey's memorial service. His siblings would not be buried in Slayton, but next to their mother where they belonged. He lay back in bed, bringing himself to the day that everything changed. He was no longer afraid of the past.

As the rain drummed on the roof of the caravan, Samson had gone in search of Mercy and Mikey to persuade them to return. He knew where they would find shelter while they waited for the clouds to pass. They had been there before. But that night he was scared because the last time they had been chased away. They were not welcome in Slayton. Traveller children were not welcome anywhere.

His childish thoughts were muddled that night. He didn't want to be left all alone, waiting for his father to wake up. He told himself that Granny Olive would keep them safe. Her caravan was warm, and each night she told them stories. He loved her tales of magical horses, cheeky elves and night owls that made wishes come true. Some days she played her Elvis records and showed them how to dance. They had to be careful not to bump her ornaments as they swayed their hips from side to side. As he picked his way through the forest, he imagined a better life.

He ducked beneath the wire fencing, being careful not to tear his clothes on the barbs. Rain cooled his skin as he approached the empty house. It was the only one with a roof; all the others were empty shells. Mechanical equipment dotted the site, but to Samson they were rusted dinosaurs waiting to come to life. He crept down the recently dug driveway, slipping in through the doorless entrance.

The wind echoed through the chambers of the empty building and Samson's heart sank. There was no sign of Mercy or Mikey. They must be further ahead than he thought. Then he heard it, the faintest of whispers coming from upstairs. They were here. He took a breath to call out, but the words were sucked back into his throat by the flash of double car headlights. Instinctively he hid in the shadows. There were people outside.

As multiple car doors slammed, it was too late to run. The building was surrounded. Nobody saw him crouch behind the boxes of tiles stacked on the dusty cement floor.

'Thanks for coming.' One man spoke with quiet anger as his flashlight strobed the walls. 'It's about time we had a police presence around here. I'm sick of these gypsies nicking our stuff. They should be run out of town.' He was thin and bearded, with dark eyes that darted about.

Samson bit his thumbnail, dumbstruck with fear. The fat man was a cop.

'Steady on now, Geoffrey,' the police officer boomed. 'There'll be none of that. We're here to shake them up, that's all. We'll soon have you all ship-shape.'

'Shush!' A third man raised a hand. 'Hear that? The little rats are upstairs.' Then Samson was scared, because he was a rat too, caught in a trap. He held back a sneeze as plaster dust rose in his nostrils. The men's boots thumped against the makeshift stairs. Big, heavy men, prowling like cats as they tried to catch the gypsy rats.

'These are temporary,' Geoffrey whispered. 'And there's no guard rail, so mind your step.' The third man stayed downstairs, blocking the exit should they try to escape. Samson wanted to cry out, but his mouth felt glued shut. He sat, quivering behind the boxes, waiting for Mercy and Mikey's voices.

'Police! Let's be having you!' the man upstairs roared, his deep voice echoing through the draughty house. There was a sudden clatter of footsteps as Mercy shouted at her brother to run. Samson prepared to run too. Any second now they would come galloping down the stairs. He would follow them. They would go to . . . But Samson's heart stalled as he heard Mikey gasp, his quick footsteps coming to a staggering halt across the landing. The builder's warning to mind his step came too late. Screaming his name, Mercy reached out to save him, but Mikey's weight must have pulled her down. From his vantage point behind the boxes in the wide echoing hallway, Samson heard every torturous sound of the two-storey fall. As their bodies hit the cement floor, it fractured his fragile mind.

It was hardly any wonder that when Ruth asked Gerard about his background he was struck with a deep sense of fear and avoidance. Now the memories came, and like examining a fossil in amber, he explored each one in turn. That night three men stood around his siblings' bodies, their features grotesque beneath their torches' lights as they declared them dead. 'I'm calling Irving,' the police officer said. 'This is his site. He needs to know.'

By the time the suited man joined them, Samson was too scared to look.

'They're just gypsies.' Irving's voice was cold steel. 'Nobody will miss them. We can't afford any more hold-ups.' As the men argued, Samson sat, his legs numb. If they found him, they would bury him too.

'It's too late to take the moral high ground.' Irving snorted as the fat man argued that he should report it. 'You caused this. How will that go down with your colleagues in the force?'

The police officer turned to the others in response. 'This is manslaughter, and you're all involved. You know it. That's why you called me first.'

'He's right,' another said. 'We're done for if this comes out.'

'Then we'd better make sure it doesn't,' Irving spoke. 'God knows, I can't cover any more delays with this project.'

Samson listened as the men made a pact. Then they talked about getting rid of the bodies, as if they were bags of rubbish. 'I'll burn them,' Geoffrey said. 'It's the easiest way.'

'I'll bury the remains,' another replied. 'It's best the rest of you don't know where.' When they were ready to move, the fat police officer spoke again.

'Wait. There's time for a prayer.' And he had granted them that one small mercy, reciting the Lord's Prayer through his tears. The wind howled as a backdrop to the one act of compassion his siblings had been granted that night. His legs fizzing with pins and needles, Samson silently joined in, his own face wet with tears.

By the time he got away unseen, he'd closed his mind to the memory. After that, he didn't speak for months. His inability to talk led to his adoption, and his new parents were insightful, allowing him to use his middle name. As Gerard, he started life over again. And now he lay in bed, his heart aching for the sister and brother he had lost.

Finally, his actions during his blackouts became clear. Through the foggy lens of his memory, he recalled visiting Geoffrey's home. All he had wanted was for his siblings to be laid to rest in a marked grave. But someone had got there first, and he had stood in Rosemary's living room, unable to comprehend the scene. The smell of blood and the deafening silence was more than he could bear. Then he had lost his footing, his face slamming into the blood-drenched floor. He recalled getting to his feet, steadying himself against the wall. He had not thought about his bloodied handprint, or calling the police for help. He had been in his blackout state, retreating even further from himself.

Then he ran, just as he had done as a child. Ran through the woods for his life. If only his young mind could have coped, his family would have been spared years of searching for the truth. Now, Mercy and Mikey would be buried next to their mother, with bluebells and daffodils and a stone angel to mark their grave.

57

Friday, 13th March 2020

'You're going to get a reputation, you know.' Richie rested his pint glass on his beer mat. 'The Criminal Whisperer.' He raised his finger. 'Or what about the Killer Hunter . . . Or maybe . . .'

'Or maybe I'm just someone who is forever ignored . . . no, *tolerated* . . .' Sarah corrected herself, 'but who comes good in the end. I'm glad karma caught up with Irving, even if we couldn't.'

She sipped her gin. She didn't want to have this conversation, because she hadn't come to terms with what she had done. But the after-work drinking session was well overdue. Even Gabby had bought a round. Sarah had never experienced such mixed emotions. Morale had been low, given what Bernard was facing. Now that Irving was out of the way, Bernard confessed to what happened on the night Mercy and Mikey died. With Irving in a coma, he couldn't pull the plug on Bernard's wife's promised care. At least she would not endure the pain of knowing her husband had suffered the indignity of being stripped of his warrant card and status, and was facing charges of arson to endanger life, perverting the course of justice and the common law offence of preventing a lawful and decent burial.

They may never know if Irving hired a hitman or carried out the murders himself. Who had been driving the motorbike? Who were the joyriders who drove past Sarah's door? Life didn't always provide answers – did it really matter now? A debt had been paid. Secrets were exposed. The children were laid to rest. MIT were leaving and taking the case with them, which would remain open but scaled down. One way or another, Irving had orchestrated Rosemary, Geoffrey and Arnold's deaths. They had found their killer. But he was lying in a hospital bed. As far as Sarah was concerned, she had put him there.

214

She had known the joyriders were coming. Had she not shouted, he would have continued to cross the road. She had relayed everything in detail until the part where Irving left her home. The car had been driven with such speed that nobody could have foreseen it. Nobody except Sarah, who had sensed it was on its way. A buzzing, deep in her brain. She had left that part out.

'You should have seen him, though,' she said. 'Simon Irving.' She carried on when she was met by Richie's puzzled look. 'I always thought he wouldn't get his hands dirty. But I could see it in his eyes. He got off on the violence. He would have done it again.' His words still rang in her ears. *I cut my teeth on people like you.* Her skin crawled at the memory of his hand on her breast. He would have come back. She had done the right thing.

'Well, he won't hurt anyone else,' Richie replied. 'Not now.'

But Irving was still alive, and that did not sit well with her. 'His presence is an assault on the universe. They should pull the plug.'

But she knew it would never happen. Not when there was brain activity in his evil mind. The coma may have put him out of action, but for how long? Nobody knew. Some people had the luck of the devil.

'I wish he was dead,' Sarah added, sipping her gin. Despite Irving's admissions, the evidence against him was hearsay. His wife denied the presence of a decoy or any indoor CCTV. It was no surprise to Sarah. How else could you live with a monster unless you were his mate in every sense of the word? An unwelcome thought occurred, monochrome against the brightness of tonight's festivities, where the pub fire crackled brightly and her colleagues chatted and laughed. She had tried to set Irving up for death by joyrider. Did that make her a monster too? Not all monsters had scales or tentacles. Some wore suits. Some even carried police warrant cards.

She wasn't like everyone else, as much as she tried to fit in. She had been touched by violence at a tender age. Perhaps she was touched by monstrosity, too. She shook away the thought, aware that Richie was staring at her with his deep, honey-brown eyes. Eyes that felt like home.

'I'll tell you one thing . . .' Richie was growing merrier by the minute as he downed his sixth pint. 'That young friend of yours will make a great detective one day.'

'You mean Elliott?' Sarah had trusted Richie enough to give him an inkling of his insights, and how he'd helped her find the children's remains. 'That's not going to happen. I don't know how or why, but he's closed himself off to it all.' She didn't know how he had managed it, but Elliott seemed a lot happier now.

'Maybe it's for the best.' Richie sounded tired but happy as he drank his pint. It was nice to see him in casual clothes, comfortable but happy as he enjoyed time off work.

'You're probably right.' Sarah knocked back the last of her gin. She slammed her empty glass on the table. 'Drinks on me!' A round of cheers went up, and she grinned in response. She could easily afford it, now the sale of Blackhall Manor was going through.

But as she walked to the bar, Irving walked with her. No matter what she did, there was no escaping him. His presence lurked behind her, the smell of whisky on his breath. At least now she knew why he'd been desperate to own Blackhall Manor and the grounds. It was to cover up any potential evidence buried there. *You should have sold it to me, Sarah,* he whispered in her ear. *You should know better than to stand in my way.* But the voice wasn't real. It was how she processed trauma, according to her counsellor. She blinked and he evaporated because he wasn't there. He was lying in a private room in a hospital bed.

For years, Irving used the secret of Mercy and Mikey as leverage over Bernard Lee. As Bernard rose in the ranks, so did his influence, which must have pleased Irving no end. Then Bernard threatened to retire to look after his wife. Offering her a place in his care home was a way of keeping Bernard in the police. Where he was useful. That's what Bernard meant about nothing being set in stone. The man wasn't evil. He was weak.

As Sarah returned to her colleagues, she basked in their camaraderie. She would do better than her DI. With Irving lying in hospital, she already had.

58

Thursday, 24th June 2020

Sarah felt physically lighter as she walked down the corridor to the CID office. Yesterday, the prime minister announced the relaxing of restrictions and the social distancing rule. The nation exhaled as he announced the country was finally coming out of hibernation. It was far from hibernation for Sarah. The emergency services had been busier than ever over the last few months. But she took hope where she could find it. Today, their new DI was being announced. Things were set to change and she was determined to remain optimistic amidst the doom and gloom of lockdown. A cloud had hovered over their station since Bernard had been charged and bailed. He was pleading guilty for the offences put against him. As for Mercy and Mikey's deaths, too much time had passed to pursue the offence of corporate manslaughter, given the builder's gross negligence relating to their demise. The site should have been impenetrable and the people involved in removing children from the building should have handled them with care. But given Irving was still in a coma, and as witnesses were deemed unreliable or dead, the prospects of any further charges did not look good.

Sarah had attended Mikey and Mercy's memorial in the local church. Olive, Noah and Gerard had stood side by side, united in their grief. Many townsfolk had turned out too. An apology of sorts. Slayton should have done better for the two young souls. Elliott had looked adorable in his child-sized suit, Elsie had cried, and the church had been filled with flowers of every kind. At least now the children would be able to find peace. By the end of the sermon, there was a sense of healing and relief.

'Noble! How's it going?' McGuire's voice rose behind her, snapping her out of her thoughts.

'Morning, boss.' Sarah fell into step beside him, her legs moving twice as fast. According to Maggie, they'd engaged in several long phone calls and a very successful dinner date. 'I didn't know MIT was here.'

'It's not,' he said with a wink, pushing his tag against the security panel for access into CID. 'Ah, so you're the welcome party, are you?' His voice rang through the office as he strode in. 'Put the kettle on, will yous? I'm parched. Tea. I fancy a cuppa tea. Who manages the tea club around here?'

Her mouth falling open, Sarah raised her hand.

'Lovely!' McGuire passed her a twenty-pound note. 'Go out and grab a nice box of Earl Grey. And a tray of Krispy Kremes, enough for everyone.'

'Gabs!' He strode towards Sarah's scowling sergeant. 'Are you so overcome with emotion that you can't speak?' He slapped her heartily on the back. 'You and me, eh? We'll have this place ship-shape in no time.' Her face was like thunder, but he did not give her a chance to speak as he turned back to the team. 'Maybe I should drop the idioms, what do you think?'

'I . . .' Sarah stared, stunned. 'So, *you're* our new DI?' No wonder he'd taken such an interest in her working practices.

'To be sure.' McGuire grinned. 'And it's been good to experience the office dynamics before I jump in.'

'Welcome aboard.' Richie joined his colleagues to shake McGuire's hand.

With a sinking feeling, Sarah risked a glance at her sergeant, whose mouth had formed into a thin, tight line. If McGuire had noticed her displeasure, he was choosing to ignore it.

'Ah! Here she is!' McGuire's gaze was firmly on the muscular young woman wheeling in a trolley laden with boxes, Buddha statues and plants. 'My moving lady. She's going to get me settled in.' He cast an eye over the office. 'My plants will improve the air quality, and the humidifier will keep out any germs. You're going to love what I have planned for the place.'

'Wait, what?' Gabby spoke at last. 'Your office is down the hall. You can dump all that . . .' she looked at his things with disdain, '*stuff* down there.'

'Oh no,' McGuire said, clearly relishing the exchange. 'How am I going to run the team from all the way down there?'

'But there's no room.' Gabby's words fell away as McGuire directed the woman towards the box room where they kept their files. 'You can't go in there, that's—'

'That's the DI's old office,' McGuire interrupted. 'Sure, his new one is bigger but where's the chi? Where's the flow?' He knocked on a wall. 'This is temporary. We can extend it. Make more room.' He turned to the woman with the trolley. 'We'll need to rehome all these old files, but most of them are covered in dust so it'll be no bother to ya . . .'

'Fucking hippy,' Sarah heard Gabby mutter as McGuire stood at the entrance of the small office within their own.

'Sarge . . .' she whispered as she caught up with her, 'why do you dislike McGuire so much? Is there something we need to be aware of?' Gabby shook her head tightly, watching his every move. But Sarah wasn't leaving, not until she knew more. Her colleagues had gathered around him, congratulating him on his new role.

Gabby exhaled tersely, hands on hips. 'I used to be one of his trainers, back when he first joined up.'

'Oh, I see.' Sarah knew that Gabby had spent a few years in HQ training school. It wasn't uncommon for officers to become trainers for a few years when they wanted a break from the cut-and-thrust of investigations. The hours were much better, as was the pace of life.

'He was a real pain in the arse. Too familiar by far and questioned absolutely everything. He only had to look at a textbook and he knew the bloody thing off by heart.'

'I heard he had a photographic memory,' Sarah responded, folding her arms. Her conversation with Bernard felt like a lifetime ago. But being clever or progressive didn't make McGuire the devil incarnate.

'They think the sun shines out of his backside in HQ.' She nodded in his direction. 'He's only been in the job a few years and already he's a DI.'

'Did you go for the job?' Sarah looked at Gabby and instantly regretted the question as annoyance tightened her face even more.

'There was no point,' she muttered. 'Not with Golden Boy in the running.' She looked at Sarah, her eyebrows raised. 'Don't you have teabags to buy?'

'Ah. Yes,' Sarah said, turning on her heel, the twenty-pound note clasped in the palm of her hand. Gabby was a great sergeant, but her people skills were lacking. She'd been fine with Bernard because he kept out of her way. McGuire was a lot more hands-on, but Gabby's behaviour didn't faze him in the least. McGuire was sanguine, while Gabby was uptight. Yet Gabby was the one she'd turn to when things went wrong. Team dynamics were important, and McGuire and Gabby's clash of personalities might just work. Either way, things were going to get interesting around here.

59

Sarah instigated the call on Zoom, wishing the meeting could be in person. Given Elsie's health, she chose to isolate. But Sarah's news should put a smile on both of their faces. As her friends logged onto the call, it felt like Christmas Day.

Sarah grinned as their faces came into view. Elliott looked like a pint-sized little man in his blue shirt and trousers, while his mother Maggie looked every inch the artist in her paint-smudged dungarees. The first view of Elsie was obscured by a black-and-white cat as she shooed it off the bed. 'Ah, they arrived!' Sarah said cheerfully, taking in the glasses in their hands. A bottle of champagne for Maggie, fizzy lemonade for Elliott and low-calorie fizz for Elsie.

'What are we celebrating?' Maggie toyed with the stem of her glass.

'I know.' Elsie's eyes twinkled as she spoke. 'We're celebrating because that good-for-nothin' Simon Irving is flat on his back – a rooster one day and a feather duster the next, as Mama Abraham would say.'

'Nope!' Sarah replied, although she was happy Irving was out of the way. But she hadn't just sent over booze, she'd sent her friends an envelope each too. Elliott clutched his in both hands, his expression expectant. In his little shirt and trousers, he looked like he was announcing winners of the Academy Awards.

'For one thing, a little bird told me that Elsie has lost four stone . . . well done!'

'It should be five.' Elsie smiled. 'But if we weren't meant to snack at night then the fridge wouldn't have a light, right?'

'Amen to that!' Sarah laughed. 'I'm celebrating too. I've bought my house. I'm a tenant no more.' It was a relief to finally own her home. Now, she could change the locks and install top-level security. She would sleep easier in her bed.

'Congratulations. That's great news!' Maggie raised a glass in response.

'It gets better.' Sarah's smile widened. She could barely contain her glee. 'I bought next door too. I'm officially a landlord. Maggie, you can open your envelope now. Unless you'd like Elliott to do the honours?'

Elliott didn't need asking twice as he opened the small padded envelope with care. A key slid into the palm of his hand, and he looked at the camera, a question on his face.

'What's that?' Maggie said, taking the key from his palm and examining it.

'It's a key,' Elliott said, looking at his mother as if she should know better.

'I know that, but—'

'You're my first tenant,' Sarah interrupted. 'You and Elliott. What do you say?' They were more than tenants. She had gifted the house to Elliott in her will. But they didn't need to know that. Not yet.

Maggie stared at the screen. 'I . . . I don't know what to say.'

'Say yes!' Sarah replied. 'The rent is half the price of where you're living now, and we get to be next-door neighbours. Unless . . . well, unless you don't want to, of course.'

'Say yes, Mummy!' Elliott squealed. Sarah knew he hated his bedroom and the memories which bloomed there. The house next door needed a makeover but it came with a beautiful garden and rooms flooded with light. This would be a new start for them all.

'I can't accept,' Maggie said, clutching the key. 'It's too much.'

'You'd be doing me a favour.' Sarah smiled. 'The reason it's cheap is because it needs a lick of paint. I thought you could help me decorate it in your spare time. You've got a much better eye for interior design than me.'

'Oh, just take the darn thing.' Elsie chuckled. 'If you don't, I will.'

'I wish I could hug you.' Tears glistened in Maggie's eyes. 'Thank you so much!'

'Stop it,' Sarah sniffled. 'You'll get me going!' Elliott bounced in excitement and disbelief, his face a picture of joy.

'You got a house in here for me too?' Elsie winked as she shook her envelope.

'Not quite.' Sarah cleared her throat. 'But I have bought you a present and you've got to agree to accept it before you open the envelope.'

'Sure.' Elsie shrugged. 'Here goes.' She clearly couldn't wait to open the envelope, and a red plastic key landed on her palm. 'What in tarnation is this?'

'It's a safety key. It belongs to the treadmill I bought you. I thought it would come in handy over lockdown.'

'A treadmill?' Elsie exclaimed. 'I don't mean to be ungrateful but I ain't no Usain Bolt.'

'This will build your fitness up slowly. It's got a screen with live classes and instructors . . . some of them are quite hunky. I think you'll enjoy it.'

'Hunky instructors?' Elsie brightened. 'Well then, thanks, count me in.'

Sarah sipped her Prosecco, warmed by her friends' reactions. Even Elliott was beaming as he asked about his new bedroom. 'It's lovely and warm,' she said, 'and you can pop next door to me any time you like.' It was comforting to know that some good had come from the proceeds of Blackhall Manor. Making good with the money was the only way she could justify the sale.

Rumours of black-eyed children had died down overnight, and YouTuber Roger Newman had moved on. Slayton was finally getting back to normal as talk of the ghostly children faded away. Sarah had managed to dampen the rumours, including keeping a neighbour's Ring security footage under wraps. The sight of Rosemary opening her front door had held Sarah transfixed. Over and over, she watched the frail woman gesticulating as she spoke into thin air. Opening the door wider, she then allowed her invisible guests inside. Little had been said of the footage, because to her DI, it made no sense. But to Sarah, it was Mercy and Mikey, arriving as a prequel of what was to come. They didn't want to harm the old lady. They had come because the couple were close to death – a time to face up to their wrongdoings in this world. She didn't need Elliott to tell her that. She just knew.

As her friends chatted online, she basked in the warmth of their friendship. She would have been lost without them over the course of the year. With Maggie and Elliott living next door and Elsie getting support, they would keep each other strong.

Living in Slayton, they would need it.

Acknowledgements

I'm so grateful to the team of people who have helped bring my latest book to you. Thanks to my editor Jane Snelgrove, and the wonderful team at Embla Books. I'm grateful to the brilliant copy editors, proofreaders, cover designer, audiobook producers and narrators, marketers, and all the people behind the scenes who have brought this book to fruition. Thanks as always to the team at the Madeleine Milburn Literary, TV and Film Agency. A special mention to my author friends, and to Mel Sherratt, Angela Marsons and all the great authors I've been fortunate enough to meet this year. Things are slowly getting back to normal in our post-Covid world, and I've enjoyed getting out and about again. A special shout-out to my husband and grown-up children. I'm blessed to have such an amazing family behind me.

Thanks also to the bloggers and book club members who have read, reviewed and spread the word. Word of mouth is a great way of supporting authors. If you have enjoyed this book I'd be so grateful if you could leave an Amazon review.

I love hearing from my readers. You can contact me via email on hello@caroline-writes.com. You can also find me on Facebook @CMitchellAuthor, on Twitter @Caroline_writes, and on Instagram @caroline_writes. Sign up to my readers' club for news, updates and a free short story here: https://caroline-writes.com

About Caroline Mitchell

Caroline is a *New York Times*, *USA Today*, *Washington Post* and international number one bestselling author, with over 1.5 million books sold. To date her books have been shortlisted for the International Thriller Awards, the Killer Nashville Silver Falchion Awards and the Audie Awards. Her 2018 thriller *Silent Victim* won the US Readers' Favorite Award in the 'Psychological Thriller' category.

Caroline originates from Ireland and now lives with her family in a village on the coast of Essex. A former police detective, she specialised in roles dealing with vulnerable victims, victims of domestic abuse, and serious sexual offences. The people she encountered are a huge source of inspiration for her writing today.

Caroline writes full-time.

About Embla Books

Embla Books is a digital-first publisher of standout commercial adult fiction. Passionate about storytelling, the team at Embla publish books that will make you 'laugh, love, look over your shoulder and lose sleep'. Launched by Bonnier Books UK in 2021, the imprint is named after the first woman from the creation myth in Norse mythology, who was carved by the gods from a tree trunk found on the seashore – an image of the kind of creative work and crafting that writers do, and a symbol of how stories shape our lives.

Find out about some of our other books and stay in touch:

Twitter, Facebook, Instagram: @emblabooks
Newsletter: https://bit.ly/emblanewsletter